COMING TO BIRTH

WOMEN WRITING AFRICA
A Project of The Feminist Press at The City University of New York
Funded by the Ford Foundation and the Rockefeller Foundation

Women Writing Africa is a project of cultural reconstruction that aims to restore African women's voices to the public sphere. Through the collection of written and oral narratives to be published in six regional anthologies, the project will document the history of self-conscious literary expression by African women throughout the continent. In bringing together women's voices, Women Writing Africa will illuminate for a broad public the neglected history and culture of African women, who have shaped and been shaped by their families, societies, and nations.

The Women Writing Africa Series, which supports the publication of individual books, is part of the Women Writing Africa project.

The Women Writing Africa Series

ACROSS BOUNDARIES
The Journey of a South African Woman Leader
A Memoir by Mamphela Ramphele

AND THEY DIDN'T DIE
A Novel by Lauretta Ngcobo

CHANGES
A Love Story
A Novel by Ama Ata Aidoo

DAVID'S STORY
A Novel by Zoë Wicomb

HAREM YEARS
The Memoirs of an Egyptian Feminist,
1879–1924
by Huda Shaarawi
Translated and introduced
by Margot Badran

NO SWEETNESS HERE
And Other Stories
by Ama Ata Aidoo

THE PRESENT MOMENT
A Novel by Marjorie Oludhe Macgoye

TEACHING AFRICAN LITERATURES IN
A GLOBAL LITERARY ECONOMY
Women's Studies Quarterly 25, nos. 3
& 4 (fall/winter 1998)
Edited by Tuzyline Jita Allan

YOU CAN'T GET LOST IN CAPE
TOWN
A Novel by Zoë Wicomb

ZULU WOMAN
The Life Story of Christina Sibiya
by Rebecca Hourwich Reyher

COMING TO BIRTH

Marjorie Oludhe Macgoye

Afterword by J. Roger Kurtz

Historical Context by Jean Hay

THE WOMEN WRITING AFRICA SERIES

The Feminist Press
at The City University of New York

Published in the United States and Canada by The Feminist Press
at The City University of New York
The Graduate Center
365 Fifth Avenue
New York, NY 10016
feministpress.org

First Feminist Press edition, 2000
Published by arrangement with
East African Educational Publishers Ltd., Nairobi

Library of Congress Cataloging-in-Publication Data

Macgoye, Marjorie Oludhe.
    Coming to birth / Marjorie Oludhe Macgoye ; afterword by J. Roger Kurtz ;
    historical context by Jean Hay.
        p. cm.—(Women writing Africa series)
    ISBN 1-55861-253-X (cloth : alk. paper) — ISBN 1-55861-249-1 (pbk : alk.
    paper)
        1. Women teachers—Fiction 2. Married women—Fiction. 3. Young
    women—Fiction. 4. Kenya—Fiction. I. Title. II. Series.

PR9381.9.M19 C6 2000
823'.914—dc21   00-061778

This publication is made possible, in part, by grants from the Ford Foundation
and the Rockefeller Foundation in support of The Feminist Press's Women Writing
Africa Series, and by public funds from the National Endowment for the Arts.
The Feminist Press would also like to thank Joanne Markell and Genevieve Vaughan
for their generosity in supporting this book.

Printed on acid-free paper by Transcontinental Printing
Printed in Canada

08 07 06 05 04 03 02 01 00   5 4 3 2 1

CHAPTER
ONE

1

Martin Were pushed a ten cent piece into the slot and marched on to the platform to meet his wife. He was twenty-three and the world was all before him. Five feet ten, a hundred and fifty pounds, educated, employed, married, wearing khaki long with a discreetly striped blue and white shirt and a plain blue tie, socks and lace-up shoes, he had already become a person in the judgment of the community he belonged to. It was eight o'clock in the morning, one of those cool, bright Nairobi mornings with a strident blue and white sky like the best kind of airmail pad, promising heat later on, bougainvillaea dry and overpowering with a familiar papery rustle, the station desperately important, loudspeaker announcements, tickets and passes, hustle and bustle, the life-line of the country as he had been taught at school, and a hubbub of young soldiers coming and going in khaki, for this was 1956 and the Emergency an accepted fact.

Of course it was distasteful to have foreigners around – real foreigners as distinct from the permanent foreigners for whom one did errands and learned lessons – and one heard that in the camps they did unmentionable things, but around town they were too ignorant to do any serious harm, on or off duty, and Martin could feel older, superior, since for him things were on the upgrade. He had a job as a salesman in a small stationery shop from which a Kikuyu had dropped out three years before, soon after the fighting started. He had a room in Pumwani from which a tenant had been 'swept' in 'Operation Anvil' and which had since been occupied by one Luo worker or another. Two members of his tribe, Tom Mboya and Argwings-Kodhek, were leading political parties in Nairobi, and people were beginning to think that Kenya would be free of British rule in twenty years. He had a hundred and forty shillings a month, of which thirty paid his rent, he attended evening classes in English and book-

1

keeping, and Paulina was coming . . . coming.

The overnight train from Kisumu had not yet pulled in. It would be her first time on a train. She could probably count the number of times she had been in a motor vehicle, even. How Nairobi and his mastery of Nairobi would overwhelm her! She was sixteen and he had taken her at the Easter holiday, his father allowing two cattle and one he had bought from his savings, together with a food-safe for his mother-in-law and a watch for Paulina's father. They had made no objection to his marrying her then, on the promise of five more cows to follow. He had built a square house for her in Gem – square was more fashionable than round – and bought her a pair of rubber shoes. He could not then have afforded the fare to Nairobi or the things to set up house with, but now she was coming and he would be a man indeed.

The train swept in, still blazing trails through society as it had been doing for fifty years. Passengers appeared in the windows of first-class coaches, white, brown and a few black, and porters hastened to attend to them. From the second-class coaches also, white, brown and black looked out, but not, of course, from the same window. The sleepers were for four or six and when you booked the clerk wrote down your race to avoid embarrassment. From the third-class coaches there emerged first the experienced Nairobi wives, hefty women with calf-length skirts and aggressively set sleeves, passing tin and wooden suitcases through windows, bunches of green bananas, squawky hens and passive children, teapots, thermos flasks and rolled-up blankets. Next in order of attack came the men, men like Martin himself but a little older, shabbier, more worried, back from leave maybe a day late and only a bag of beans between them and payday. After them the rearguard, the mothers-in-law and the young brides, not very pushing, not very much equipped. He could not see Paulina but was confident that in days to come she would be one of the first to emerge, stouter and more impressive then, masterful of chattels and babies, a woman in her own right.

At last Paulina came into sight, clutching a triangular bundle in a cloth that would not go on her head through the doorway, and a tin box with a handle. She looked thinner than he remembered – remembering with hands rather than sight – and pale, with deep shadows under the eyes. She was wearing a faded blue cotton dress

2

and a white headscarf. Her rubber shoes were scuffed and brown. She put the bundle down while he shook her hand discreetly. They exchanged the formal greetings that were expected and the formal answers that were also expected. He could see that she was not well and that the journey had frightened her, but would have been shocked if she had answered in any other than the approved 'very well' form. She could see that he was weary and came near to knowing that he had been doing without bus fares and midday tea to save the money for her journey and to get the house ready, but she said nothing.

'Quickly,' he whispered, 'you must see where we are staying. It is all ready for you.'

He was ashamed to say that he must be back at work by half past nine, that his boss had been sarcastic at the idea of such a youngster being married, thought he was pitching a yarn. He helped her to set the tin box on her head and the bundle on top. There would be flour and vegetables in the bundle but not enough, by the look of it, to last them till the end of the month. They stood, jostled by the crowd, to give up their tickets, then he began to walk swiftly, Paulina following.

The front of the station was full of taxis and cars meeting trains. People thronged together. Ahead of them lay a street of tall buildings and rushing traffic. She supposed it was normal for big cities to be like this, but still had difficulty in keeping up with Martin, as she wanted to leap away from the kerb each time a car came close and felt, being new and strange, that she must be the one to give way whenever she came face to face with someone hurrying in the opposite direction. She waved to two of the women who had sat near her on the train and was greeted by a woman from her father's home carrying a big bunch of bananas to market, but Martin would not let her stop to talk. They turned down a wide road to the market and then passed shops and a church and school and a little mosque – Martin thought it more impressive than the other way between the public convenience and the factory wall, but for her it was only more confusing – until they were going down a hill with car and bicycle repair shops and little factories at the side and crossing the filthy little river at the bottom. Here she had to set down her burdens to go and retch at the side of the road, and Martin even offered to take the suitcase in his hand, but she was ashamed to be seen with him carrying it, and said she was better,

3

if only he could lift it up for her. And so, rather more slowly, they climbed to the top again, where more roads crossed, and passed a big arched gate with strange writing on it and figures carved and gaily painted. Martin told her it was where the Indians came to put their dead away, as they had no land round their houses. That struck her as a bad omen but she only looked and walked on.

They were crossing a piece of open ground to another road with houses of a kind to the right and a thick hedge on the left. Some chickens strayed on the road, which was smelly with piss and excrement lying in a ditch, and she looked with fear at the houses, of which she had seen the like in Kisumu, but not so many in one place or lying so close together and so dirty.

'Well, nearly there,' Martin said cheerfully, and led her across the gutter and into one of the doorways, past staring half-clothed children and a woman who was swilling glasses in an enamel basin and emptying the water in front of the house so that it left a narrow channel down to the gutter. She put the glasses down on a tray where the children making mud-pies in the wetted area could hardly fail to dirty them again.

The house was square, if it was right to speak of it so when it was not one house but many. The wooden door was open and the stale air struck her as they went in and Martin bent to undo a padlock on the third door on the right. 'There,' he said proudly, and she stumbled down a step and reached helplessly towards the bundle on her head which he gently laid down for her. The room was dark and airless and she sank back on the bed which he had made up neatly to please her. Bolting the door, he moved forward to embrace her, then, feeling her cheek hot and her breath sour, he threw open the wooden shutter, letting in a little more light from the space between their room and the next house.

The room was about eight feet by ten. The walls were painted and whitewashed – there had been a recent order, he told her, for landladies to do it – and the floor was of rough cement, of which he was very proud. The bed lay against one wall and the small wooden cupboard beyond it held cups and plates. A folding table stood under the window and there were three wooden chairs. In a corner by the table stood three suitcases in a pile with half a dozen books on top, and

4

behind the door a lamp, a charcoal burner with a couple of cooking pans and some charcoal in a cardboard box. There were even two pictures on the walls, with lines of figures underneath, an enamel basin, a teapot and a newly washed shirt and pair of trousers hanging over a string. Martin was always neat and clean.

'I am exceedingly tired,' she said, casting frightened eyes around. He poured water from the teapot into a mug and handed it to her to drink. Afraid to spit on the cement floor, she drank a little of it without the ritual and then held her mouth, feeling sick.

'I hope you are pleased,' he said. 'I got it ready just for you.'

Indeed, she knew he had; a cupboard, a basin, a lamp, a teapot, even a tablecloth. She was very lucky. She should offer thanks. But how could she tell him it was the noises she feared, coming into the room across the partition, floating through the bare rafters below the patched tin? At present there was only the drone of old ladies' voices in the back and the clatter of pans, but at night she knew there would be high words and screams and giggles and cruel laughter set loose in the house that was not a house, and the words would be the more menacing in languages one did not know. And how could she complain of this when she did not know how she knew it?

'I shall have to vomit,' she said.

He took her outside then and showed her, not a patch of private ground, for there was none, but the stinking latrine blocks where you had to remember which side was for men and which for women and pick your way among the mess. He explained how to pull for the water but it did not seem that anyone else had bothered to do so, and in any case water often got finished early in the day, he said, because of the increase of people. She saw the taps up above the big cement washing blocks that someone put water in, somehow, and you got it out without paying; but if they did not put enough in, what were you to do? And where was she to cook and gather firewood and do her washing? Yes, she knew in fact that town people bought charcoal to cook on, but these were other people, not the likes of her who could not conceive of burning money, and who used charcoal only on special occasions like a funeral or a demonstration of cakes by the club women. And how could you leave your clothes outside with so many strangers going by and the children passing water and throwing things?

In her father's *dala* there was no latrine – a dirty habit, people thought, to build one, and everyone knowing where you were going – but Martin, having been at school, had built one in his homestead which they used at least for long calls, but that was only for people who belonged, not strangers. The good brown earth would absorb the dirt and still smell leafy and familiar, at least in the dry season, not like this heavy black soil that held the water, or the slimy cement.

'I must go,' he said hastily, when she had brought up a little bile and washed her face. 'You rest. I will be back about five o'clock.'

Five o'clock! Till nearly nightfall she would be alone.

'Then you will get to know some other people. Bolt the door. You will be all right.' He closed the door quietly. 'Let me hear you bolt it.'

Shakily she drew the bolt and then lay back on the bed, after wiping her feet clean on a cloth from her bundle and putting the cloth beside her in case she should need to spit again, as it would be unthinkable to spoil the shiny new basin. She drew the blanket over her and shivered.

Later, she leaned to look under the bed. There was nothing there but a cardboard box with newspapers; no mat. So they would have to go on sharing a bed as he said they would, like Europeans. But if there was a baby, or other times if she was unwell? He hadn't asked why she felt sick: of course it would not be right for him to ask. But it was three months now. Soon it would begin to show and then they would be able to speak about it.

She dozed, still shivering. A clang overhead jerked her awake but she soon realised, from the scolding woman's voice that followed, that it was only a child throwing a stone on the roof. She supposed one would get used to it. Being married was, it seemed, a whole history of getting used to things. There was a dull ache in her belly and a bad taste right down her throat. She would have liked to make some gruel to warm herself but was frightened to light the charcoal inside the little closed room, and also she was tired, so tired. Although one or two of the women on the train had spoken civilly to her, everyone could see that it was her first journey alone, so that hawkers seemed to shout and stare longer in her direction than in others and she dared not go right off to sleep for fear of losing her luggage and the precious envelope inside her dress with her ticket in it and the five shillings her elder brother had given her when he saw her off at Kisumu. She had brought maize and bananas to eat on the way but gave most of it to the children on the next seat, she felt so sick as well as shy.

She did not know how long she had been lying there – the light from the little window was not enough to tell the time of day by and she did not yet know that she would learn to tell the time school closed by the succession of cheeky faces peering through – when someone tapped at the door. Her throat blocked with terror. She knew no one, and people one knew did not in any case tap on doors.

Then a woman's voice called in her own language, 'May I come in?'

'Who are you?' she asked, trembling.

'My name is Rachel Atieno. I live in the next house. I met Martin going to work and he said you had arrived, so I came to greet you.'

Paulina pulled herself to her feet and unbolted the door, still not sure whether she was doing right. But as soon as she saw the woman, plump and homely, carrying a teapot and a plate covered with paper, she thought how wrong she had been to give up hope. God has his angels everywhere to guard us. She gestured for the visitor to enter: the first guest in a new home: it was something of an occasion.

'So you are Akelo?' asked Rachel, shaking hands as soon as she had put her things down on the table. 'So we are going to be neighbours. Good.'

'I am happy to have a Luo neighbour,' faltered Paulina. 'I thought I should be all alone.'

'Oh, in Nairobi you are never alone. There is a lot to do and to see,' answered Rachel. 'Have you had tea since you came from the train? No, I was afraid not, so I brought you some.'

Paulina fetched mugs from the cupboard and they drank hot sweet tea and ate brown, doughy *mandasi*, still warm.

'I was afraid to light the *jiko*,' she whispered.

'Yes, it is strange at first. And you know you must never light the charcoal here indoors without opening the window: it can send you into a faint.'

Paulina shivered again.

'You are younger than I expected. Did you travel by yourself?'

'Yes,' said Paulina, astonished now at her own achievement. 'I am sixteen.'

7

'Sixteen? Yes, they are in a hurry to get you settled these days. And pregnant?'

Paulina blushed and nodded. 'How did you know?'

'You get to be able to tell. I have these myself' – she showed a fist to indicate five. 'Two are at school and one will be ready to start next year. My husband is a driver, so I get a rest sometimes when he is on long distance. But he has odd hours so he likes me to be here all the time with a pot of food on the go. And I make these *mandasi* every morning and sell them to the corner shop so as to help myself a bit. You'll settle down too. But right now you be careful.'

'Careful?'

'Yes, indeed. So skinny you are and vomiting in the mornings, I can tell by your skin. And all the upset of the journey. Still, it's the first time for him too. He doesn't know better.'

'He said he would take me out in the evening to meet people. I suppose in a town there are lights.'

'Lights? Yes, plenty. But plenty of barbed wire too.'

'Barbed wire? What for?'

'Well, for emergency. Surely you know, child, that there is fighting going on. And though there is not a curfew for us' – she stopped to explain what a curfew was: the day would come for Paulina to remember that talk and how innocent she had been – 'there are times and places the Kikuyu cannot go without a special pass, and guards to see they don't. So you see a woman on her own must be . . . careful. Now you know what kind of district this is?'

Paulina didn't. She shuddered as she was told about the bars and the prostitutes and these old multiple houses owned often enough by people who had no other home, people who counted slaves among their forebears and sometimes did not know where their ancestors were born. And yet Martin thought himself so lucky to get this house because of something called 'Anvil' which happened when he was newly working in the town and staying with an uncle. She was amazed when she later went to see the uncle's house – two good-sized rooms and a tap to themselves because he was working for the municipality. But still people had crowded in from home looking for work when they heard that so many jobs were going on account of the Kikuyus being taken away and locked up at 'Anvil' and even before, and so she

8

supposed it was right that Martin should move away on his own, even with the noises and the bad air floating over the shared rafters.

2

Rachel left so as to be ready with the children's lunch and Paulina, comforted, slept a little, but the ache in her back from sitting hunched up all night seemed to grow worse whichever way she turned. However, she put her things away and changed her dress before Martin came home. He took her to be introduced to some of his friends along the road and they had tea there, and then he showed her how to get the charcoal alight outside the house and put just enough on not to cause waste when the *ugali* and greens were cooked.

He was in a hurry to get her to bed and she lay, bilious and sweating, in his arms but could not get to sleep long after he was snoring. There was music and shouting from a nearby house, but the traffic had grown quiet early because of the curfew. The night noises were unfamiliar – dogs snarling, women screeching in a language one did not know. She tried to massage her belly to ease the pain. There was no way of telling if it was near day, the ordinary house light being so dim and the glare in the street so strange. When men came marching by and talking loudly Martin also awoke and explained, when she asked, that they were bus drivers coming off duty at Eastleigh Garage and that they deliberately talked loudly in Swahili to show that they were on lawful business, with passes, and had nothing to hide.

Before he could go back to sleep she felt bound to tell him – for though it was against custom she felt outside the place where custom could help her.

'My husband, I feel pain.'

'You are tired with the journey and the strangeness. It will go off. I know you are a strong girl.'

'Martin, I do not fear the pain but I fear for the baby.'

'It is a long way off for us to speak of a baby.'

'It is three months now, Martin, and I do not wish to soil anything.'

'Lie still there now till it is light and I will try to get someone to take you to hospital. From this place it is not possible to do anything at night.'

All night she lay still and started to bleed, and brought her box so

9

that she could sort out cloths and bind herself, but as soon as a streak of light appeared in the sky he went out looking for a vehicle. Rachel's husband was away but she persuaded a friend of his to let them use his van on a promise to pay twenty shillings on the fifteenth of the month, and as soon as the sky began to lighten they climbed in and rattled through the town and up the hill to King George Hospital.

It took them about half an hour explaining and writing things in Casualty before she was taken to a big room full of beds where Martin was not allowed to go with her. They put her into a kind of chair and wheeled her up and then dressed her in a stiff, cold gown and napkin and pulled screens round the bed and prodded and pummelled her. They gave her something to make her sleepy and the ladies said afterwards that she had been taken out of the ward on a trolley, but not for long. She woke up about midday feeling sore and intensely hungry, but the bleeding was less. They brought round great tin plates of *ugali* and beans but she could not bear to eat the stuff. Many women had food of their own and one gave her a banana. She could not understand much that was said, though a woman in the opposite bed addressed a few words to her in Luo, but an instinct told her that the talk in women's wards, which in later years she came to know, was always much the same.

She managed to call a Luo girl among the trainee nurses and was told that although she would not get this baby she must be sensible: there was nothing to prevent her getting another but she must not strain herself, especially at the first and third month. Martin came at four o'clock, bringing her tea and bread, the tea in a tall flask that somehow kept it hot, and he said that he would see her next day and she must not upset herself: there would be plenty of time for a baby. Food was brought while it was still light, the electric lights were turned off early and she slept heavily, though aroused at intervals by the clanking of trays and trolleys or the cries of women in distress. She was not thinking forward or backward, except for disappointment that the child was gone and an underlying comfort that she was young yet, there was no hurry.

No one had explained to her when Martin could come again, but she could see for herself that there were fixed times for visitors and for different kinds of staff. The pain had receded but she was still very

10

tired. They brought gruel in the morning and ordered her to go and wash her face and made her sit out while the bed was tidied. Some women were crocheting or doing one another's hair. Then the nurses started running about, straightening things and whispering 'Doctor, doctor,' until a silence fell on the ward as the visitors entered – a European doctor and a younger Asian doctor and a very special old white nurse in blue and white and some younger African nurses grouped round them. They went from bed to bed talking and pointing. When it was her turn they called a young nurse to interpret and ask her about the pain and the bleeding, nodded to one another, made some marks on paper and passed on to the next bed. The Luo nurse whispered to her, 'You can go home now,' but no one moved until the group had left the ward.

Then the nurse came back to her and whispered urgently, 'Come on, come on now. We have so many cases wanting beds. They say you are all right, now. We kept your clothes here, didn't we, since it was an emergency?'

The clothes were fished out from the locker and Paulina was sent to put them on and hand back and check what had been issued to her, only they let her keep one of the soiled dressings. They gave her a card and some aspirin tablets and showed her the way to the main door.

At the door she still felt lost, but one of the Luo attendants came up to her: 'You'd better wait till your people come,' he said. 'Have you got money for the bus? No. Have you got the key of the house? No. You see you can easily get lost here.'

But she had been told to go and trained to take orders, and it was always better to go from a place of death and danger than to stay. She had been in Kisumu several times and found her way round without knowing the names of places and had hardly noticed that Kisumu had grown bigger since she first visited it. How could she understand that Nairobi was a city or imagine that it would take a day to walk across from edge to edge and be impossible to remember all one had seen on the way? She had to get out.

3

The road out of the hospital lay through the quarters, completely closed houses of corrugated iron which must have been intolerable in

11

hot weather, so dark and noisy. Somehow she had the idea – she had been two years in primary school and had attended a few homecraft club meetings since her marriage – that medical people wanted lots of light and air. Even for a country girl it seemed odd for hospital staff to be given such houses, where children ran pot-bellied and with shirts at half-mast, failing to cover the strings of waist beads designed to ensure that their private organs developed properly. The side-road opened into a massive highway full of traffic, with barbed wire in some parts and residential buildings between tall trees. She remembered having come uphill to the hospital – did she really remember, did the heave of the trade van over tarmac mirror the still-unfamiliar jolting and panting of the country bus pulling itself up a muddy hill, or had Martin told her? In any case she took the downward slope and so saved herself what might have been days of wandering amid the scanty and picturesque population of the old European quarter. Perhaps simply she remembered from Kisumu and from the conversation of many house servants on home leave that the official quarter is always up and the labouring down. To call them west and east would only be confusing but it still applied. She started to walk down. The sun was already high but it was not hot as at home you would call a day hot, only her head was still muzzy and she was not used to walking so far in shoes.

She went on walking down though other roads seemed to crisscross, and after a time she became conscious of clanking and rattling noises on her right. Of course, the railway. This was the one thing she was sure of. After some time she found someone who knew her language to direct her to the station. There she could sit down safely and maybe get a drink of water and from there she would know her way.

About two o'clock in the afternoon she reached the station, her feet fumbling on the pavement by that time, drank some water from the tap in her cupped hands and curled herself in a corner of the waiting hall. Perhaps she slept or perhaps she didn't but to move seemed impossible. She shrank herself even smaller inside her wrapper, took off her shoes and carefully sat on them, then slipped from full consciousness. A couple of men tried to speak to her but they were answered only by a frightened stare and she fell back into a confused dream.

12

When she was jolted quite awake by someone banging petrol cans one after another on the floor she knew at once that it was time to move. She must get home before Martin came from work. She had not learned the town capacity for moving from one place to the next without returning home. Looking at the sky – thank God the sky is the same everywhere, that is why it has the same name as heaven – she realised it must be about four o'clock. She set off on the right road but was soon entangled with crowds of little khaki-clad boys coming out of school. Round the corner another school was discharging, great tall girls in blue tunics with yellow, gauzy scarves like butterflies, boys with yellow turbans. They were so pretty and so happy-looking compared with the bitterly intent and hungry faces of the black children that she could not help pausing to watch. She came nearly to the market and then hesitated. This was where she had begun to feel so bad only two days before and she remembered why and choked at the memory. By the time she had reviewed her experience of the baby, the house and the hospital, she had lost her longer recollection and took the wrong turning. Crossing the road by placing herself behind a large woman who looked at home and following on her heels, she found herself isolated by traffic on the station side of that seemingly endless road that followed the railway *landhies*.

People were pouring down the road on foot or by bicycle, the first section of that interminable crowd flowing out of shops and offices. This in itself made her think, though she recognised no landmarks, that she was on the right lines, going towards where people lived. The *landhies* consisted of good block houses with watertaps outside, all with letters and numbers: they were stoutly fenced from the road and each gate guarded by a railway policeman. She walked on and on, recognising nothing but fearful of crossing against the current of men walking. Round a corner they came to Kaloleni and she thought for a moment they must be European houses, so new and neat, till she saw the faces of people going in and out, many of them Luos. Most of the Kikuyu people, had she known how to recognise them – only those with the yellowish skin and high cheekbones were easy to tell, but the powers that be always seemed to know – were going on to a place called Bahati, 'Good Luck'. Funny name for a ghetto, but then she still did not know what that meant. Kaloleni with the football stadium, then Makongeni and Mbotela, then the big new church, set like a small town church at the edge, just before the bush began. But of course they knew – one hoped they knew – that soon the houses would grow further and further on and the church be where it belonged, in the middle of the city. If they had not known that, how could they have borne to change it for the old St Stephen's which had given way to LEGCO and later Parliament, but gave way only inch by inch, refusing to fall down, while week after week the blasting alarmed the faint-hearted and enlivened the bearers of wild rumours. Martin had seen it and told her about it.

She knew for certain now that she was on the wrong road. She was afraid to go on and almost too tired to turn back and she determined to consult the first Luo with a kindly face. By good fortune the first person she met at the gate of Makongeni Estate was an elderly lady who could only be a Luo, tall, long-skirted, carrying a Bible sticking out of the top of a plastic shopping bag.

'Excuse me,' said Paulina shyly, 'but I am a stranger here and I am looking for the house of Martin Were from Siaya. Can you direct me?'

'Were?' said the lady thoughtfully. 'I do not know one from Siaya. Does he work on the railway? And how is he related to you?'

'No, he does not work on the railway. He sells envelopes in a shop, but I do not remember the name of the shop. He is my husband.'

'He is your husband and you do not know where he lives? Now, child, tell me the truth. Is he a friend you are looking for? Have you run away? I cannot help you unless you tell me.'

Paulina felt suddenly too weary to bear any more. She held on to the gate but because of the barbed wire she could not lean against it. All Nairobi in those days was full of barbed wire. Everything was designed to keep you out. Breathlessly she explained about the miscarriage, the hospital, the long walk.

'Granny, please help me,' she implored.

'Come in first,' said the older woman, and helped her across the compound to a two-roomed house where a couple of children were sitting at a table doing their homework.

'Florence,' said the mother, 'greet the visitor and then go and make tea quickly. Use the primus, do not wait for the charcoal. This sister is sick and she will stay with us tonight. Peter, go and see if Brother

14

Samuel Obura is in, now before it is quite dark. He works at a printers' and may be able to help.'

The children obeyed. The house was neat and clean. Paulina found herself sitting in a soft chair with crocheted cloths behind her head, giving her name and the rest of the story, while Susanna, from behind the door, prepared the vegetables and asked the right questions.

'And when you say he is your husband,' she persisted, 'is he a husband that the Lord has given you? Were you married in church, or did you just go to him as girls go nowadays?'

Paulina began to cry again.

'We are not married in church,' she replied. 'It is so expensive. But he has given my father three cows and some other presents, and my father will have no objection if we have the church ceremony after he has finished paying. But we both read. I was baptised as a baby and Martin has been confirmed also, but they said my reading was not good enough for the confirmation class. Surely God would not take away my baby just because I do not have the ring.'

'No, I do not think God would take away the baby to punish you. It was a bad time to travel, that is all, and your people should have helped you on the way. But since it has happened there will be something for you to learn from it. And of course the hospital people should not have pushed you out without finding out where you lived. It was too soon anyway. I will ask Drusilla to have a look at you.'

At that point tea was brought, with fresh bananas, which revived Paulina greatly, and after tea Samuel, a huge, smiling man, praising the Lord in every second sentence, came to greet her, but though he worked in a printing shop he did not know Martin by name and she could not tell either the name of the place of work or what street it was in.

'I thought all Luo people were brothers in a big town,' she dared to say. 'That you were sure to know one another.'

He laughed again.

'Have you any idea how big Nairobi is?' he said. 'If you went to the big location of Alego and said to the first person you met, 'My sister is married in Alego, probably you know her,' it would be just the same. In the old days when there were frontier guards it was their business to know, but not without your telling them the name of the village and

15

the clan. But we have brothers indeed, brothers and sisters in Jesus. Ask us for those and we can hardly fail to know where to find them.'

He made her describe the house and said to Susanna that it would be the other side of the river, near the little church. Susanna was inclined to agree, but she reminded him that there were houses like that down below Eastleigh also and on the other side of the city at Kibera. But Martin would not have been so crazy as to expect his wife to walk all that way with her loads, so perhaps it would be Pumwani after all. But they could not make sure till morning. It was not safe to walk after dark without being able to explain exactly where you were going. And Paulina felt comfortable and content to wait, though she knew Martin would be worried when he did not find her.

Then someone brought Drusilla, a saved sister who was a midwife and had felt the call of God to remain single and work at her profession, helping and witnessing to other women. Paulina found it hard to understand how a woman who, though not very young, was still marriageable could make such a choice. In custom there was no place for the unmarried. She was led to the bedroom for a private examination and Drusilla pronounced her well enough, though she could have done with another twenty-four hours in bed, and again reassured her that she would be able to have other children. She also urged Paulina to repent and then all the hardships of the past two days would come to make sense.

Drusilla had to run back to a case nearby and Paulina was embarrassed to find the master of the house waiting to get into the bedroom to change out of his overalls and heavy boots. However, he greeted her in a fatherly fashion and talked to her while supper was cooking. It appeared that the other three children were grown up and away, so they had the house to the four of them, except for a sister-in-law who was visiting her sick husband in hospital in Nairobi and a niece who was trying to get training after finishing her primary school exams, but they were both out and would be escorted home later. He stressed over and over again the risks of Nairobi for a woman on her own. After supper and prayers Paulina slept on a mat with the daughter and the niece while the sister-in-law occupied the spare bed and Peter somehow fitted himself into the kitchen.

In the morning everyone was in a bustle. Susanna had a market

16

stall, so she was up and ready even before the school children. Their father was getting ready for work. Only the sister-in-law was minding the house, so the niece was detailed to show Paulina the way across the railway line and down through Shauri Moyo. This she curtly did but then disappeared into the flurry of new buildings. Even Paulina began to wonder what kind of job-hunting she had in mind.

From the railway line she came to an open space which was the site for the Baptist Centre and from there a line of solid brick houses bordered the road down the valley and up again, with the more ragged outline of Pumwani beyond. In the gentle morning sunshine, the eight o'clock rush to school and work already beginning to subside, Paulina walked gratefully. The houses looked respectable and she came upon a little Koranic school where curly-headed boys in white robes and caps sat reciting round their *maalam* and rubber tyres lay about for recreation. At the top of the hill the other side looked more familiar, not like homes exactly, the buildings were too big and close together for that, but like a market in the country with a petrol pump, a shoe repairer, a grocery shop with a sewing-machine on the pavement, but further along the barbed wire reappeared and the notices on which one could always make out the big letters, KEM, KEM.

Coming to the top, however, she was back at the old problem. All the houses looked to her exactly alike. The first one she approached with a polite enquiry, 'Do you know a Mr Martin Were? Does he live here?' was full of the smell of beer. Dirty glasses were lying all around the big room that was opened to her and a woman came out, tousled and red-eyed, who did not answer but sent her away with a foreigner's galling imitation of her accent – '*ok awinji, ok awinji*' – and screamed with laughter. At several houses it was the same. At one a young boy tried to grab her and she started away, crying. She came round to the big hospital – since there was a hospital here why did they take her so far away? She did not realise that it was for women who had real babies. And she tried to speak to the barefoot girls in pink starched uniforms behind the barbed wire but they turned away, and she thought they were afraid of being punished if they spoke to people outside. She did not yet know how much there was to be frightened of in Nairobi, and that in the mission house a few doors away women with difficult pregnancies were given a room to stay in in case they should be caught by curfew if their pains came on in the night.

She came round again and started up a side road where a flock of doves rose suddenly from a house where they were kept and startled her, and she drew back because this road was not paved and she remembered the made road and the chickens and the foul-smelling ditches.

It was noon again and she started from house to house along the paved road past the church.

'Excuse me. Do you know a Mr Martin Were? Does he live here?' But most people did not understand her and all shrugged her away, and she stood for a while in the shade to watch the Kamba people so deftly fashioning with adze and hammer little giraffes and zebras and lions out of wood as they sat on logs outside the house, and the women polishing them till they shone. She had never herself seen a giraffe or a zebra or a lion, though Martin had once seen a number of giraffes from the train and one of her grandfathers had been famous for killing an elephant, but her school-fellows found it hard to believe nowadays.

She forced her way forward and the houses seemed to multiply as she went from one to the other, and she stumbled, and did not observe a woman in the uniform of the Prisons Department (as she later found it was) watching her closely from the main road. The woman had been dropped from an official vehicle and it looked as though she were visiting relations in the village (as Pumwani likes to call itself) while off duty.

'Hey, you, come here,' she shouted loudly in Swahili.

Paulina did not understand but she knew where the message was directed all right.

'What are you doing, going from house to house like that? Distributing leaflets? Begging? Don't you think we've got enough prostitutes round here without a kid like you? Where did you go to school? Who is your father?'

Paulina understood more of this, by instinct rather than reason, than she would have thought possible a day or two before, but she still had no answer to it. In fact there were no passes, other than school identity cards for non-Kikuyu women, and it was not hard to recognise those who had for any effective period attended school, so

18

she replied with her usual, 'Excuse me, do you know Mr Martin Were from Siaya? I am looking for his house.'

'Oh-ho, *an ang'eyo MISTER MARTIN WERE,*' answered the lady loudly in bad Luo. 'In fact I know everybody you might want to see round here. You just come with me, old dear.'

And muttering under her breath she dragged Paulina along, inwardly protesting at this rough treatment but outwardly quiescent, since any lead to Martin seemed better than none. They cut along some unmade back paths which seemed vaguely familiar to Paulina and then out beside the little white-washed mosque which she had certainly seen on her first evening stroll in Nairobi.

'*Chiegini ka,* near here,' she burst out.

'Oh yes, no doubt, very near, *chiegini ah-i-i-i-nya,*' mimicked her captor, dragging her past the white-washed stones that marked out the territory of the Police Post and pushing her against the counter. 'Complaint? Charge? Question?' asked the duty officer rapidly, and the uniformed woman poured out such a stream of accusations in Swahili that even a local Swahili speaker might have had difficulty in keeping up with it. The general tenor was that the stranger was behaving suspiciously at a time when a search for escaped prisoners had created a tense security situation, that she refused to answer questions and that she pretended to be a halfwit for evasive purposes.

Having asked Paulina her name, father's name – he did not credit her with a husband – and residence, without listening to her tremulous story but writing firmly 'no fixed address,' he shoved her into a cell, turned the key in the lock and returned to his records after passing the time of day with the prison officer. (She actually had a cousin holed up in Pumwani evading an abduction charge, and this was one of her reasons for resenting all strangers and any show of weakness.) Paulina curled herself into the corner of the cage furthest from the door, crying quietly, and was soon asleep.

At nightfall the European inspector took over. Curfew area – unrest over escaped prisoners – tribal mixtures – new workers replacing those in detention – political activity – all these factors required a firm colonial hand. No one seemed surprised by it at the time, not even the young white men who found themselves patrolling five acres of seething rumour with bush telegraph wires to every corner of the colony and beyond (for the richest witch-doctor was the Tanzanian with snakes drawn on his house, and an up-and-coming young Ugandan called Obote was active in political meetings at Pumwani Memorial Hall). Some of the young white men were well-intentioned and some were also clear-sighted, so this particular officer was very disturbed to find a girl asleep in the cell and nothing that looked like a charge in the rigmarole handed over by the duty officer.

'Protective custody, sir,' said the sergeant, seeing how the land lay. 'Doesn't seem able to look after herself.'

'What girl can, with you lot around and her under lock and key,' growled the inspector. 'All right, I admit you know the area better than I do, but interference with female suspects is one thing I won't have. Get her into the car . . .'

The man's eyebrows lifted: he dared not ask the question that came to mind.

'Get her in the car, I said. Driver and myself. No hanky panky. Get on.'

The sergeant unlocked the cell, prodded the girl awake, enjoyed her moment of terror as he gestured towards the European and the car. Wearily she allowed them to put her in the back. The inspector sat in front with the driver and explained carefully in good Swahili, but it was lost on her.

'Now, don't be frightened. I can't have you left alone at the station, so I'm taking you to the house of a lady who'll take good care of you. You don't have to come back to the station unless you want to and I shouldn't advise you to. Come on now.'

It was not far, retracing part of the way she had followed that afternoon. They got out and hammered at a heavy wooden door. An elderly European lady looked out of the balcony overhead asking what was the matter.

'Police, ma'am,' the inspector answered respectfully. 'We've got a young girl who appears to be lost. Wondered if you could possibly put her up for the night. She'd be safer here.'

'Of course, of course.' They came down, the grey-haired one with twinkling eyes and the younger one with glasses and thanked the inspector for his concern and then led her up the long staircase and into a room that was simple enough not to be alarming. The older lady

– Ahoya she was called – talked to her in Luo at once and found out the whole story, translating it bit by bit for the younger one, and they fussed about because she was alone and had lost the baby and brought her rice and meat to eat, showed her how to use the bathroom and made her up a soft bed on the floor with blankets and pillows. They prayed that next day she might find her home and then switched off the magic light and left her to sleep.

In the morning, while the young one made ready to go to work by bicycle, Ahoya brought the car out and said they would look around before it was time for the men to start work.

'It is not very far from the mosque, I have seen the mosque,' Paulina insisted, 'and they would not let me go that way.' Ahoya quietened her, saying they would start the search there, and within a couple of minutes she recognised the house and Martin just leaving it.

4

Martin was thunderstruck. Ahoya introduced herself, reminded him that Paulina was badly shocked and needed to rest but had been kept safe, repeated to her the church and meeting times and drove away. Martin had not said a single word. He took the key out of his pocket and pointed towards the house.

'Oh, I'm so glad you are here,' cried Paulina. 'I was so frightened. But they wouldn't let me stay in the hospital. I walked and walked.'

The key was in the padlock. As the door opened he gave her a hard push over towards the bed so that she fell to the floor, grazing her knees and knocking her forehead on the wooden frame.

'Slut! Whore! Is that what you came to Nairobi for?'

'But they would not let me . . .'

'Too busy about the city, are you, to sit at the gate like anyone else waiting for me to come? If you had bothered to find the way you would have found the house locked, wouldn't you, wouldn't you? And spent the rest of the day wandering about Pumwani making enquiries as you call it – wouldn't you? Wouldn't you?'

His hand slapped across her cheek and again across her shoulders.

'Want to come and live in Nairobi as somebody's wife, do you – do you?'

His fist was pummelling into the small of her back and he began

21

pulling at the bed as though to overturn it on top of her.

'Two nights. Where did you spend those two nights?'

'With Susanna and her husband in a place called Makongeni – I'll take you there . . .'

'And that is how the white woman came to bring you?'

'No, no. The first night Susanna found me. She is a saved sister. I can take you to the church. You will see. And the second . . .'

'The second day you couldn't get any of those great friends of yours to come to Shah & Sons, Printers, Reatta Road, to find me? You couldn't get anyone to telephone? You can't bloody well remember five numbers.'

He kicked her buttocks.

'Martin, you never told me. The name, the number, you never told me at all. Oh-oh. And there is still bleeding.'

'Bleeding there may be. Can't even keep a baby for me. Can't even be sure it was mine, can I? – Whore! – Bitch! – How did you get here with that white woman?'

'I recognised the mosque, but then instead she pushed me into the police station and they locked me up and the officer took me to the white woman . . .'

'Police station – you went to the police station!'

She screamed as he came flailing towards her but in Pumwani people are accustomed to screaming. She was discoloured with bruises now and dragged herself to lie face downwards on the bed to protect her face and belly from the rain of blows.

'But did you not look for me? Did you not tell other Luo people to look?'

Look! He had spent two evenings till midnight wandering in search of her, but he would not demean himself to say so. Ask his friends? Let them know she had not come home? He would rather leave her to die than do that.

'Ignorant bitch! And you don't know I have to go to work, keeping me arguing like this?'

He slammed the door behind him, padlocked it and pocketed the key. He was already sweating profusely and there was blood on the sleeve of his shirt.

She continued to lie there sobbing. Then she thought she should bathe the sore places and wash the torn dress but there was only an inch of water in the bottom of the pail. She poured a cupful for drinking and dabbed at her wounds with the rest. She put on an old faded dress, did her best to tidy the bed that was now her prison and slipped under the blanket for warmth.

Would he send her home? She supposed so. Would her parents consider her disgraced enough that they must take her back? How would she ever get the child again if he did not come to her? Or would she die of his beatings here where there was no tribunal to appeal to? Would they have to move? She had heard that in town people might be afraid to face their landlord after fights and quarrels.

Indeed, she was almost as ignorant as Martin called her, for he certainly could not afford to send her home or the risk of sending her unaccompanied.

She lay there, more dazed than dozing, she did not know for how long. No water. No charcoal. There was a little hand mirror in the cupboard and she looked at the dark bruises on her cheeks, but they were less swollen than her back and shoulders. She had opened the window a crack to see in the mirror, then closed it again, but now there was a tapping on the shutter.

'Who is it?' she called, fearful that he might be testing her by sending visitors.

'It is Ahoya. Don't be afraid,' came the welcome voice in Luo. 'Are you all right, Paulina?'

'I am all right but not very,' said Paulina shamefacedly, pushing at the shutter, 'and I cannot open the door.'

'Yes, I thought so,' replied the matter-of-fact voice. 'He has locked you in. Did he beat you also?'

'Yes, he beat me also.'

'And that is the first time?'

'The first time. He used to love me.'

Ahoya laughed gently. 'Well, he does love you. I could see it in his face as he caught sight of you. But I thought also he would beat you, for it is a shame to him to have you lost, though you did not mean it so. Have you anything to eat?'

'No. I do not need anything, thank you.'

'Or any medicine?'

23

'No, I shall be all right.'

'Be sensible, child. Every wife who comes to Nairobi from the country has problems. Do not think it is the end of the world. Every young man has problems too. Probably all his friends and workmates have been telling him he is too young to marry and now he begins to wonder how he will manage. Don't you know that if you had been married in the old way your husband would have given you a token beating while the guests were still there? They say that is so that if you are widowed and inherited you will not be able to say that your new husband was the first person ever to beat you. So don't start to wish backwards. You praise God that He has given you a husband to love you just as I have been able to do without one.'

'You too?' asked Paulina, wondering. 'You too, like Drusilla, you are not married and yet you seem to understand so much?'

'You have met Drusilla, have you? Well, she is a very great friend of mine. And Miriam, who lives quite near here, is another. And we all know that God can look after us in all that is needful. But you, who have a husband, also need food and medicines, and I will bring it myself so that no one can accuse you of having men visitors, but you can give the tray to Amina in the front room and I will get it collected.'

She rushed away and Paulina at once felt comforted. After half an hour Ahoya came back in the car. She handed through the window a tube of ointment and a tray with thick slices of bread and jam and a cold orange drink on it.

'Now if he smells the ointment, tell him I brought it and he can come and ask me any questions he likes. But now I must hurry. I have a meeting on the other side of town.'

Paulina heard the car start. She ate carefully, forcing herself to finish, and when Amina tapped at the window to take the tray away they exchanged such small courtesies as can be managed without a com mon language. Paulina slept until the stiffness softened into a small ache all over her body, and Amina gathered her cronies to tell them:

'That Martin, soft he may have looked and spoken but my goodness, did he go for her! And the mother's milk hardly dried on her lips, poor young thing. We'll see that she learns to give him something to think about, won't we just.'

Martin was late for work, was cautioned for being untidy and made several mistakes in calculation. By the time he got home at 5.25 p.m. he was ravenously hungry, wearied by two sleepless nights and spoiling for a row. As he opened the door Paulina raised herself cautiously from the pillow and sat up.

'Lying in bed till now?' he roared. 'And no food ready!'

'There is no water and no charcoal,' she replied meekly.

'No . . . You employ me as a bloody coolie to bring you water?' he shouted. 'Don't you know where the water is?'

'But you had the key, Martin. I couldn't get out.'

'Carry my own key, fetch my own water, cook my own food! What the devil am I married for?'

She began to make for the pail to fetch the water, leaning a little crookedly where her back hurt most.

'And another thing,' he shouted. 'What about the thermos?'

'The what?'

'The thermos. The jug I brought you tea in at the hospital. That was borrowed. I suppose you left it at the bloody police station?'

'No, no. I never had it. It was at the hospital. I didn't know it was ours.'

'Ours? Damn all is ours. It's got to be paid for, do you hear? What are you going to do about it?'

He lifted his hand to strike again, but Amina and her friends started making a lot of noise in the front room and he let his hand fall. The bruises showed even in the dim light and he had not remembered hitting her so hard in the morning.

'Maybe I could learn to sell vegetables in the market like Susanna.'

'You – market – that's a good one. You'd get yourself marched off to police again or to mission again or to bloody holy brothers and sisters again before you learn to get ten cents for a twenty-five cent bunch of carrots. You don't get out of my eye-range again, that's all.'

'As you say, Martin,' she replied gently and dodged out to get the water.

When she returned he was stretched on the bed, eyes ostentatiously closed. She made her first domestic decision as a city woman and made her way to Rachel's kitchen to borrow some charcoal. Rachel took one look at her and handed over a little tinful.

'We'll talk tomorrow,' she said.

25

By the time she had cooked the vegetables and *ugali* Martin was fast asleep and snoring. She shouted and tugged his shoulder, then covered the food on the table. She used the last glow of the charcoal to heat a little black tea and then sat down to wait. After some minutes Martin opened his eyes, washed his hands in the basin she had set ready and sat down to eat without a word. Then, after vanishing for a brief moment which could hardly have been sufficient for a trip to the latrine he padlocked the door, put the key under the pillow, pulled off his top clothes and retired to bed. She ate sparingly and piled the dishes in the corner, then put out the lamp and, pulling her wrapper closer round her, squatted on the floor. After some drowsy time he called to her.

'You will catch cold there. Better come to bed . . . Get those cold feet off me,' he grumbled. Then, 'Don't worry. If you're a good girl we'll get another baby next year.' A few minutes later he was snoring again.

<h1 style="text-align:center">5</h1>

In Nairobi Paulina thought herself a woman but she might well have been a standard eight schoolgirl of middling ability – she did not even know that there were already two schools in the country where African girls might be educated beyond that unimagined height. She was not slow to learn, considering how little time had been allowed her for learning up till now. She soon began to get used to it.

She had one advantage – a mixed one – over many Nairobi wives in that Martin came home every evening and never slept out. He was hungry enough to want to come home every day unless there was an evening class or a trade union or political meeting after work, and that never went on till dark. He was hardly more than a boy himself, a hearty eater, and for a couple of months after meeting the expenses of her journey, the hospital fee, car hire and the replacement of the flask, he had to do without the midday bun and cup of tea which he sometimes allowed himself in the first half of the month.

He stayed close to her because he still desired her, was proud of her and yet had a lingering doubt about the time of the miscarriage which made him afraid to leave her alone. He could not, of course, bear to lose face by checking her story with Susanna or Ahoya. He was too cautious to venture out much after dark, although the curfew did not strictly cover non-KEM. Primary school did not teach you much about Kenya tribes. Everyone knew Kikuyu, but Embu and Meru did not mean much to outsiders. Yet now 'KEM' was becoming a kind of entity, not embodied in the old lady who collected the rents next door but omnipresent and threatening. Still, a curfew meant guards patrolling, looking, perhaps hoping, for trouble. It meant, at times, workers walking to work between cordons of armed European boys lining the road – so young and helpless the boys looked, you wondered how they could possibly know who to shoot at if occasion arose – and it meant that the person being searched for was someone whose language you didn't know, whose motives you didn't fully understand and whose aims, though they might be partly good in trying to change the way things were, you had not been invited to share in.

And trouble there could easily be in Pumwani, leaving aside the struggle between the powerful and the apparently powerless. One Sunday morning a Luo man was found knifed after a dance at the Pumwani Memorial Hall. He lived in the corner house and Martin had often chatted with him on his way to work. The investigation was never brought to a conclusion. Another time one of the old Kikuyu ladies was taken away for questioning. It was rumoured that they were going to hang her, but just in time the person they thought she was was actually captured and she was allowed home, not much less loud-mouthed and demanding of her family than before, so that people of other tribes shrank back.

A woman must not go into a country bus alone, Paulina was warned, or a reason would be found for 'questioning' her privately. She ceased to wonder about these things, but kept strictly to time, sought from day to day the food that was needful, made the best of the narrowness of her room with no chickens or goats or fields to tend. And then there was Ahoya encouraging her to attend Luo meetings in the little church of St John, with those other women who did not understand the Sunday Swahili services very well, and to look forward to joining the sewing class when she could afford the simple materials.

Little by little she was coming to know Swahili. Martin encouraged her and bought her a New Testament which she could compare with the Luo *Muma* word by word, though her reading was so slow that she

27

still could not think of keeping up with the book in church. But by passing the time of day with her neighbours and accompanying them to the shops and vegetable market she became daily more fluent. She also got to know several of the Brethren women through Susanna's introduction and observed intently how they managed their house-keeping. They all spoke beautiful Swahili and it was one of the measures of unity of the intertribal group. They encouraged her to do the same 'so that she would be able to witness when the Lord called her'. She laughed, but tried to please them.

At first Martin gave her money every two or three days and told her what to buy, but she was learning from the older women what to do – not to waste twenty cents on salad oil for cooking, which ended up sticking to the sides of a long bottle, but to keep a bottle in store and use it sparingly, only taking care to put it away so that she would not be forced to lend. She learned not to rush to the market straight after payday but to wait till the price had died down, and she found that in Nairobi people expected meat once a week and toilet paper and soap for dish-washing, since even the air was gritty and public. She found a patch over behind the old racecourse where she could raise a few vegetables. They were not so secure as at home – if people wanted to take them how could you prevent it? – but they helped out on lean days. She learned where to go to meet people from home who might be bringing a bag of maize or flour or at least a message on the bus.

She learned, too, that not all Nairobi women were like herself. Not all of them had husbands, to start with, or they had husbands who were away, they claimed, because of the Emergency. But even those who had husbands often received visitors at odd hours – for the men without women far outnumbered the women without men – or sometimes went trading at the market without telling their husbands what they earned. They bought clothes or cigarettes or perfumes, for they said in Majengo a woman could not keep her man against all the professional competition if she did not use means to keep herself beautiful.

One woman Paulina knew paid over everything she earned to a medicine man who promised to bring her a baby, but they got transferred to Machakos and moved away before Paulina could ever find out whether the medicine worked. In any case in Machakos, people said, there were even more powerful medicines. She had not thought of buying any herself. After all they loved one another and she had nearly persuaded Martin to confirm their marriage in church, so she had no doubt that it would be fruitful.

The only thing she asked Martin for in those first months was a brassière, and he laughed very much and asked what a country girl would want such a thing for, but when she bore his laughter patiently he was sorry and bought her one for six shillings at the end of the month. As she became more confident and he caught up slowly on his expenditure, he began to take her out more. They went to the museum on a Sunday afternoon and saw real leopards and giraffes, only dead and standing up, and birds and butterflies and implements from different tribes. She enjoyed it and begged to go again. They also strolled through the town gazing into the windows of the big shops, where a dress could cost more than a month's wages and a man's suit half a year's. They went out to Ruaraka by bus to visit a friend who lived at the Breweries, and she got a feel of a country district different from their own. They walked in City Park and out among the big houses where people like Martin's employers lived and ladies strolled in soft tissues scandalously bare at the waist.

But in spite of all the beautiful things in the city there were scandals and quarrels among the elders, the City Council, Martin said. And in Uganda there was trouble too about the King and Parliament. And trouble over Suez where the big ships used to come bringing the things for Martin to sell in the shop. There seemed to be no end to what one was supposed to learn and to be interested in.

CHAPTER
TWO

1

Paulina had begun to learn to crochet when she was in Gem and she practised hard as soon as she could persuade Martin to buy her thread and a hook of her own, so that by the end of the first year she had white lacy covers for the table, the suitcases and the top of the cupboard, and they were sufficiently admired by other people to get her requests to make more, so that she was able to produce thirty or forty shillings each month by making cloths to order. This weighed in Martin's decision to keep her in Nairobi and not send her home the first year to bring in the harvest. His plot was small enough for his schoolgirl sisters to be able to manage it easily in return for his paying their fees. He was nervous about leaving Paulina at a distance and eager that she should get a baby soon; so at Easter, with news of a place called Ghana ringing in their ears – a new country, people said, which had not been there before, which surprised Paulina – they went together to the home place for three weeks, and then came back together, and though his mother and sisters must have been disappointed to see no signs of a child, they were kind and said nothing.

The elections had come and gone in March, freedom seemed to be nearer, and, though 'KEM, KEM' were still common signs, there was no more talk of shooting and few people taken away. From January, Martin had read in a newspaper, Kikuyu could move about freely in Pumwani, but the habit had been lost. The newspapers had been running a series called 'The Return of the Kikuyu' and had given a lot of news about the election candidates, though Tom Mboya was the only one whose public addresses were regularly advertised 'Under the Standard Clock'. Mr Moi and Mr Ngala used to stay at the little guest-house by the church when Parliament was in session and people were surprised that they still felt at home in this simple and smelly place. Ahoya went away – she was getting old now – but the short one with glasses and a bicycle still stayed at the mission house and other Europeans came and more classes started.

After the holiday Paulina had hope of another baby. She was wretchedly homesick during the months of nausea for the open fields and familiar small talk of home, but she stuck it out. One morning she came home overtired from digging her small vegetable plot and resolved to rest in the afternoon. But there came a clang of boots, a banging at the door.

'Who is it?' She started up nervously, afraid to open.

'Police, police. Open up.'

'How do I know?' she faltered, still half asleep and throbbing with anxiety.

'You know because I say so,' somebody shouted, kicking the door.

'Open, open,' shouted Amina from the other room, and pleaded with the men – 'You see she is not well and she does not understand very much Swahili. Her husband has forbidden her to open. That is why she questions.'

Trembling, Paulina drew the bolt and was pushed out of the way by the three policemen who crowded in. They overturned the bed, shook the cupboard until a couple of glasses broke, strewed the contents of the boxes over the floor, then, with another shove and injunctions to make more haste another time, they were gone. She never knew for certain who they were looking for, but two or three Kamba people round the corner were arrested and it was supposed that they must be hiding someone. She leaned back against the upturned leg of the bed where she had come to a halt. Her back was grazed and sore but they had not really hurt her. She started to tug the heavy wooden bed with its crisscross of rubber straps back on its legs, but felt a sharp pain and laid it down again. The fibre mattress and bedding had slipped off on to the floor and there was the print of a dirty boot on the sheet. She sat down on the mattress to get her breath and Amina appeared in the still-open doorway.

'Are you all right?' she asked abruptly.

'A little bit all right,' replied Paulina.

'You are lucky. They might have made it much worse for you. Do you forget that the Emergency is still on?'

She did forget sometimes. The elections and the gradual disuse of

31

the restrictions that were still technically there on the boards (but the boards in Swahili were hard to read) made people feel so much better. Besides, Emergency for her meant living in the town. She had never known Pumwani before and might not have found it very free either.

Amina's strong arms pulled the bed into place and repiled the suitcases. She was tactful enough not to make the bed up, though Paulina would in any case have been too weak to resist her. Then she lay down again, refusing Amina's offer of tea or to go and fetch someone to help. Ahoya was gone, and only Ahoya would have spoken her language and understood.

By the time Martin came home one look at her face was enough to tell him that this was serious, and he swallowed his resentment and ran to the mission house himself, but by the time he returned with Bibi Tett it was clear that nothing could be done. This time they did not go to the hospital and he was gentle with her, putting all the blame on the police. She did not dare tell him how bad she had been feeling before they came.

2

In November the time came for them to confirm their wedding in church. He bought her a white cotton dress and scarf as well as a shiny wedding ring. They had a few friends to tea and felt progressive and important. She thought she was beginning another baby but she said nothing about it to Martin, and when two months later she began to bleed again and he found her in tears because of it he beat her and told her she was imagining things. He sent her to his home in February 1958, long before the rains and time for digging and she stayed six months, till the harvest was gathered in and her mother-in-law reported favourably on her hard work and obedience.

At first she loved being home again, to wake in the dark when the cowbells began to tinkle, to dig by moonlight and in the hot mornings to busy herself with the chores of food preserving and storing: to eat in the evenings under her mother-in-law's arched roof, with Martin's younger sisters and brothers clustered round, full of talk and questions, as there was no adult male present to overawe them, and sometimes a sickly calf snorting in the shadows. She had taken one of the cats into her own little house because of the rats, and became very

32

fond of him, naming him Pusi, as some people said it in Swahili. The physical work was good for her – she rounded and developed, ate well (for it was not a home where one went short, even before the rains), observed the taboos carefully. She was able to make a short visit to her own mother, who questioned her sharply about Nairobi life, but her mother-in-law, though disappointed at the lack of a child, was more tolerant and the atmosphere of the home was serene.

And yet – and yet she was not the girl of the house any more, but someone's wife, and friends of her own age came to see her with babies in their arms, or some of them were training as nurses or teachers, but not many of these came visiting. She hugged herself at night and brooded to herself in that afternoon time when there was not much left to do; and when the letter came – a week late, because the school it was addressed to had already closed for the August holiday – she was eager to be off and away.

Martin came again to meet her off the train. It was two years since the first time. She had finished growing now. Her breasts were firm and her eyes knowing. This time her goods were more expertly handled and she had brought a lot of food: so much that he had to give a man two shillings fifty to carry the sacks on a handcart. She had been crocheting industriously even on the train – like a Kikuyu, people said – and this time he did not have to walk home with her, but returned to the shop while she organised her woman's business.

Back in the house she unloaded the goods and set about storing them. Cold as Nairobi is in August, she needed air, if not exactly fresh air. There hung about the room – how small it looked compared with the houses of home which never need to be cooking-place or wash-place or grainstore as well – a faint strange scent which she could most easily identify as coconut oil. Surely Martin would not use such stuff on his hair? Yet from day to day they all used new things, she reflected, remembering how she had taken that long-disused brassière, now tight, out of the box for the journey, how knowingly she had opened and closed the windows of the train, how secretly she had gazed at skincream in shops and flimsy combs in bright colours.

She arranged her things, filled the water containers, bargained for a little charcoal with the odd change she had left over from the journey. She greeted Amina and the other house neighbours. Rachel was still

33

away completing her harvest. She was just getting ready a midday snack preparatory to lying down after a sleepless night of travel when a head paused outside the window, a graceful head with beautifully plaited hair and a nylon wrapper.

'So you have come,' said a teasing voice in beautiful coastal Swahili such as one used to taunt an ignorant country wife.

'I have come but I think I do not know you,' said Paulina plainly and turned to the charcoal stove.

'Oh, you have come, and you are the wife of the house?' continued the voice.

'Yes, I am Mrs Were,' announced Paulina, glorying in the foreign name that had once sounded so odd.

'Oh yes, Mrs Were,' tinkled the voice, 'and you are the mother of who?' and with a peal of laughter she was gone, the ravishing face, the high, brittle voice, as it sounded to Paulina, and sickly sweet smell.

There was another gurgle of Swahili talk, fast and flowery, as the woman passed the front of the house. It was too hard for her to follow – they could always make it too hard if they wanted to.

'Who was that?' she called as she heard Amina coming down the corridor.

'That? Oh, Fatima. She has come to live in the corner house. Don't take any notice of her. She has more words than sense. I am glad you are back,' called Amina, a hefty woman whose own liaisons were discreet and long-lasting.

But Paulina's heart sank and she did not rest well, although she was determined to keep herself alert for the rapturous night to come.

She looked her best and cooked her best and Martin was happy to have her back. They discussed decorously all the news from home and the night was long and full of promise. But somehow a scent of strangeness hung about the room and the stink from outside did not cease to trouble her.

Her crochet work prospered and she began to ask whether they could not think of moving into one of the brick houses that were easier to keep clean and where you would have four walls to yourself. And because there was no chance and not enough money either, Martin would grow angry and go out in the evening. The house was not so oppressive for him as for her since nowadays he habitually came home

34

late – sometimes it was overtime, sometimes an evening class. People were not so nervous in the evenings as before and occasionally he came after the radios had stopped playing, smelling of beer and not hungry, although he could not afford to drink regularly and did not neglect the housekeeping money or his own appearance.

Eight months passed uneasily in this way and with no sign of another baby. She did not catch him with another woman and he did not sleep out except on two occasions when he told her he was going to a wake for a fellow clansman on the other side of town. Each time he borrowed from her ten shillings which she had put aside from her work money to buy more yarn for crochet. Of course she could only get them back by paring the food money, and one day when the charcoal man was dunning Martin to pay the bill and he therefore swore at her for sitting idle with no tablecloth in hand, she found it hard to bear and made a pretext to go and sit in Rachel's house a little while, but she never went anywhere he could not keep her in his sight.

Fatima returned to jeer at her a number of times, and twice when Martin was home in the early evening she put her head, shiny and evil-scented, right through the little window, begging him to take a stroll with her outside, since she had accounting problems to discuss which might disturb Mrs Were or even wake up the little ones, since they were so quiet that they might be thought not to be there at all.

Martin froze and told her to go to a proper accountant. He had not the time or knowledge to take on outside engagements, he said. But Paulina could not tell from his face whether he was really shocked or only offended, and she knew by now that this kind of invitation occurred commonly in front of Majengo wives and as often as not was eagerly accepted.

She bore it and looked aside. He hardly ever walked out with her now but he found little reason to quarrel with her either. In April she went home again to look after the farm; it was arranged almost without words between them and he did not see her to the train.

She busied herself as usual but the crop was scanty and the work seemed harder than before. One of her sisters-in-law and a giggly friend of hers who had been to school in the town tried to persuade her to get a baby by another man. Although custom was not too hard on this practice she felt a revulsion that it should ever have been mentioned, and twisted the ring on her left hand till the friend remarked pointedly that it took more than a few prayers to get the job done. Besides, she knew that the fault was not Martin's, but did not want to discuss the whole painful history with others. Then a remote clansman began to bother her and she found it difficult to keep him away, with no man of the family to hand, though her mother-in-law threatened him with curses if he did not mind his manners.

Months passed in the trivial intimacy of time spent at home. There was always something to talk about – a birth, a death, an illness, an exam, a marriage, a change in the bus route, a new shop open, someone building a new house – and yet rarely anything to think about. Things happened – bridges were flooded, buses collided, schools were upgraded, but in the total picture nothing changed. In Nairobi you got less personal news and yet things changed all the time and you did not need a newspaper or a radio to tell you so.

Paulina would never forget that sunny Id-El-Fitr of 1957 when the air blazed with freedom. Nobody said that anything had happened. You just knew the tide had turned. Things were heard in the air all round you and you could not pinpoint which language you heard them in, even the women knew them, even the standard eight children knew them, and so there was no need to mention them. But for the village someone up above might have decided on a standard seven exam instead of a standard eight, English in class three instead of class five, and yet in the home where you talked and talked nothing ever changed.

On her way back to Nairobi she stopped in Kisumu to visit a neighbour who had gone to take a course in the Homecraft School. Paulina loved it – the neatness, the cleanness of the little rooms, the ovens, the embroidered cloths, the strictness of timekeeping for married women inside the tall fence (like a boarding school, as she imagined it, so safe, so orderly, so free of painful choice). How she would love to go there and keep her home clean and well-provided. She enthused to the teachers about it and they said she was welcome to apply next time. She found it hard to leave. But the train was going and she had bundles to pick up in the care of a home friend now married in Kisumu, and Martin would be waiting. He had written that he was moving house. It was small, but away from Majengo. He hoped she would be pleased with it. So in another way she was eager to go.

3

It was August 1959. There were still troops at the station but not as many as they used to be. Martin was there, just as he had been three years before, but a trifle smarter, a little more self-confident. This time they swung away from the OTC bus station, after passing the Sikh School and St Peter Clavers, up to where Duke Street crossed River Road and down to the river valley there, where the Indian flats begin that stretch right up into Parklands.

'Where are we going?'

'Near Kariokor Market.'

She knew the market, called, as a section of every big town was called, after the place the Carrier Corps had rested. You had to pass a number of pleasant little houses – the Indian evangelist used to live in one: she had met him and his wife at some church service – and then opposite were the remains of the old City Council estate which could easily be taken for a barracks, never intended for family houses but only sleeping places for men at work. A cold fear descended upon her – was this what she was expected to come home to, a red-brick box with only a tiny back window the size and shape of the stables she had seen set up for the horses that year she had been taken to the Show? She sat down on her suitcase and could not prevent a tear trickling down her face.

'But you *wanted* to move,' said Martin, making the familiar opening move of an argument. 'You wanted to get out of Pumwani. What did you think I was finding to please you? Government House?'

The bed filled most of the room. The cupboard was jammed at the back and the boxes were piled under the bed. The table was gone. The chairs were folded against the wall so that you could squeeze your way past to the cupboard. The burner and basins fitted behind the door once you shut it from the inside: the width of the bed prevented it from being fully opened. Her sacks and baskets of food remained outside.

'Have to hang them up,' said Martin gruffly, 'like we do in the kitchen at home. People hang their bicycles, even, from the roof. No other way.'

37

'There are too many. They can't possibly fit. Oh, how I have tried to make it nice for you, and you bring me this! My covers . . . tablecloths . . .'

'All in the boxes. Don't worry. Have to make ends meet – we'll find someone to store for us if needs be. I've only just come here; don't know many people.' And with that he was off.

A few other women were washing in basins outside the row of houses and one was cooking gruel for a couple of children. They did not speak till Martin was gone, then the nearest came over and introduced herself. She was a Mkamba and staying only briefly with her husband. The children lived in the country, she said, and went to school. She travelled only with the two-year-old. Life was too hard in the town, but she had come to get money, a new dress and medicine for her mother-in-law. On your own, she supposed, without children, you could put up with it. In the lines they were mostly men alone or young boys sharing a room, but in good weather you could do a lot outside.

Paulina was not very communicative. She pulled out the two chairs and set her goods on them, off the dusty road where the chickens pecked and the sanitation was no better than in Majengo. She fitted what foodstuffs she could into the cupboard and roped a bunch of bananas over the rafters but she could not deal with the heavy sacks of flour and beans that a handcart had helped them to bring. At last she dragged them on to the floor where the chairs had been and left the chairs outside, resolving to lay them on the bed if she should need to go far away. Then she bolted the door and lay down to close her eyes on her troubles.

Martin came with some rope and boxes and tried to hoist the heavy sacks while she made him tea, which helped her to feel a little more at home, but he couldn't manage it, so they moved some of the produce into cardboard boxes which swayed perilously above the bed and he went to ask an uncle of his to house the sacks and came home with two hefty schoolboys to help carry them. So they managed, but of course when she went next month to refill the boxes from the sacks they were lower than they had been. 'It must be the housemaid,' they said.

One of the first women Paulina ran to for comfort was Rachel, but Rachel had problems of her own. Her ayah had just been delivered of a baby. Ordinarily, of course, she would have sent the girl home in disgrace long before, but she had concealed herself for a long time and never showed very big, so at the end Rachel was really taken unawares. In any case the girl was so clever, and in her refusal to talk dropped so many speaking hints, that Rachel was half persuaded that it was her husband's baby and that the girl would have to stay on as *nyar ot*, a junior wife from her own clan. In that case it would not do to stir up trouble, especially as he was grumpy and unheeding of her complaints about getting the work done. Perhaps, in fact, he suspected himself. But when the time came the baby shocked them all by being palpably white – pink, that is to say, and wrinkled, brown-eyed, of course, but with unmistakably gingery hair and a long nose. One of the young soldiers? A policeman? By force or for money? The girl remained silent and apparently unmoved, but Rachel's husband was so furious – disappointed, perhaps? – that something had to be done. Paulina found the girl rocking the baby back and forth on the step with a sly, secret smile. Rachel had given her an old towel and a dress for it. It was a girl and was going to be called Joyce. But of course she could not take it home. There it would be an alarm and a laughing-stock, something that society could not absorb as the lighter-skinned tribes had sometimes absorbed their bastards. And she could not stay here for fear of the master's anger. But where else could she go, unskilled and cumbered with the child? Within a few days a solution presented itself to the satisfaction of all parties. Amina came over with a splendid shawl for the baby and sat down to negotiate. She was getting into middle life, she said, and had no child. In a coastal family light skins and long noses were quite acceptable. If the father were not pressing his claim – the girl mother looked down with a grimace – she would adopt the baby and bring it up at her own expense, but it must not be claimed back. It would never know its parentage.

Rachel was openly relieved. The whole situation was an embarrassment to her. The girl made a half-hearted plea for money but obviously she too had a burden to dispose of. She agreed to give the child up provided – and her insistence surprised everyone – she should be brought up as a Christian and retain the name Joyce. To this Amina cheerfully agreed – after all, it was a white baby. A form of agreement was drawn up by someone from the mosque in characters none of the signatories could make out. The child's mother was given a new dress and the train fare to Kisumu and departed the next afternoon with a heavy bundle which she had somehow managed to conceal in a friend's house. She was the more shapely for her recent confinement, a big strong girl with thin ankles and sullen eyes, more smirking with the pride of achievement than chastened by her public shame. Even Paulina felt it could not be long before she was back in town.

Amina proved unexpectedly expert with powder and feeding bottle and soon afterwards approached the pastor about baptism for the child but bowed to the rule that since there was no Christian parent Joyce must make her own profession when she could read and write. The baby made a good pretext for Paulina to come and see Amina from time to time. Little by little she built up a picture of a world quite remote from her own, a world of gay wrappers and jingling bracelets and perfumes and spicy dishes, where slim men with bony features came and went, for what purpose one was never quite aware, and of town houses where these urbane traditions from the coast somehow collected themselves despite the bare crumbling walls and the outlandish cold. Even some of the stories burned themselves into her mind, lively fantastic stories with expressions in them that no nice Luo girl would use and that, had you asked her, she would not have thought she knew the Swahili for, and long afterwards she drew on them to amuse the children she looked after and to reprove their carelessness in the national language.

4

Paulina used to sit outside crocheting and contriving a profit from her crochet despite the dust and the smells from ordure and market refuse, and sometimes she went to Rachel's with her work or to Susanna's, and kept on and on about Homecraft until Martin wrote letters about it and found references for her and helped her a bit with reading and writing. So in March 1960, with the Kenya African National Union newly formed and politicians beginning to show their teeth, she set off for home to see to the harvest and from there in August she joined the Homecraft Training School in Kisumu. By the

40

time she left, Joyce was sitting up and already had a coquettish air, with little gold rings in her ears, a bangle on her arm and someone to play with whenever she required attention. And by the time training started the name of Jomo Kenyatta was loudly in the air and his picture – which she had never seen before – on the front pages of the newspapers. The Emergency had ended officially in January, though a lot of people were still in detention, and in March KANU was formed, with a lot of jockeying for position and a row over whether Kenyatta could officially be its leader while still detained as a public enemy.

In May the African Elected Members, with threats of resignation, insisted on being allowed to visit him, and somehow overnight he turned out to be *Mr* Kenyatta, referred to on the radio with guarded respect. And of the KANU people Martin's idol Tom Mboya had once more emerged as a leader – even Jaramogi admitted it to his face after all the manoeuvring to keep him out of the Kiambu conference. People said he had traded in the People's Convention Party for the secretaryship, and indeed no one heard of the PCP again, even the Nyanza branch which had only just been formed. Martin was present at that Adult Education Rally at Bahati where Tom finished his speech, debonair and controlled as ever, and then rushed away to the meeting which had been arranged to exclude him. There was challenge in the air, not to say scholarships to America. The least one could do was to learn to bake cakes in a real oven and sing Swahili songs.

Paulina was the youngest woman in the Homecraft class, and they cold-shouldered her because she had no child and very little education. The European praised her – which made it worse – because she was not leaving any baby behind and was eager to improve her home. The others lectured her in private. There was nothing wrong with their homes. They needed no improving. The object of the course was to get a job as a club leader so as to teach other women and make money. You could embroider tablecloths and make money. If you lived in a town you could even make cakes for money.

She pointed out shyly that she had already sold some crochet work and had helped Rachel make *mandasi* for sale when she was without an ayah, only to be daunted by the array of tablecloths shaken out before

41

her and the learned discourses on styles and prices. In a week or two, however, the women learned to get on together. Some were frankly grateful to be away from the demands of husbands and the labour of child-rearing, some congratulating themselves on refuge from a petulant mother-in-law or importunate neighbours while the husband laboured in Mombasa or Eldoret. A few were frustrated and made the most of free afternoons. Some were worried about their children, gleaning from the bus station news of coughs, bruises and extra school demands. Joanna wept openly that she knew her girls would not eat properly while she was away, but girls they all were, and her husband so mean that he would not let them eat corn on the cob (the soft young maize vanished too quickly for his liking and all must be stored and ground for flour), so she looked for work to help her along against the day he would decide to waste no more school fees on daughters. Janet was widowed and had a son at Maseno High School to provide for. A saved Christian, she had refused to be inherited. Paulina loved to hear her witness to spiritual things. At the same time, she reflected, second husbands would rarely contribute to school expenses, so Janet was not really worse off for her refusal. Tabitha, who was always grumbling that she should have got into High School (High School if you please! Not one girl in a thousand had the chance to go to High School) had to leave before the end of the course because her youngest child, whom she had abruptly stopped breast-feeding at ten months in order to enter, died of diarrhoea. The staff said it was a pity she could not finish because she would have been such a good teacher.

Life in Kisumu went on evenly, sunny in the morning, scorching in the afternoon, with a wind suddenly blowing up before dark, thunder storms sometimes and dust devils nearly every day. Occasionally they were allowed to cross the road in the evening to see films of football matches or life in foreign countries at the Victoria Social Centre. Grown-up people would be playing games with a bat and ball in the open courtyard inside, and there was a bar in the same building and a library, but only for English books. Sometimes there were dances and from the security of their cottages they could hear the band playing late at night. Paulina had never seen a 'cinema' before. But she was good at netball when she got over her shyness. It was not customary for married women to play with schoolgirls, however large and old, and she would not have liked Martin to see her doing it.

She found her way round Kisumu quite soon. It was a manageable kind of place for anyone who preened herself on knowing Nairobi. She was already familiar with the old railway station and further along the lake the new station was being built. From there you could walk along the lakeside towards the place where hippos come to the surface, but not easily, for the lake level was rising and you could see trees and a few buildings sticking up out of the water. It made her feel uneasy, thinking of the old story of the unwelcoming village swamped under the lake, but she could not think of anything very wicked she had done and in any case the life of the town seemed to go on undisturbed.

She measured out the inland end of the town, past the Catholic church, and explored in the other direction up past the little park as far as St Peter's, where she had twice gone with ladies of the St Stephen's congregation because a young white couple were trying there to overcome the legacy of recent days when Africans had not been allowed in that church. But the centre of the students' social life was, of course, the market and the bus station beside it, where news could be gathered from one's home, one's mother's home and even from Nairobi. Something lively was always going on here, and all the communities of Kisumu gathered to do their shopping – which interested her now that she was seriously learning about cooking – so that as well as the essential maize, beans and *alot* you could get an avocado pear for fifteen cents or a grapefruit for ten. Foreigners did not demur at paying twenty cents each for eggs and more than a shilling for a pineapple.

Here women who lived in the town would keep their stalls going from day to day and those who came from outside with a sackful of produce or a couple of bunches of bananas would haggle over them with the licensed seller. Whole smelly busloads of fish would come up from Uyoma, and it felt a bit like Nairobi when people surged round the buses selling biscuits, sweets, handkerchieves and medicines. But because the people were fewer of each group they mixed more. The Nubian ladies with their ample robes and superb basketware knew Luo as well as good Swahili, and the little Ahmaddiyah missionary, an Asian with an earnest face and a lambskin cap, would always stop to discuss his Muslim interpretation of the Christian Bible with anyone who would take him seriously. Ja-abu was always about with his enormous trumpet made of pieces of gourd and thermos flasks and tubing tied together with bits of cloth, his cheeks so distended that they sagged limply when not gathering in the tremendous wind required to blow a blast as of doom, his feet heavy with bells swaddled in sacking so that the ankles would not be rubbed, a merry song of local application for anyone who paid him and a not so cheerful one for those who refused. The Church of Christ in Africa, a new thing since Paulina had left home to be married, was always out and about at that time too, Bishop Matthew eager to entice former Anglicans to his side, but Paulina did not see reason to change: she sided with the Brethren – although she had not come forward to be saved herself – against those whose greater love militated against church discipline. (She twisted her wedding ring often enough, wondering whether it would be strong enough to stave off disaster, and pondered the promises of Sarah and Hannah as against the wiles of Pumwani.) Now two years old, the new church was already threatened by a split in its own ranks, and soon to lose the old blind archdeacon and a serviceable vehicle. The conflict had led to burnings of churches and neighbouring congregations vying with one another who should sing the same familiar canticles the louder, *Jubilate* in one classroom overlapping the reading of the gospel in another. But Paulina valued the neatness and form of the old church, particularly the Kisumu buildings in contrast with the simple country ones, and felt she understood their order and hierarchy. There was little of the rebel about her.

Her course results were good and she was appointed club leader at the centre nearest her husband's home. There was even talk of setting up a second centre, which would have brought her earnings to a fabulous total in the as yet undemanding village economy. Naturally there were strong objections from the committees to her appointment, but the European leader brushed these aside. To appoint a slip of a girl? One who was not sidetracked by old-fashioned ways and was still full of enthusiasm. A childless woman? All the more time she would have to apply herself to the work. A young woman *away* from her husband? But all the women were away from their husbands. That was Luo custom, the European explained, and they preferred it so. The wife was then like a single woman, occupied and earning money.

(A fat lot she knew about it.) A person without influential relations? Of course. That was to be the mark of the new society.

The inevitable happened. Balls of crochet cotton disappeared from the stores or turned up, tangled and muddy, in the corner of the classroom where the club met. Rumours ran round about a liaison with the lecherous brother-in-law who had pestered her before. A crazed old woman was encouraged to hang about the homestead telling stories of unresponsive wives who had been threatened with barrenness. But Paulina's mother-in-law backed her up, out of liking for the girl and appreciation, also, of her contribution to the home, and she mastered her temper and got good results from her club and literacy classes. She never went back to Kariokor.

5

The seasons and years passed, in the dry one harder digging and less palatable food, in the wet one heavy mud dragging at one's feet on the way to the club and women staying away because they were busy in the fields. And news coming in all the time – meetings, conferences, appointments. Martin had a lot to say about these when he came, but he didn't speak much of his personal plans and ambitions. Black men were coming into power but white men were still the ones you went to see at the Town Hall or the hospital. Once a year he came home to spend his leave. Once a year during recess Paulina travelled to Nairobi, but there she was more like a visitor than a wife. Martin had moved to share a single room with a friend and had all his meals out to save the expense of entertaining. The friend obligingly found another place to sleep when Paulina arrived and she cooked for the three of them, scrubbed and crocheted and visited her old friends, but the focus of her life had changed. Martin was getting fatter. He drank beer but no spirits and had improved his position in the firm after getting a certificate. He did not beat her when he had evidence that there was still no baby on the way but threatened that he would do so if she was not faithful to him. She did not ask him for any pledge of faithfulness in return. What would be the use?

Her house at home was neat and comfortable. She had bought a new bed and mattress, a food cupboard and some upright chairs as well as helping her mother-in-law, out of her income from the club. She did some crochet and a little sewing for other families and made regular trips to Kisumu for shopping. She wanted to ask Martin to help her buy a sewing-machine but hesitated because in some places, she heard, this was the gift given to sweeten the first wife for the arrival of the second.

All this time the vision of *Uhuru* was growing larger and larger. Delegations came and went to London for complicated talks. There were black ministers. There was going to be a black prime minister. It was a bit hard to imagine, but after all they had got used to having a black bishop long before there was a secondary school headmaster who was not foreign. One by one Emergency restrictions, which Paulina felt she knew more about than anyone in her home place, were broken down. Kenyatta was first moved, then freed, then elected. At home people got restless. Stones were thrown. A European was left to die when his car fell into a river near Maseno, although someone had dived far enough down to get his watch and his clothes. Institutions were confused with the foreigners who ran them. When a college bus overturned, villagers refused to help right it till assistance was called from outside. Several students were worse injured than they need have been and one girl lost a leg. Paulina could not understand it all, though they listened regularly to the shopkeeper's radio in the market. People one looked up to were changing and moving, but the country and the country people did not seem to change much and she could not make out what was the advantage of being free. And yet she had become free, in a sense, of Martin, and she had changed. She provided for herself, lived by herself. Although she had obligations to him she neither hungered for him nor expected him from day to day. She made decisions for herself, of course, what to buy, what train to travel on: whether there were more momentous decisions – resolutely she closed her mind to them and considered how to teach the women about changes her supervisors said were coming.

All 1960 Martin waited in hope. Paulina would finish the course. She would be a credit to him. She would have an income and then, surely, as a grown-up person, she should have a child.

He moved to Makadara with the intention that his house-rent, charcoal, lamp-oil, would be saved by sharing with another man, and, perhaps, a little bit, to please Paulina when she came. Bus fares would be needed, at least on wet days, but surely they would pool their vegetable and maize meal and very little would have to be bought for cash. But somehow it didn't turn out like that. Aduogi was often behind with rent and always seemed to be waiting for a bag of maize meal that had not come from home. One night, coming in late, he kicked the lamp so that it broke, and Martin had to pay for a new glass and then for all the oil, since he needed light to study by and Aduogi insisted that a small tin with a wick was good enough for him. Once their supplies were finished Martin stopped sharing food with him. Then there were textbooks for evening classes and his younger sisters were getting into higher classes at school too. He was a bit disappointed that Paulina had not offered to pay for them. Of course she didn't need anything from him, but then they were no longer earning their fees by having to harvest for him. He visited Fatima occasionally in her room – she was skilful, but domineering as well as expensive – and after all he was still a married man, so he never let her come to his room in Makadara or in Kariokor either. He wished that he had never let her come in Pumwani. Perhaps she had put the evil eye on them.

6

In April 1961 he went home on leave and expended all his affection on Paulina, who had done so well, but although she wrote to him whenever someone was travelling to Nairobi there was no hint of a pregnancy. In August 1961 she visited him and he went home again at Christmas and the next April, but to no effect. In May 1962 he came back to Nairobi to find the house dirty and rent and charcoal owing, so he kicked Aduogi out. He was now earning three hundred and fifty a month after passing his exams and decided he could afford to live alone.

He could afford it since – the thought nagged him – he had no dependants other than the sisters wanting school fees. That was enough. Paulina could sew their uniforms for them. But although he could go out for a few beers on a Saturday night, for a cheap film show or a lecture or an evangelical meeting on a Sunday afternoon, get an occasional newspaper or a copy of *Drum* magazine, though it was no longer such a struggle to appear at work in a clean collar and tie or to

47

put in a contribution at a Freedom meeting, still it was a dull sort of life, trudging home to wash and make tea and perhaps sew on a few buttons before it got too dark, revising a few pages of marketing or salesmanship if no one came to call, beating your head all day about paper sizes and type specimens and fitting cards to envelopes. Once he had found it exciting: now he saw it as only the footslogging of the new world which others were beginning to penetrate with motorbikes and Mercedes. If he went to visit his uncles and cousins they were always agonising over nursery school fees, starting fishponds, contributing to cattle-dips, sending students overseas: one way and another pride and pocket were constantly touched.

So he was quite pleased one Saturday when Fauzia came to call. She was a kid sister of Fatima, staying at an aunt's house near his while trying to get into a secretarial course. She did his ironing for him and accepted a Coke from the corner shop, chattering away about her schooldays at the coast and the superior facilities of Nairobi.

She came more often. The aunt beat her, she complained, and the colleges were always asking for more money before offering a place. Somehow she was soon staying the night. He put his foot down when Paulina came in August 1962, and had to pay the aunt to keep her mouth shut, but he was not sorry when Paulina, so neat, so prim, so dutiful, went away again and Fauzia returned, giggling, perfumed and with a sound Swahili erotic education to warm his bed and spice his food. After all, she was a young, clean girl who might give him a child. He was nearly thirty. It was his right to have a child and he was not going to pay dowry again without being sure.

Martin began to grow fatter and to talk more. Fauzia was attentive and not more demanding than one would expect of a young girl not long out of school. In the daytime she visited her people and they sometimes gave her dresses and things. The room seemed to be full of little pots and jars, but he didn't mind: he had been starved of a feminine presence for so long.

In November Fauzia's aunt made a formal call for which tea and sweet cakes were produced and the table laid with Paulina's crocheted cloths. The bed was concealed behind a highly coloured hanging which was to be made into a dress afterwards.

The aunt spoke at length in flowery Swahili which Martin did not

48

try too hard to follow about marriage customs and the formality of gifts. She had a great thirst for knowledge, she said, and was eager to find out in what way Luo and Christian custom differed from her own. Martin reluctantly handed over two pounds in an envelope and asserted that in his custom dowry could not bring good fortune unless the former marriage was first terminated by the infidelity or sterility of the wife or the agreement of all parties. Of course, he added, his mother, brothers and his unfortunately bewitched wife all willed his happiness, and the greatest sign of God's blessing was the gift of children, which could convince the whole family that he had found favour before the Lord. He had every intention of taking formal steps when his brothers and his former wife could see for themselves that love could override all barriers of tribe and creed.

He was very careful not to commit himself, and the aunt took her leave suggesting wordily that generosity was the quality most likely to evoke the desired gifts of God. The little room seemed to grow cold as Fauzia escorted her aunt away, chattering shrilly. Only a couple of chairs had enlarged the furnishings since Pumwani days and Fauzia had brought her own boxes to store her clothes in. The makeshift curtain looked thin and likely to fade – he had paid more than it was worth – and he had no serious thought of taking this butterfly creature home to mud floors and the care of heavy children. If he had any plan at all it was, vaguely, to retain the child and let her go her way. He did not get much reading done nowadays and there were no signs of dowry payments accumulating in the Post Office Savings Bank.

Deliberately he went out to visit some relations and talk about the constitutional conference and the state of the parties. He had been careful not to let them think of Fauzia as anything other than a casual girl friend. They would not find that worth mentioning in their letters home. Meanwhile Fauzia's aunt had opened the envelope and reacted with indignation to the small amount she found in it. Fauzia wept and cajoled that night, but he could not put much heart into consoling her. She stayed away for two days but then crept back; it was the middle of the month and times were hard.

At Christmas he resolutely went home, taking a dress-length for his mother and a teapot for Paulina, but she was prostrated with a bad period both days and he returned to Nairobi with anger boiling up in him. Fauzia was not in the house when he arrived, stiff and red-eyed from lack of sleep, in the early hours of the first working day. She later explained that she had been frightened to stay alone in the house and had gone to her sister's. He did not ask which sister.

CHAPTER
THREE

1

The new year, the great year of Independence, dragged on. Martin shortened his leave at home because there was a lot of work and he could use the extra money gained for the forfeited days. He gaped at the great ceremonies of June, the reversal of the order of his schooldays, the known world turned on its head. He even took Fauzia out to see the fireworks and the decorations and that was how people from home got to know about her and sent word back. Because of this, he supposed, Paulina did not come in August and sent no word, but she sent no questions or recriminations either. Nor did his mother send to ask why she was getting no money from him and no greetings. As the year wore on he began to ponder things that Fauzia's aunt had said, as though people themselves could control the gift of children or women be unwilling for it, and wonder how the girl who seemed so young and guileless had yet learned the lessons of her girlhood so well. He began to examine the dresses, the wrappers, the bangles, when she was out at one of her Moslem festivals and to wonder who paid for them and how much.

And so he told her that when he took another wife she must be a Christian who would leave her hair unplaited and her ears without ornament, who would dig in the fields and plaster walls and leave her children fat and naked. But she only laughed and said she must enjoy herself a while longer.

Martin was still in essence the Luo boy he had been when he got married seven years before, whose whole world picture revolved round an idealised 'home' to which he would return in plenty and comfort after making his mark on the big world. The fact that Paulina was herself an important person at 'home', despite his disappointments, reinforced that picture, and she had made the house itself far more fitting to his expectations than most of his friends' wives. And yet there was a tension in the Nairobi air that left him not quite satisfied. Home might suffice for the primary education of sons and the marriage of daughters but the city was better for higher education and careers. A civil servant at his own level of employment would get a second-class train ticket – second-class, mark you – to show the continuation of his urban dignity right up to Kisumu, but then the home bus services were not very reliable and the markets were sometimes without bread or bottled beer, and one had come to rely upon the dry cleaner . . .

In June 1963 a group of women rather bigger than the usual number of Paulina's club went to Kisumu in a hired bus for the celebration of internal Independence, feeling so safe, so mutually protective in spite of their squabbles, so moved by the half-understood thing that was happening to them, that there was a compulsion in them to be present. They went again in December for the full Independence celebrations and there Paulina spotted the little white girl who had been in Pumwani, with two children now and a black husband, and, though they did not really recognise her, they greeted her civilly in Luo and exchanged congratulations on the occasion. She was worrying about how to teach the women the National Anthem, since their Swahili was so bad, and about the new flag. But between the two trips something had died in her: word had come for certain that Martin was living with a coast woman and he did not write at all any longer or send anything to his mother, and though she knew that it was not surprising and that he had been patient a long time, her heart sank and she twisted the ring on her finger. But still her mother-in-law refused to admit it to be the truth, so though the older women envied her training and were eager to belittle her and expand on what they knew of Martin's life, she composed herself and went on with her duties.

2

A week after *Uhuru* Day she went on an ordinary shopping trip to Kisumu. Apart from the new flags flying, everything looked very much as usual. One went into the same doors and bypassed the same doors as before, not by any law or antipathy but just by habit and familiarity. She accomplished her errands as usual, lingered a little over some dress materials and reached the bus stand only to be told that the Lucky Strike bus had already left.

'Left? But it's hardly two yet and it never leaves till half past.'

'Kisumu time. It has already left.'

'He's lying,' put in the turn boy of another line. 'If it had gone there'd have been a lot of people waiting like you.'

'If it *hadn't* gone there would be people waiting, but you see because it has . . .'

'The bus hasn't gone. It's being repaired. It will be back soon.'

'No, it's not being repaired. It's being washed in the lake. And the people are in it. So it may not come back.'

'Of course it will come back if there's a chance of more passengers.'

'If it were being repaired the people wouldn't stay on it.'

'The people went on Soni because they were afraid Lucky Strike wouldn't be back on time.'

'So it may not come back at all?'

'No, perhaps not.'

'And Soni is really gone?'

'Yes, that I know for sure because I put my in-laws on it. But wait, wait, something will turn up.'

She waited till four and knew that no bus would start so late. The early morning dark held fewer terrors but the evening dark was for 'rogues'. She could have gone to the Homecraft Centre, perhaps, or found enough money for the Christian Fellowship Centre Guest-house, though it went against the grain to spend hard-earned money on food and beds. But she did not like the idea of sleeping away from home and continued to hang about in the unlikely hope of a lift being offered.

And there was Simon. When one came to think of it Simon was there at every turn in Kisumu. He always seemed to be in front of the Town Hall rather than in his own office, or at the station or at the Victoria Social Hall arranging about a meeting. What more natural than that he should be at the bus stand after duty, gathering news and passing the time of day. She always used to see him when she went to the Town Hall, which she sometimes had to do with a query about personal tax or to leave a message with the husband of one of the club ladies who worked there in the licensing department. Simon was a clerk in the health department but nothing seemed to keep him to his

53

desk. He had been at school with her elder brother and claimed to have recognised her at once. He was courteous and tidy, the sort of man who always wore a jacket even in the hottest weather. He generally seemed eager to talk to her, perhaps because his wife Martha was keen on going to Homecraft Centre too. One day Martha had come to the Town Hall and taken her home to tea in one of the new municipal houses. She seemed shy and nervous, though several years older than Paulina and a mother of three. So when Simon urged her to stay with them if a lift could not be found, and went on till nearly nightfall asking this driver and that if he could not help her, it seemed natural enough to go with him. Enough people must know by now that she had looked hard for a way home. All the same she was a little uneasy. She was astonished to find no one at home but the little serving-maid who was sent off to buy food.

'Oh, Martha must have taken the children to a film at the Centre. She'll be back in half an hour. Just make yourself at home.'

So she sat primly on the edge of the sofa, suppressing the knowledge that a Luo woman does not go out with all the children when her man is due home and the meal not ready. The girl brought beer and rice and hot cooked meat from a hotel and then made her way to the kitchen to prepare her own meal. Paulina began to protest, but Simon was too strong for her. Was she not an old friend and a guest? Why did she shame him because Martha was careless enough to stay out? Was he not lonely and hard done by enough? And as she sat mesmerised while lie after lie poured over her, he plied her with food and drink and compliments, he drew closer and for the first time broached the logic of it – she was a married woman denied a married woman's rights and respect, in custom she should seek a child where she could. She had the right. And everyone knew that she had not delayed in the town on purpose. There would be no shame. And she knew that there would be shame but not, for a barren woman, the public evidence of shame, and she bridled at his comfort and cast her eyes down and ceased to resist. As he took her she felt neither liking nor commitment but a kind of inevitable propriety, and before she slunk out in the morning, trying to avoid prying eyes, she knew without words being said that she would come again. She could not pretend that she could any longer do without.

3

She caught the Soni bus when it returned for the morning trip – there was still no sign of Lucky Strike and someone suggested it had gone off on private hire with a party of Youth Wingers. People at home confirmed that it had not appeared the day before and accepted her story that she had slept at Homecraft, but of course neighbours who were at the bus stop receiving guests and goods and letters by hand nodded and chattered among themselves and she never for a moment supposed that they were deceived. She told her mother-in-law that in order to complete her shopping and arrangements for the group she would need to stay over in Kisumu once a fortnight.

At Christmas time her husband came as usual. She was ill at ease and feared he would suspect her new well-being, but he was desperately tired and had had a little too much to drink so, though he murmured about hearths and babies, they had little time to come together, none for private talk. He swaggered out to the Boxing Day afternoon bus with three other young men returning to Nairobi almost without seeing his wife as a person and relieved that she had not asked questions about his life in Nairobi. She was, for the first time, glad to see him go, incurious about what women he might take up with, accepting at last her role as an absentee wife, hugging to herself the knowledge of perilous compensations.

The whole year passed like that. Martin did not come on leave. He sent word that he was going instead on a tour organised by his evening-class teachers. When recess came she did not go to Nairobi either. She sent word that she was attending a Singer sewing class in Kisumu. She did attend it for as long as she could provide the required materials, but she stayed with Simon of course. He had made an excuse to send his wife and children home for the school holidays, and an aged deaf aunt was staying with him while attending hospital, to save face. Once a fortnight Paulina had spent a night with him, in his house when Martha was away, other times in a friend's house he had fixed, where people coughed and giggled as they walked through to the room prepared for their use. But her hunger was now so great that she could forget the other people as soon as she had taken her place on the bed that was so generously provided for her benefit. If she saw

Martha in the town they passed with a curt greeting. She felt less tired these days and more sure of herself: she was a little fatter and took more care to oil her hair and her skin. It was not surprising that people talked a bit. There was that club member whose husband worked at the Town Hall with Simon. And one communion day the pastor's wife made the long journey to their local church on the back of her husband's bicycle on purpose, it seemed, to bear Paulina off for a little talk on the responsibilities of community leaders and the discipline of Christian marriage which rarely (she said) allowed husband and wife to be together all the time since for progressive, educated people doing work and getting money was a natural preoccupation. But Paulina managed to head her off, discreetly bemoaning the concubine in Nairobi and the jealousies of the less able women in the club. All the same her mother-in-law was aware of the questioning and began to treat her more coldly.

The next Christmas Martin came. He did not let them know beforehand but appeared off the bus on Christmas morning, red-eyed, lean and angry. Rumours had reached him in Nairobi and had been confirmed when by chance he met a brother of the friend who had allowed Simon the use of his bedroom, and the man taunted him with the knowledge. Blows had followed, and then some hours in a police cell, the need for a bribe and the loss of a day's pay. What was worse, Susanna had heard about it and brought some of the Brethren to plead with him that his own behaviour had put Paulina into temptation, and that he should bring her back to Nairobi, forgive and forget. Fauzia had naturally had something to say about this and had stained his treasured suit with greasy dishwater. Though of course he did not divulge these details at home, Martin had loss of dignity to avenge indeed, and felt very sure that he had been patient with his wife's ignorance and infertility. That she should now be so ungrateful as to deceive him was provocation intolerable to any man.

He beat her heavily and kept her home from church. This was not experimental like that long-ago beating in Pumwani: both had matured since then and grown apart, so that he rained down his blows more methodically, she tried to avoid them with the cunning of a now separate and defensible person. She appealed to the headman to testify to her industry and modest behaviour at home, but the headman shook his head, spat and said that it was not his business to interfere in domestic matters. Martin spent Christmas night in a bar while Paulina, bruised, and frightened as she had never yet known fear outside Nairobi, cowered behind a barred door. He then made a round of the homesteads, denouncing her and disowning her. Many of them received the news with a sidelong grin and several husbands assured him that they had had enough of clubs in any case. Before leaving on the bus on Boxing Day afternoon Martin broke two of her chairs and threw the clothes out of her best suitcase and took it away with him. He gave his mother five shillings and took a chicken and a pot of ghee for his wife in Nairobi. He did not mention any children or speak of bringing his Swahili wife home.

4

For three days Paulina stayed quietly in her house. She knew that this time she could not win. She also knew what she wanted. On the Monday after Christmas she reported to her supervisor's office in Kisumu that her husband had assaulted her because he was taking another wife, accused her of infidelity and tried to set the club members against her. She had tried to bear an unsatisfactory marriage for eight years. Now she could bear no more. She would like a transfer to Kisumu where she could live in a municipal house and educated opinion would defend her. She was legally married and could not accept a polygamous arrangement.

The European was sympathetic but not unwary. She did not want any disgrace associated with the clubs. Paulina forestalled her by offering to undergo a pregnancy test. (She had learned a lot coincidentally with the Singer course.) She lived quietly in her mother-in-law's compound, she said. What possible cause could her husband have to malign her if she were not pregnant by another man? The test being satisfactory in a manner of speaking, the supervisor sighed and gave in. The last thing she wanted was a quarrel breaking out in one of her most successful clubs. There was no job available in Kisumu immediately, but a few miles along the Ahero road there was a new centre with a small house available and plans for expansion. She would move Paulina there and instruct her in her new duties at a regular salary.

Paulina had already sent a message to Simon to warn him to keep out of sight. At home she found three balls of crochet cotton, two dresses and a towel missing from her house, but she packed up her other belongings without comment, gave her mother-in-law ten shillings so as to achieve a reasonably dignified exit, and piled up her furniture by the wayside to wait for the bus. There were enough sympathetic hands available to get her away without mishap.

When Martin reached Makadara Fauzia was away. She stayed away for three days and claimed when she returned that if he could spend holidays with his relations she could spend them with hers. She was fed up, she said, with fights and expenses and bad tempers all coming from a place called 'home' when she was doing her best to make a comfortable home for him here on a pittance.

That was enough. He beat her, this time, slowly and methodically, while her plaintive Swahili cries for assistance fell on deaf ears among those who had been taught, like Martin, that true disaster can only proclaim itself in the tribal language. He threw her things piecemeal into the road, which suddenly filled with black-veiled women ready to pick them up and lead away their weeping sister, filling the air with dazzling imprecations meanwhile. The neighbours did not exactly fear the curses but stored up the juiciest for future use.

The landlord came to complain, but this time friends and sympathisers prevented a fight. Martin was glad enough to get away and enlisted the help of the firm's van to take his things to Kibera where a cousin of his, a very junior clerk, had got into desperate financial straits his first Christmas in work and was glad enough to share the house and expenses through the coming lean months.

5

January 1965, the beginning of the second year of freedom, was a time of newness for the country, such newness that for people who could read and write little seemed strange any more. Some were disappointed that big houses and farms did not, as by magic, fall to them, but most were comforted that someone they knew or called kin had met with promotion, land or first-grade housing, and if those people were preoccupied and much away from home that also was part of the new order of things. So for a young woman of twenty-four to move alone to an official house, for her to gather women together and issue programmes to them and buy in stores and collect fees, this also was an acceptable part of the newness. She herself accepted it. Month by month her days grew more full and her home more pleasant – decent is what she would have said – as her regular salary and income from sewing and crochet came in. She had to buy food as she dared not send home to Gem, but at first she did not have many visitors except just for tea, so she could manage on about twelve shillings fifty a week. She soon started a garden but would not expect much from the poor and waterlogged soil. She could not get enough firewood either and often had to buy charcoal.

Though she did not write letters except about work the news filtered through to her mother and Martin's mother and Martin, and people came from home expecting bus fares and blankets as from a big person. The facts of separation were accepted without comment (for after all not everyone can be a teacher and have a house to herself) and Simon began to come regularly, discreetly, so that her routine was tidy and tolerable and she did not often feel lonely. There was that one club trip to Nairobi which she saw afresh with a countrywoman's eyes – parks, Parliament, big shops, not at all the homely Nairobi she had known, though she managed to leave the group for long enough to get in a few visits. She went to call on Amina and Rachel but Rachel had moved away, they told her, and she found that Joyce was already in school, had slimmed down and carried herself gracefully. She spoke Swahili very well. Paulina managed, between compliments to the child, to drop a casual query to Amina.

'Martin is no longer in Makadara then?'

'No, they have moved to Kibera.'

'They?'

'Yes, he and the young man he was sharing a house with. Did he not write to you?'

'I did not know till last week that we were coming here,' muttered Paulina, stretching the truth a bit. She had not known what dormitory they would occupy but the outline of the visit had been arranged for months. 'And I have no time to go to his place of work.'

'With freedom or without freedom, with a job or without a job,' enunciated Amina carefully, 'you are not going to get a baby that way.'

59

Paulina thought it over on the long night journey back, whenever she was not showing the others how to stow their bundles away or find their way to the toilet. Martin could, of course, have taken steps to get his dowry back (he had paid the three cows only, no other instalments) but in fact his threats did not go beyond bluster and the church ceremony was an extra hold on him. His coast woman had still not given him a child and there was still some hope of Paulina's proving fertile, since she had conceived more than once. Her family insisted, too, that he should give her another chance to get a child. Her own mother had visited her and made stern enquiries about the accusations against her, but they were proud of her position and glad that she could sew for them and send a little money, so they did not pursue the matter. She heard nothing from Martin himself but one of his workmates made a formal call whenever he came to Nyamasaria for the weekend.

6

A few days after returning from Nairobi she got a message that her father was seriously ill and she should go home. It did not take long to leave word with the class members, send a note to the office and get ready to go. She had not been home since Independence – since her conscience had clouded – but she knew it would be no different. The home was pre-eminent in the lives of its people and since it had never been subdued it could not, either, be liberated.

The buses were still sparse and she had three-quarters of a mile to walk from the stopping-place. The high banks beside the main road were full of wild flowers, the side paths were familiar, the earth brittle in the dry season, the stalks still not cleared. There were familiar faces, but not so many at mid-morning: school was in session and it would be market day at Luanda. Some women would have made the long trip there. The gap in the hedge that marked the way into the homestead came in sight, but suddenly it seemed, after all, different. A knot of people greeted her quietly – there were far too many for a normal time, but at least they were not crying. He could not have died yet. And she had brought the money for the hospital if need be: it could not so suddenly be time to die.

The difference was that her father was there, dominating all their thoughts, demanding attention as he had never done during his lifetime. It was nearly four years since she had seen him. The homestead was ordinarily a place of women and children. They had their own routines and satisfactions. It was something special when father came – she remembered sometimes preparing a chicken for him, when she was still a girl, or helping her mother smooth the earthen floor into better shape. He had worked, till his retirement the year before, on a sisal plantation beyond Nairobi, in the great bare plain that spread eastward towards the coast. She had never been there, nor had her mother, and she had very little idea of what his work was. Sisal was tricky stuff to handle, could cut your hands to pieces. Her grandfather used to make rope quickly by hand out of the long fibres, looping the knot round his toe. That was a long time ago; she remembered her grandfather's funeral and quickened her step. Father never seemed to make much money out of this tedious work, month after month, with few stories or excitements to tell about when he came on leave. It sounded to be a bleak place, close-built, mean little houses, one shop on the plantation, church services in the rudimentary school-room, now and then a wandering musician to gather the Luo people together, nodding to the song and throwing pennies, or Kambas gathering for their mysterious, exhausting dance, up and down, up and down, up and down, with football whistles endlessly screaming. And out of it they got school fees for a time, uniform, a few clothes, tax money, and the set of chairs which was the pride of her mother's eyes.

Her little sister was running now to greet her, and she could make out her brother from Kisumu, already arrived, leaning against one of the poles that supported the overhanging thatch of the house, and her mother detaching herself from a group of women at the doorway, coming to bid her welcome. She and Martin had once seen her father off at Nairobi Station on his home leave, but he would not come to their house for a meal: he did not want any delay in going from that strange country to his own, and of course there was nowhere they could get him a place to sleep.

Her mother, always small and wiry, was sagging with weariness. Her feet were bare and she set them flatly on the ground, one at a time, like an old woman. Her dress was soiled and the *shuka* tied crosswise on her shoulder gave her the look of other tribes, where the women

61

were more puny and servile than among the Luo.

'How is he, mother?' Paulina asked, as soon as the greetings had been exchanged. 'Has he seen a doctor? Do you want us to take him into Kisumu? What can we do?'

'Oh, you youngsters,' her mother replied quietly, 'you think there is no death, only doctors. There is nothing you can do for him except be near – and stop the people singing over him. They did that yesterday when they thought he was sinking and really it was hard for your brother to make them stop. Poor man, he didn't himself know whether he was alive or not.'

Paulina entered the house and found the sick man lying in the centre of the room where the rope bed had been lifted so that he could see visitors by the shaft of daylight from window and door, rather than lying in the dark and secret recess. He was so thin and shrunken that for a moment she hardly recognised him, thinking back to the grandfather who had been more constantly at home and whose gradual retreat from flesh had not, in childhood, alarmed her. Father had always been straight-shouldered, unbending, laying down the law as far as her recollection of him went. He used perpetually to wear a cloth cap and an old-fashioned shirt like a military uniform. Now to see the sparse white hair uncovered, the skinny shoulders in a tattered singlet that still did not disguise the heavy development of muscle there had been, the thin chest wheezing, was to lament a shaping force of which she had never been much aware before. Perhaps, after all, he had been subdued by his employment and for that reason had kept it a world away from home, so that the home remained intact.

'How are you, father?' she asked, knowing now that the bus fare and the doctor's fee would not be needed.

'As you see me, girl, as you see me. Is it Florence? I can't see very well in this wretched dark house.'

'No, father, I am Paulina – Akelo.'

'Akelo, you have come after a long time.' He spoke with an effort between long pauses. 'And Were – is Were with you?'

'No, father, he has not yet come. From Nairobi it is a long way.'

'But if you can come . . .'

The effort was too much, and he turned aside, coughing.

'Now you must not get tired talking, Baba Akelo,' one of the older

62

women insisted. 'She will come back and see you after she has had some gruel. She has just come from a journey.'

'Ah yes, gruel,' murmured the old man, and hopefully they brought him some, in a mug with a handle as the gourd was too heavy, but he turned aside and left them holding the cup.

Paulina obediently went to drink her gruel in the kitchen hut and to hear the news of the course of the illness. Her older sister, Florence, arrived later in the morning. Her other brother was making a long-distance delivery and had not been contacted yet. All day they drifted in and out of the house, talking softly but each time with less and less risk of disturbing the dying man. About four o'clock a shriek from Paulina's mother, who had been sitting silently beside the bed, alerted them to the other sudden silence. The struggle for breath had ended.

Immediately the house was filled with wailing and voices outside took up the lament till it spread beyond the home itself to the whole neighbourhood. People began to slash and twist branches from the trees and run up and down with them, singing and weeping. Paulina found herself weeping and singing with the rest. Fragments of old praise songs which she thought long forgotten came to her unbidden. She did not understand all the allusions made by the old people, but the pattern was familiar and it gave tongue to what she felt.

People were bringing chairs, stools and benches from all around and arraying them outside the house ready to place inside for the wake as soon as the body had been prepared and arranged. One of the uncles was brandishing a sharpened stick as though it were a real spear and making mock rushes as though to attack bystanders in a frighteningly realistic way: it was easy to believe that in the old days more deaths had resulted from the celebration of one, when armed warriors would campaign to the edge of the district in honour of the name of the lately dead. As soon as it could decently be done, Paulina's brother summoned her and sent her about the purchase of tea and sugar for the crowd from her own money, while he sent out messages for his own wife and other relations to come urgently, mustering all those who would be travelling or could send a verbal message by road transport: he also sent for the nearest market carpenter to come and see about the coffin. An uncle set aside a beast for slaughter next day, as night was already approaching, and, after tedious labour over

63

refreshments in which the neighbouring women shared, Paulina settled herself in a corner of the house for the long night of singing and story-telling in honour of the dead. Her mother was sitting rigidly in the best chair, her cries now stilled, her eyes sunken with weariness, her feet twitching from time to time out of exhaustion, her face a mask of extreme dignity. She was ennobled by her loss in the eyes of all around. It was as though after thirty years in that homestead, seventeen of them in which she reigned supreme, her father-in-law and his wives now dead, her husband constantly away, the decision hers to plant, to harvest, to store, to sell (only once he had renewed the house in that time and arranged about the dowry cattle), she had momentarily become the household head, a person to be consulted and deferred to. Of course she had grown-up sons and so would not need to be inherited by another husband. Soon the sons would be in charge and she would retain just enough of her gardens to support herself and the youngest child as long as support was needed.

Paulina had got used to a regular routine of work and sleep and the obsessive requirements of ritual left her drained and light-headed, even apart from the emptiness of unexpected grief. The next three days and nights were a blur to her: constant cooking and washing of utensils, new visitors arriving with new loud bursts of lamentation and considerable appetites. They made the actual burial the next afternoon, as her other brother managed to arrive in the morning, with his wife, and the hole had been prepared against his arrival and the coffin quickly knocked up. A lay preacher came to lead the service and speeches were made before the grave was filled in. They kept silence, as was customary, so that the dead could recognise – although the box was already screwed down – if any bewitcher was at hand. But witchcraft was powerful in Ukambani, someone murmured afterwards, and none of *those* people was around here. Perhaps they had resented his superior strength, or else resented the withdrawal of it on retirement. After all, he was an elderly man and, as the preacher said, we all come to our time. Only custom has never recognised that time as natural. Perhaps that was why you had to keep watch the customary days, in case death should still be prowling and find you vulnerable, asleep. Or perhaps it was just because no home could find sleeping-mats for so many, or accommodate them without breaking the complex rules of avoidance.

Paulina, her eyes smarting from the now unaccustomed woodsmoke, noticed that her mother, under the guidance of her sisters-in-law, was now wearing a clean dress and had put on over it her husband's favourite shirt. No one now expected her to tear her clothes off in farewell to the body of her husband, as used to be the custom. You took from custom what suited you, and so it had always been. The gap was now being beaten down in the hedge so that the ritual shaving could take place outside, and she knew that some of the younger people would refuse, submit only to a token cutting of the hair. What did it matter? Of course for women, nearly always wearing a scarf, it was easier than for men, but if, obscurely, the sacrifice of her hair would appease her father's spirit, then it was a small price to pay. The saved ones, after all, gave up their beads and plaits and see-through nylon dresses in the name of Jesus: it was not so very different. There was nothing new about the conflict of opinion. When Tuda, in the story, refused to go to South Nyanza to mourn his nephew Dodo, killed by an elephant, on the grounds that in a place where elephants were so dangerous he might get killed as well – and then what would become of the lineage? – the story-teller did not rebuke him. It was conceivably a point of view.

The days passed, the meat was finished, and they killed a few chickens so that the men, at least, could eat and be satisfied. Even the most modern women would not break taboo on such an occasion as this. Her mother did not brew beer and her sisters-in-law had both been away, so they served only tea and gruel instead. Paulina's dress was stiff with sweat – she had brought only one change and there had been little time for washing – her eyes red, her bare scalp prickly against the limp and smoky chiffon of the scarf. Her hands were scraped and sore from the continual breaking of sticks to feed the fire. She was so tired that she was getting people's names mixed up, and the uncles asked perpetually, 'Where is Were? You sent a message? Does he say he is coming?' And she had to say every time, 'There is much work. I think he may not get leave.' Her mother said nothing but looked at her reproachfully, for when a woman's father dies her husband must come and sleep with her at home, when the mourners disperse, to signify his protection and the continuing of the line.

65

So on the fourth evening she told her mother that she must leave next morning, for she had already stayed away longer than she had asked permission for.

'But there are still a lot of people and the sugar has run out again. Who will see to the visitors?'

'I know, mother, but you must see me as a man who has to go back to work. I have no one else to support me, and I have given the customary time. My brothers' wives are not working. They will have to help.'

'And the sugar?'

What supposedly sorrowful guest had been complaining to the widow about sugar at a time like this?

'Mother, I have nothing left that I brought except just the bus fare back to Kano. I will arrange with Tito to send him twenty shillings at the end of the month if he gives you that much sugar. But I have no fields to dig, mother. If these people all come empty-handed they cannot go on for ever being fed.'

'But it would be a shame to my husband if we do not feed them. And some have brought me money or things to eat. However, if your people expect you I cannot stop you going.'

The sisters-in-law were not very pleased, but Paulina and her brother left together on the early morning bus. They were sitting awkwardly, wedged among the baskets of produce, on opposite sides of the aisle, he two rows in front, so that they could not have talked much even if they had not been so stiff and sleepy. Several passengers recognised them and offered condolences, but others, who had started at three in the morning, remained huddled under sacks or old raincoats against the night chill and the weary day ahead.

'You do not think Were will come?' asked her brother, when they climbed out in the early morning bleakness of Kisumu, a few pink wisps of cloud still visible over the western hills.

'I'm sure he won't. You didn't put the announcement on the radio?'

'No, I thought our people would all hear by word of mouth, and the expenses are enough, God knows.'

'He turned me out, after all. He will not feel free to come.'

'Hmm, perhaps not.'

He was still hostile, suspicious.

66

'And you know I have to work, just as you do. The sisters will manage the rest of the guests. I have done what I could.'

'Yes, you worked hard. Virginia thought you had forgotten how to live at home: she was pleased to see you taking part. I will leave her there for a time to keep things in order.'

'She won't be pleased at that.'

'No, she won't, but mother cannot be left alone, and as our first child does not start school till January there is nothing to prevent her staying.'

'Well, enough. I must be getting back. We haven't met for a long time.'

'You know our house in Kisumu. There is nothing to stop you coming there.'

'I will try. And anyone at the Centre can show you where I am. I don't suppose you often get out, but when Daudi is driving he could often stop in.'

'I'll tell him. Now to face the music at the works. I never realised we should miss the old man so much.'

'Yes, we thought he wasn't there but perhaps in a way he was there all the time.'

'Well, we all have our way to make.' And he left her, without tenderness but at least with a limited courtesy. That was one thing about funerals: they made you face up to other people.

7

Then back to the round of too wet and too dry, day in, day out, until well into the second year when, as though by a miracle, her periods stopped and she had difficulty retaining the water and felt a little queasy when it was hot. She wondered whether to go to a doctor, to her mother, to the supervisor. In the end she told nobody. As her figure filled and rounded the men about the place took a little more notice of her, the women found her happier and thought she was beginning to enjoy the fruit of her labours. Her morning sickness was carefully concealed from them and her longings were not remarked on as she generally ate alone.

Nobody ever questioned her about Simon, whom she referred to casually as 'my in-law' if introductions were necessary. Perhaps some of the neighbours thought that he was her husband visiting from Kisumu, but many close to her knew that she was a wife of Gem and did not doubt that she lived alone on account of her childlessness. And some certainly knew Simon through his work or because of kinship, but they said nothing. Even the two saved women in the group were not unkind to her, though they told stories pointedly sometimes of broken marriages miraculously healed and children born after long years of waiting, for her ways were quiet, like theirs, and Simon came and went so inconspicuously that no one was forced to challenge him.

After the third month she began to sew herself looser dresses. Simon was sated these days, and took her quickly and carelessly, and it was not till the end of the fourth month that he asked her and she replied. He was glad, but he told her, and she already knew, that Martha's people would not stand for his taking a second wife and that he himself did not want to get into conflict with Martin – after all, no one could blame him for wanting a fertile wife and he might even wish to claim the child.

They were speaking quietly in bed in the little house. It was hardly ten o'clock and there was still the noise of heavy traffic along the Kisumu road. Paulina had never felt more alert, more detached, more sure of herself. She stepped out of bed and put on a robe and a pair of rubber sandals.

'I thank you for the child, Simon,' she said. 'It is what I wanted. Whatever quarrels may come, no one can doubt that the child is mine. You also have had what you wanted, and there is no need to become involved in my quarrels. A child of mine does not have to look to a father who will not stand up for him. Go now. There will still be buses running. Tell my friend Martha that you were kept late by a workmate wanting to talk in a bar. She has been patient with you. She will not start to make a noise now. Repent towards your blessed in-laws if that will make things better for you. But go, just go now. I have a longing to be alone.'

His eyes showed relief as well as offence. Wordlessly he put his trousers on, checked his pockets and closed the door quietly behind him. She could hardly hear his footsteps as he walked away.

Paulina was now carrying herself heavily, and the ladies she taught at last began to whisper behind their hands. In the sixth month she

68

started attending clinic and the young man from Martin's office stared uneasily when he came at Christmas time. She put in a request for maternity leave to begin in March 1967 but she did not go away. The baby was born in hospital in Kisumu in the middle of the month and she called him Martin, and then Okeyo, after the father who had recently died.

She came home on the second day. 'Home' was the community work house in Kano and soon it was thronged with visitors. After that short absence in which the world was turned upside down for her she looked at it with new eyes. Lying on the metal bed where she had slept alone for the last five months, with the baby beside her in a basket-cot which, defying superstition, she had bought in advance and padded herself, the new mother looked about her with pride and hustled little Margaret Odongo, who had been helping her in the house for more than a year and was now promoted to a canvas bed and a salary of thirty shillings a month, about her multifarious tasks. The cement floor had been swept clean and there was a reed mat in the bedroom. Flowered cotton curtains hung at the windows and a wooden suitcase held the baby's clothes while her own hung in the wardrobe, with the most precious of the cups and plates in a box below. There were two oil lamps and she could hear the clink of mugs being washed on the concrete slab outside. Water was carried from a communal tap – there was no longer the daily trek to the river or to the muddy pools of the rainy season – and ten could be seated, at a pinch, in the sitting-room, though the three-foot table covered with an embroidered cloth would only be used by the most highly honoured visitors. The new sewing-machine, guaranteed to pay for itself in the next year, stood beside the wardrobe.

Paulina lay back and watched the flies buzzing in and out of the open window shutters and a ray of light full of dancing particles striking the end of the bed where a new towel, for handing the baby to visitors, was neatly folded. She had pushed the cot well back out of the glare and a square of net kept the flies off. She was wearing a cotton dressing-gown over one of her old dresses and lay stiffly, sore from the stitches and the heavy bleeding, casting a new eye of ownership on everything around. The customary gifts of meat for the new mother were simmering on a brazier in the outside kitchen. Simon had sent his deaf old aunt to the ward with an envelope containing a hundred shillings. Her brother had brought twenty shillings and a shawl for the baby. He was nearly eight pounds, still red, with damp curls of hair and a piercing cry. Her breasts were beginning to stiffen and he fastened on them fiercely, hurting her. There was nothing she lacked.

Two days later her mother came, having heard the news, bringing her youngest daughter, now in standard three. Both of them fell on the baby, giggling and cackling till he cried. The mother respected the house. She stayed with distant cousins in Kisumu and came out on the bus each morning. She looked bent and old nowadays. Her wrapper was never quite clean. Her shoes were cracked and she needed new ones. The little sister needed a pen for school and Paulina knew she ought to have new blouses too, and promised to make them up later on. She would have kept the child during the school holidays but her mother would not agree, though she did not give any convincing reason. She asked if Martin knew about the baby – if he would come – if Paulina would go to Nairobi – but asked nothing else, as though afraid of her daughter, awed by the neat house and the sewing-machine. But still she was happy that a flood-gate had been opened and Paulina, softened by her joy, was glad to have made her happy and submitted to her blessings, while the little sister stroked the basket-cot, the woven bed-cover, the new soft towels and the cotton napkins.

After a month Paulina returned to her classes and demonstrations. The women were happy for her and she was more respected. If a man occasionally banged or shouted at her door after dark, that was not to be wondered at, and he would soon hear a chilly command to be off. Margaret enjoyed the new dignity of looking after the baby and Paulina was not too far away to breastfeed him regularly and make sure that all the utensils were clean and covered. She took in dressmaking and fitted herself out smartly with the proceeds. Margaret was decently clothed also and the pieces made odds and ends for her little sister and the brothers' children at home. Her life was full, so full that when a young widower from a road haulage company came proposing to set up house with her – he had three-year-old twins, and did not want to leave them with a young wife even if he could afford to marry with dowry again – she shrugged him away without even considering the proposal. Okeyo was still sucking, and she was a married woman with a husband busy in a far-off place.

Two years passed and Paulina's first delight in the new baby sobered into acceptance. She loved him and kept close to him but he did not fill her life. A Luo baby was meant to widen the social circle, not to constitute it. Sometimes, when she had flu in the wet season or had to teach after a sleepless night when the baby was restless, she wondered if there was any end to this way of life.

CHAPTER
FOUR

1

But the world went on, with or without Paulina's attention. In January 1969 Argwings-Kodhek, the Foreign Minister, died in a car crash. She was sad. He was a big man in Gem and she had seen him sometimes when she used to live in Pumwani and he would hold Congress meetings there which Martin and his friends went to. Rumours flew back and forth but she didn't make much sense of them: after all, lots of people die in road accidents. But when the funeral procession came, and of course Martin was one of those following it, it did not make the expected halt for the viewing of the body in Kisumu but drove quickly round the town and out again towards the home place. The townspeople were angry and disappointed. In the homestead in Gem a police burial party fired a salvo of three shots into the air and sounded the Last Post. But though so many Kenya Police and Administration Police had turned up, apparently for that purpose, among the VIPs, local people forced themselves repeatedly through the cordon to get as near as they could to the grave. And as though death needed still to feed on death the very next day someone called Eduardo Mondlane was assassinated in Dar es Salaam. Paulina had never heard of him, but the politicians shook their heads and talked of the loss to Africa. Kenya was a hard enough idea to get hold of. Africa, to Paulina, was a name on a map. But perhaps before she went to Nairobi she would not even have recognised the map.

All year there were political quarrels going on, especially at the coast, and newspaper reports of 'unrest'. The radio in the Centre went on and on about these things until you could not keep them out of your mind. In May Parliament annulled the Affiliation Act. This Paulina noticed ruefully as the end of something that might have been meant to help her, while so many high-sounding pieces of legislation controlled her life without her ever knowing it. Even with the act, it was hard enough to get fathers to take any responsibility for their children outside marriage: those whose wives were working often enough avoided responsibility within marriage. Only a fool would expect voluntary provision. At least Paulina had never had the illusion that anyone was going to help her maintain Okeyo. She could not really see what all this talking in high places had to do with it.

Kano had kept the old hedged homesteads more exactly than the other locations, and also a bigger share of the old plumed head-dresses: teams of male dancers bedecked with feathers and bells and intricate chalk patterns were often to be seen going off to the funerals and other public occasions like the Kisumu Festival. Okeyo used to get excited, chattering and pointing till she restrained him, so that the Kikuyu shopkeeper remarked sombrely, 'He's a real Luo: more keen on a funeral than anything else.'

There were small outings and events. In July 1969 Paulina had to take a group of women to Kisumu to see the annual show on the Saturday, the last day. They kept the hired bus waiting and at midday were only halfway round the sights: it had been difficult to get them together at all after the mock battle in the arena from which some had fled in terror, but once reassured they continued to march round resolutely. And then, after the radio news, a hush fell upon the ground for a moment, and people began to weep and wail and brandish sticks and branches. Tom Mboya, the voice said, had been shot in Nairobi and rushed to hospital in a critical condition. By the time the news came that he was dead they were already being shooed out of the ground.

At the same time Paulina was shepherding her party back to the bus, Martin was sitting in his room at Kibera glued to the radio. His eyes were hot and hard. Nancy dared not speak to him when he was like this. He had promised to take her shopping and there was a pair of shoes she was determined to get out of this month's money. Too bad that a big man was dying, a handsome and powerful man too, but people died on the radio or in the newspapers every day. It was not like anyone you really knew or had a duty to. Nancy was fed up.

She was eighteen, a Pumwani-born girl with a light skin and soft curly hair. Her mother was a Kikuyu. They did not know who her father was. When she was a baby her mother had been moved from Pumwani down to Bahati with the other 'free' Kikuyu. She had a vegetable stall there and grumbled constantly about the closeness of the houses and the harassment, so Nancy started with a determination to get away. She was lucky enough to get a place in high school but had to leave after the first year because she was pregnant. Her mother took the baby and it died soon, but they couldn't afford to pull strings to get her into another school, so she drifted off to live with a school teacher who had promised to get her admission, but he never paid the fees for her and was afraid his headmaster would object to his having so young a girl in his house, so he was trying to push her out. At this point Martin, who knew the teacher through evening classes, was setting up in a new room at Kibera, since the cousin he was staying with was getting urgently married, so the teacher introduced Nancy as his cousin and a bargain was struck.

She liked Martin, who was a bit soft, and kept in reserve the possibility of really marrying him, since there was some mystery about his first wife and they had no children. On the other hand he was quite old now and might not get much more promotion, and people warned her she would be expected to learn Luo and have dozens of babies. And surely, Nancy thought, a pretty girl these days could at least expect a car before being burdened with a big family. Martin was still doling out the housekeeping money at ten shillings a time and going with her to buy a dress or a handbag in case she should be cheated over the quality or add a margin to the price. But today she was really mad at him, sitting there over that radio as though he were going to cry and taking no notice when she pulled her wrapper tighter and made ready to go out.

Three Luo men trooped in. They shook hands, barely speaking, and huddled over the radio also. At last there was a low moan. She was rattling water in a tin basin outside and barely understood who had made the sound but the import was clear. The man had died and they sat there staring at one another like mad things.

'*Wawuok mondi*,' said Martin abruptly, and had to pull himself together to repeat in Swahili the common refrain of the Luo husband, 'We are going out for a bit. This will be a bad day,' he added. 'Do not go out at all. Bolt the doors. If we need beer we will buy it when we come. Do not go out, mind you.'

They filed out without even formal farewells. Their minds were far away. These Nyanza people, she saw, could never pass up a funeral. She would be in for it now – beer drinks, collections, long faces, crowds to feed. 'Not go out' indeed. Who was he to give her orders? What was she in the house – well, after all, what? She had not been asked to be a wife. She had not been asked to be a servant. It was something like 'she can go and give you a hand while you are moving'. She had cooked and washed, scrubbed the floor and warmed his bed. She did not go out visiting with him or put herself forward when his friends came. Well, what future was there in that? A couple of dresses and some strings of beads, that was all she had made out of it. Well, food and beer, true enough, and a few things for the house. But come here, go there, lock up, take care, that was just like being at school. And for more than a year no one had talked about going back to school.

The noise increased outside. There was weeping and wailing in Luo. She knew enough to recognise that, but others were crying also and in a house across the valley a couple of people were shouting.

Nancy made haste. Her dresses, her 'jewellery', her little bit of make-up, her spare slippers were all bundled into one of the sheets. They had bought the sheets to use together, after all. And the cloths? She would surely be justified in taking one of each kind. And the money for market tomorrow? She would need that, of course, for the bus fare to get to her mother's. She wanted to be fair. She bolted the back door and slammed the front door Yale lock. He would have a key, surely? If not, he would have to break a window. Let no one say she had left the house unguarded. He had not treated her badly. But a Luo was a Luo and herself she was a new Kenyan.

Nancy walked down the road. Cries and shouts seemed to come from all round her. She pushed her way to the main road. It was still thronged with people. She stood at the bus-stop and someone told her it was no use waiting for the buses would not be able to get through. Not able? Did one death make all that difference? She could not understand it, but there was no going back to the locked room so she allowed herself to be carried along with the crowd. By the time they got to the mortuary it was impossible to move. All the hospital roads were blocked. She glimpsed one of Martin's friends on the far side but he could not even see her. Her big bundle was ripped open against a fence. The sandals fell out and it was impossible to recover them under the trampling feet. She would be knocked breathless before she could reach her mother's place, and it was four months since she had visited her mother. Who could say whether she might have moved? Where else was there to go?

In the crowd she spotted one of the boys she had known at school. He must have finished form four by now and looked very smart, as though he were working.

'Hi, Peter,' she called.

'Hi, Nancy, you're looking super. A bit of a crush here, isn't there? Where are you heading for?'

'Just back from safari. I'm trying to get to my mother's in Bahati, but it's a struggle and I don't know that she will expect me in all this.'

'Sure she won't. You know my brother's place is not far from here. Why don't we put your things there and then decide what to do? It looks as though your bundle is getting torn already.'

'That's a good idea. I'm not working at the moment so I'm quite free really . . .'

The house was full of boys and girls and Nancy felt immediately at home.

Martin reached home about eleven o'clock that night. He had had a few drinks with friends here and there and some roast meat but what he had gone out for – to find what had happened, what had been found out, what was to be done – still baffled him. The young men had started out together in need of solidarity in their grievous loss but neither hope nor enlightenment had come to them. He remembered meeting Tom at a students' fund-raising meeting once and Tom had said, 'Oh yes, I've seen you passing Alvi House. You work near there, don't you?'

Tom was always like that – never forgot a face, never at a loss for a kind word. Oh, bugger it all.

He had his key all right and opened it on a dark house. She should have put the lamp out with matches even if she'd gone to bed in a sulk. She didn't wake when he called and when he felt the bed it was empty.

76

Fool of a girl. Just as likely to get herself assaulted in all this crush. But when he groped in the cooking-recess for the lamp and lit it after wasting half a dozen matches, he could see clearly that she had gone – dresses, shoes, everything. Well, no loss. He ran perfunctorily through the cupboard – his things were safe anyway. She wasn't going to set up another man with his shirts and shaving tackle. The shelf of cups and pots was not stripped either. The radio was in place and so was the charcoal iron. If anything had gone it was nothing out of reason. The Alego girl who had been so eager to marry him had had everything packed up when his cousin came home and found her getting ready to leave. This time he would cut his losses.

He fell into bed in his underclothes and extinguished the lamp. He felt nothing for Nancy. She was better gone. He was too old and cynical for a kid like that and it didn't look as though he would ever have luck with women. Right now he didn't feel like it anyway. Thirteen years since he got married. A wife of thirteen years' standing should have been well trained and able to comfort him now. Out of those years, half he had hoped and prayed for freedom – no, not for freedom, *Uhuru*, which everyone knew in Swahili, but for *loch*, self-government, something he understood. Whether or not there had been what people meant by *Uhuru*, for six years there had undoubtedly been *loch*. And was this what it had come to, the striking down of the best and the brightest?

2

Nancy didn't leave enough of herself behind for Martin particularly to miss or resent her, but she had left a mirror, a little framed one which could be hooked on the wall, and he noticed this and examined his face during one of his thrice-weekly shaves. In fact it was the first time since the assassination he had felt steady enough to do it himself. There was always a fair-weather barber under a tree to do it for you if you didn't feel up to it.

Although his paunch had grown a little, Martin's face was thinner than it had been when he was a young man, though not much lined. Still the basic convexity of the Luo features remained. His eyes were a bit bloodshot – he had needed to keep half in a stupor to get through those days at all. His hairline was receding slightly. He was thirty-six,

77

three years younger than Tom had been, and what had he achieved? The household was plain but decent. He could provide bedding and dishes for several guests. His library had expanded from the left-over school books to a neat row of professional texts and Kenyan documents. He knew how to use the resources of the town for what he wanted – a reference book, a haircut, a likely pick-up or a chance to observe the top people. He did not see himself as maturing but as deprived of the chance of maturity, a childless man who could not keep a wife, whose house at home was shamed and whose house in town could never be home. He had long since ceased to wear the silver-gilt wedding ring he had assumed that day at St John's, Pumwani. It could provoke too many questions.

But he was growing all the same. He had adjusted from a vision of freedom in which the figure of a mythical leader, released from prison, hovered distant and glorious like the queen, to an actual country in which shops and houses changed hands, the wage structure remained very much the same, and the man you addressed as 'sir' haggled just as before over discounts and overtime. He found himself correcting even foreign customers about the size of envelopes and index cards. Greatly daring, he found that he could enjoy a film better in the comfort of the Kenya Cinema than in Starehe Hall, and that the extra few shillings earned him command of the luxurious foyer and the darkness in which dreams come true. He actually went to a bedroom in the New Stanley Hotel, high up, helping a salesman to hump his bag of samples, and had a drink there, ordered imperiously by phone. On good days he could even remind himself that there were big people in the country who were still bachelors, so he need not be so worried.

In one way working relationships were changing. Asian customers started speaking to you differently, 'Bwana' or 'my friend' instead of 'you there', and some unnecessary handshakes. But working hours did not get any shorter and excuses were not tolerated for lateness or slacking off at work, though a little more leniency than before might be shown for attending funerals or school interviews. Births and weddings hardly came up on the list of special requests – one might have thought that birth and marriage would take on more significance now that everyone was born a Kenyan but somehow it was not so. People had once been underdogs on a communal basis but now if you were an underdog it was somehow your own fault. Martin was glad he had realised it in time.

Tom had realised it too. Tom was a person who fitted fully and easily into that new world and yet could still express his ideas in Luo or Swahili with equal fluency. Tom remembered people's names and remembered their natural hopes and fears. He didn't make a virtue out of parading round in leopard skins; he knew there was nothing shameful about cutting sisal or inspecting drains. He knew the risk: since Pio Gama Pinto's death, if not before, he could not fail to have it always in sight. But now he was dead, and who knew how to get things done any more?

It took a long time to arrange about his funeral, and still no one knew what had really happened. In the meantime Miriam Wandai, that shrewd and saintly old maid whom Paulina had known as a Nairobi neighbour, had died and was to be buried at a brother's home the same day that was finally fixed for Tom's funeral. Paulina heard this from the Brethren, but all eyes were turned to Rusinga Island and the great ceremony to take place there, so few people found time to ask why Miriam was not being laid to rest in Butere churchyard and near the schoolhouse which bore her pioneer name.

From mid-morning Paulina and her neighbours waited by the roadside and no news came. Okeyo was happy with a new shirt and kept them amused playing with a cardboard trolley one of the schoolboys had made him. The expected cortège did not appear from Nairobi. Probably a lot of people wanted to stop and touch it. The sun grew hot and people went back to their homes for umbrellas and scarves and water-bottles. It was rumoured that the widow's car had had an accident in the Rift Valley and that delayed them, but no one knew where the rumour (which turned out to be true) came from as no loudspeaker van was sent to give news. Eventually, late in the afternoon, the cavalcade came into sight and the people at the roadside made their show of mourning, but the cars hurried past without acknowledging their salutes. In Kisumu there had been trouble, passing drivers later told them, so they shut themselves in their houses without waiting for the procession to make the long sweep back to the Lake shore.

But Okeyo was lively and full of new words and games he had

learned, so that Paulina could not bring herself to feel sad, and though she remembered how much Martin had admired Tom Mboyo she had her own life to live now and could not assume the guise of mourning. Months passed the more quickly as in each the child learned a new skill, until October came.

Martin did not go for the funeral to Rusinga Island. There ·vas a man from South Nyanza in the same company who obviously had the greater right to claim leave – as Martin had claimed his for Argwings's burial. And, after all, what would the big funeral do? The ceremony was to keep the spirit at peace and bring blessing to the home place. But Tom was at home everywhere, and the spirit was not at peace. Martin heard later how the cortège was held up by an accident and people had waited for hours in the hot sun without getting news. And then they had been beaten back with batons from trying to touch the hearse, and when some local fight had broken out in Kisumu tear-gas had been used, as though people were being punished for their reverence. And yet even the gas had broken down barriers, for people had crowded in anywhere, even to Asian houses, and had been given water to drink and reassurance that the congestion of nose and throat would pass, and it could be seen that the discomfort was the same for white or black, KANU or KPU.

3

With Nancy gone the room in Kibera seemed cheerless and inconvenient for housekeeping after a long journey from town. Everywhere Martin looked seemed cheerless too, Luo faces blank with dismay, the newspaper columns full of the trial of Njenga which seemed to get no nearer to the mystery of the murder, while Njenga himself smiled loftily through it all, like some half-activated idol.

It was Amina who actually brought to a head Martin's decision to move again. He met her one lunch-hour searching for dress materials in River Road and she greeted him mockingly:

'Oh, Bwana Mkubwa, do you still remember staying in my little house? You were a slim boy then and Paulina was just a slip of a girl. Now you have a big tummy and a full purse, I bet.'

'Too big a one for the purse to fill, in fact. But I don't know that I've been more at home anywhere since I left your house.'

'Well, everything moves on. I'm down at Eastleigh myself now and Joyce is a big girl in standard five. Why don't you bring Paulina to see me?'

She knew very well why not, but there was no harm in prodding a little.

'Paulina's working near Kisumu. She doesn't get down here often.'

'Well, we must go where the money is. And number two?'

'There isn't any number two, my elder sister. We are Christians, you know.'

'Even so, I thought there was a pretty little coast girl persuaded you otherwise.'

'Oh no. That was long ago, and she was not pretty enough to break a law for.'

'Well, well. All the better for Paulina. You don't feel like taking board and lodging with us while you're all on your lonesome, I suppose? Nice rooms, furnished, water laid on.'

'That would be a bit beyond me, I expect, Amina. In any case I must have my own kitchen, in case . . . for when . . . well, you know what I mean. But I wouldn't mind getting back to Eastleigh. The bus service is better, shopping easier. I suppose you wouldn't know of a room?'

Amina promised to call at the shop next day and by the end of the month it was all settled. She didn't exactly get anything out of it but she enjoyed pulling strings and getting to know other people's business.

By this time man had actually landed on the moon. The landing took place ten days after Tom's funeral and few Kenyans had any thoughts to spare for it, although President Nixon declared, in a record that was soon selling cheap in Nairobi's supermarkets, that eyes and hearts all over the world were directed to that spectacular feat. Perhaps he was already more nearly tuned into the launching pad than to minds and hearts. A lot of the world still saw the USA as a land of gadgetry where you could watch a president's assassination on TV without being able to do anything about it. A week later the papers were reporting the death of Mary Jo Kopechne in Edward Kennedy's car.

At home, preparations for the election continued. People were asking about conditions under which the new system of 'primary elections' would be conducted. Commentator after commentator advised a political stocktaking, pressed the public (like Philip Ochieng' in the *Sunday Nation* of 20 July, which Martin certainly read from cover to cover and Paulina absorbed in a different way, for skins were becoming very thin in Kenya just then, very sensitive, reacting to hints and radiations that would have needed blunt statement to penetrate the protective grease and red ochre of custom) to 'face squarely the real problems of tribalism, corruption and economics – problems whose very existence it needs the brilliance and candour of a Tom Mboya to gloss over successfully'. And over it all hung the grotesque figure of Njenga, grinning in the dock like a cartoon character and spared the one question which would have made sense of the trial.

4

Paulina waited patiently by the roadside. Okeyo did not often have her to himself. He tugged at her hand, laughing and chattering. In spite of the restricted life she had grown up to expect, she found Kano dull after living in Nairobi where there was always news, always something you could walk out and see on a Sunday afternoon. Here it was the same group of classes, day in, day out, the same orders to the child ayah, day in, day out, and although her little son had taken away her reproach, he was a burden on her alone, and she sometimes wondered for how many years he could go on till he realised that he had no father, and although the father-figure of Martin hovered in the background he did not come, would not come.

So on a sunny Saturday afternoon just to stand by the roadside and wait for the procession was a kind of relaxation. The Mzee had long promised to come to Kisumu. This time he had come for the purpose of opening the new hospital, and some of the hope she had had in those young days in Nairobi was coming back again. After all this time the future was for everyone, and her child had been born in a country that stood up for itself.

The noise came down the highway from the far distance, the noise of many cars and lorries and something like drums. How could they be beating drums without singing or instruments in accompaniment?

82

The first lorries came into sight, full of figures in strange masks. Perhaps it was meant to amuse, but it looked frightening. Some of the children cried, but Okeyo was jumping up and down with excitement. The road was long and straight. Many people had gone into Kisumu for the celebrations. Only a few of the bitter ones had remained indoors. So there was a straggle of spectators, not continuous but bunched near any roadside building. As the lorries came into sight, Paulina and her companions saw the knot of people on the horizon break and run. Perhaps someone had used rude words there or tried to get too close for safety as they had done when Tom's body passed for burial. It seemed natural enough that something like this should happen. As the lorries with uniformed men passed, car after car followed, full of people in ordinary clothes, and guns pointed from the windows and from time to time a stammer of shot came from the motorcade as it dragged on, and the people backed, but few ran away, assuming this to be some harmless demonstration. Okeyo was still bouncing in delight, crying 'Bang, bang – bang, bang', and then suddenly he had slipped out of her hand and was running forward. Clumsy, not used to being in charge of the child herself, she dived forward, but before she could get hold of him he fell at her feet, blood oozing from a hole in his forehead. She snatched him up and began to run, heedless of the noise behind. A door of the schoolhouse was open and she dashed in after the others, who stood round her in a respectful group, silent.

'Get a doctor,' she shouted. 'Don't just stand there. Help me to get him to hospital.'

'Mother,' the oldest man in the group plucked up courage to say to her, 'mother, don't you see the child has no need of a doctor? He is dead.'

'But it is a very little wound. Hardly any blood.' Yet as she looked she knew that it was true and began to wail loudly, rocking the baby in her arms as others took up the lamentation.

'Mother,' said the old man again, 'No one will be going to the hospital today. From the hospital this thing started. In Kano we shall treat our wounded and bury our dead. Do not think you are alone.'

For an hour they continued to mourn, almost unconscious of the hubbub left at the roadside, the shouts and groans, the frenzied search for someone out of sight, the rustle of dispersion, the final silence. Cattle were hastily stalled that day, some left unmilked. Sermons that should have been prepared that evening burst out next day as frenzied intercessions. Homework that should have been marked that weekend was caught up in a frantic expurging of comment or question. By Monday morning the quietness of routine beggared belief. According to the Luo expression, the country had eaten its people. At last.

'We must go to our homes,' the old man said. 'If they find us here after dark there will be trouble. I have been in the military in the old days and I know. The neighbours will not leave you alone, mother, but we who live at a distance must go.'

With two old women he accompanied Paulina to her house and the women made tea while the others dispersed silently. The old man's face was deeply lined. It was as though the skin had not so much sagged over the retreating flesh as been taken in, sewn and cross-stiched like the seat of a boy's shorts which the tailor has mended, thrusting his machine back and forth to reinforce the patch bulging underneath. Every wrinkle was impressed on Paulina's eyes as she recognised in the lines of experience and pain and kindness the truth of her son's death. As they helped her into the house she glimpsed her own face in the mirror, staring now with grief but basically as smooth and unlined as Okeyo's own, and wondering how much more one has to take, how many more years, how many desertions and deaths, before it could show and command respect. And as she fingered Okeyo's face and clutched at his body, she saw that this too was calm and unused. The puckered skin of healed cuts, the bulge of a remembered burn, were not in him. Except for the little wound he was perfect, and that one would never go through the straining together of a healed wound. He would go to the earth, like herself, unperpetuated and unfulfilled.

5

They heard no more that night but next morning, sure enough, loudspeaker vans came to tell them that a dusk to dawn curfew was in force. One neighbour had had two fingers shot off and a quarter of a mile up the road there was another house of mourning. They had no idea how many others there were in Nyalenda and Kisumu town, for people who came and went on duty did not speak of these things or show any emotion. Inside the house they began to discuss the funeral.

Most of the neighbours knew, wordlessly, that the child was not Martin's and there would be no burial plot in Gem for him. She could go to her own home, but her father was dead and her elder brother, though often in Kisumu, was even more often away with one of the transport lorries. Who would pay the expense of the funeral? To hire a lorry, even if the money could be found, was to draw attention to oneself. To stay away for the night was to break curfew. They talked and talked to her. It is only a child. It does not matter where a child is buried.

'It is like a war,' said the old man. 'We left our dead in Ethiopia and in Burma. We had to. So no harm will come of it.'

A corner of a public plot was found and prayers hastily said. No one sat up for the wake. Curfew was in force. On Tuesday Paulina returned, stony-faced, to work. No one spoke of these things. The women did not come to class in large numbers and even the market was visited only for essential supplies, not for sociable gatherings. Only an irrepressible youngster, living with his uncle in Kisumu town on schooldays, brought home the story of how one of his schoolmates had burst a milk-packet blown up with air at Kibuye market on the Sunday morning and the market had emptied to the sound.

Okeyo was dead. She sent Margaret back to her people, giving her the bus-fare, careless of what might happen to her on the way. She gave away Okeyo's clothes: she would not need them again. Perhaps his death was a punishment for being born out of wedlock. She brooded over it alone. There was no good discussing it. All around her babies were being born out of wedlock and legitimate babies were dying. She continued to wear Martin's ring, remembering again and again that quiet ceremony at St John's Church where he had confirmed their marriage and put it on her finger. And yet even that time she had lost the baby. Everything was topsy-turvy. At her father's funeral, she remembered, the oldest uncle had been concerned about the breaking of the roof-pole, to show that the house was now without a head. They had decided to leave it because they could not find any young boys who knew the role they should play in the ceremony. But now in the empty house there was, so often, no lack of children, and the house of promise remained empty. Would it, after all, have been different if Martin had come for that funeral, to fulfil her rights? And yet, if Okeyo had been his son, would he not still have died?

Martin did not go to Kisumu for the opening of the hospital, for he was at work, and public events were often cancelled or delegated, so that you did not risk losing work-time on them, and when he heard about the curfew and the shootings and the detentions he felt that he had always known about it, though he had never heard a gun fired in anger, only those painful, empty shots over Argwings's grave. It was four days before he heard about the death of Paulina's son, and then he thought that if he had brought her back to Nairobi with the child it would not have happened. But he said nothing. And he did not go for the elections or for Christmas, for what comfort could he bring to his parents when after all these years he no longer had even the pretence of a child to care for their old age?

A break came in December when the Kisumu curfew was shortened by two hours and the new elections were patching over the gaps in the ranks. One of Paulina's friends introduced her to a top bank official who was going to Nairobi on promotion and needed someone with experience to look after the house and children. Paulina was glad to go. Although domestic work might be a step down in status it would be a break from the deadly monotony of Kano. She would get a glimpse of the 'Upper Hill' end of Nairobi life and perhaps a chance to visit old friends too. She travelled by OTC the same day the Okelos were going by car and the mother picked her up from the bus station. Already, driving through unknown streets for unimaginable distances, she was sinking into the blessed anonymity of the big city.

She sorted linen into drawers as though born to it, mastered the working of the stove, conjured up supper for the children out of tins, while their parents, exhausted by the shift in status as well as place, went to eat in a hotel. There was a room for her built in the garden, left a bit greasy by the previous occupant but still sound, cleanable and private compared with the old Pumwani room. She felt at home at once. Okeyo belonged to the past. He had never had a home. He had no nickname to identify him with family and clan. Perhaps she had never had a right to him, after all – it seemed so natural to be alone.

That talent for order which Martin had hoped to cultivate in her as a wife would serve as well for the job of housekeeper.

In the daytime, when the Okelos were out at work, servants from the neighbouring houses would come to pass the time of day. The Luo people asked only general questions, names and places. None of them referred to recent events or the curfew. Other people, asking, unspecifically, 'How is Kisumu?' would relate the necessary answer, 'Well, but not very well', to the detention of Jaramogi or to Tom's death, all those months ago. They didn't seem concerned at the little news they had received about the curfew and the shootings and she locked these things away in her heart.

6

Paulina never knew who in Nairobi could have heard of her move, but on the second Sunday Martin appeared at the little house, neat, polite and distant, like someone sent with a message. She could not spend long with him as the children were to be taken to tea in a neighbour's house, but he expressed formal regret for the death of the child and asked for news of family and friends. For the first time she was able to express to somebody in words the numbness of Nyanza after the shock that had burst upon it that Saturday, the indignity of the curfew, the hardly believable acceptance of death, the terrible silences. Martin had lost weight, his cheeks were hollow, his eyes deep and staring. He told her he had not been home. There seemed no point in it.

'We can't do anything,' he kept saying, 'we can't do anything.' He shook hands and promised to come again. He had left Kibera and got a room in Eastleigh, but he still worked for the same company, as outside salesman now, which got him a few extras and more chance to see the world than the man at the counter.

'I did not think,' he said, 'when I first brought you to Nairobi, that there would ever be a time you would feel safer here than at home.'

'I can make a home here now that I am alone,' she said practically. 'I like the people. There is plenty to do.'

But he shook his head, murmuring that only Gem was home, which seemed odd, since she could have no welcome if she went back there. She had to bring the children back from the tea party and get them

87

ready for bed, so there was no time to brood on it.

She often slept in a corner of the children's room if their parents were going to be out late, and sometimes she made extra reasons to sleep there when men banged on her door in the night and troubled her. She always told them to go away because she was not allowed to receive visitors, and for the time being did not find it hard to do so. The child's death left her hyperconscious of sin and Martin's nearness reminded her that she had not been the first to break faith. She did not ask him about the coast girl.

The months passed. The elections and the curfew were forgotten. Jaramogi, in detention, was not spoken of. But Tom's death, the previous year, was always remembered, and his photograph still appeared in shop windows and picture-framing booths. The papers said that Njenga had been hanged for the murder, though somehow, amid all the other alarms, the fact had not reached the news at the time. But no one took any account of Njenga, for the circumstances of the murder remained as hidden as they had been that final Saturday, when Kisumu Show closed down and Okeyo had been a dancing little boy, not understanding why grown-ups glued their ears to the radio, and there had been another day when they lined up by the roadside to watch the hearse pass and yet he came back unharmed and demanded meat for his supper and astonished everyone by his cleverness. It was better not to remember.

Paulina seldom got the whole day off to brood over things, but she sometimes found her way to church at St Stephen's or St John's and discovered that some of her Brethren friends were living in smart new flats and driving cars. In the old Pumwani streets there were not many people she knew now – a few of the shopkeepers, the younger of the landladies. Amina had moved. She had a house in Eastleigh, people said, and took in boarders, which was more profitable than just letting the rooms. She had got big ideas since taking in the coloured child but the rest of the women were not too hard on her for that. They agreed that Pumwani was not a good place to bring a girl up in and that Amina had done well for herself. The girl had been sent away to boarding school, where she told people that her mother had had a white husband who was killed in the Emergency.

The months came and went, cleaning, washing, minding children.

That other rocket had nearly burned out on a trip to the moon, but people were blasé about it, counting another world already colonised, the spectacular risk of those few men in space hardly commanding a prayer meeting or a special edition. From Gem there came constant news of death – not suspicious, exactly, but as though ill-omened. The Okelos discussed the news with relish and attended services where appropriate but did not let it distract them from the steady social climb. These days death announcements took up longer and longer radio time, so that people from all over the country were expected to forgather, and time was left for them to do so, except when the successive cholera scares, from 1971 on, put a temporary halt to the practice. The expense of Paulina's father's funeral looked negligible beside the new demands. The Asian habit of inserting photographs with the death and *in memoriam* notices was beginning to spread to other communities, so that it became from year to year a bigger burden on the bereaved and a secure comfort to the press through the years of rising paper and printing costs.

Early in 1971 Jaramogi was released from detention. It did not make a very big headline, but every Luo heart was the lighter for it, though he looked old and ill. There was talk of offering him a Parliamentary seat at the coast if Nyanza politicians did not vacate one for him, but it all came to nothing, as it had for an earlier detainee from Sakwa. Martin never let anyone forget it.

The Zanzibar plot was very much in the news and Uganda in a state of flux. Suddenly on Madaraka Day it was announced that nine men of different tribes and professions had pleaded guilty to plotting to overthrow the government. For a week the hearings and confessions in the Sedition Trial continued to dominate the news. By the time of the nationwide loyalty rally at the end of June, for which people travelled from all over the country, weapons were forbidden and refreshment rooms requested to provide a 24-hour service, the 'sedition' shock was over.

Paulina knew about the trial because radios up and down the road carried the news and everyone was talking about it, but it would not have occurred to her to go to the rally and the Okelos did not go either. Martin went and reported that he had never been so squeezed, deafened and generally shoved about in his life. He was not happy or sad or excited or disappointed but only reassured: everything was going to stay the same. On 4 July the Chief Justice made his loyalty pledge. The reporting was in so low a key that Paulina would not even have noticed his leaving office three days later if Martin had not pointed it out to her.

Martin always knew about the whispers. Whispers of a ruby mine, whispers of oil in Northern Province, whispers of Obote, with a big price on his head, being openly seen in Dar es Salaam – that same Obote whom one used to run into in Pumwani Memorial Hall. Whispers of hidden violence in Uganda – whispers, whispers, whispers.

It gave him something to talk about when he came to see Paulina, since they were not very free with family news. His mother died at the end of 1971 but he never suggested that Paulina should go to the funeral. Much as she liked the old lady, Paulina accepted exclusion, knowing that she had not fulfilled a daughter-in-law's duty. Martin was decorous, not particularly shaken by his mourning. There was nothing monstrous or untimely about the death. Paulina dared not ask him whether the little square house was in good repair, who slept there now and kept her gardens. One of the little sisters was a nurse and still single. The other had left school early and married in Uyoma. She supposed that nephews must have been brought in, all these years, to fetch firewood and water and do the herding. She had kept her mind away from it. Here no one brought her maize to grind and she cooked daily with the insipid white flour out of packets. Some days she finished work too late to feel like cooking, and so she kept a loaf of bread in the cupboard, like a European. But the regular, dull work kept in control the feelings surging inside, just as Nairobi kept going with its surface chatter and safari rally cars charging about at the very time that, if the confessions in the Sedition Trial were to be believed, a violent plot was simmering just below the surface.

Paulina sometimes got a ride into town if the children wanted to go shopping with their mother on a Saturday and marvelled at the new buildings and the sophistication of the city centre. There was something of the same excitement now that she had felt fifteen years before on seeing the city for the first time – the pleasant sunshine, the continuous change of spectacle, the bustle and the hard-learned possibility of belonging. Only what was gone was the hopefulness of a first start. There might be a new start, but the gush of feeling and the certainty of birth would never come again.

7

The days passed. Mrs Okelo, who complained bitterly that her boss would sometimes keep her twenty minutes late finishing the letters, and always on a day when they had to go to a party and it would take her three-quarters of an hour to get ready (not that she enjoyed parties, she insisted, but for the sake of her husband's career they must go), never seemed to be aware that time existed for other people. Even when Paulina had gone to her room after giving the children their supper and tidying up after them, she would call her back with instructions for the next day, a shopping list or a search for something that had been too safely put away. In the mornings – especially the crotchety mornings following the parties – Paulina might have to call the parents when the cook had breakfast ready, ferret out the green shoes to go with the green dress and remind about the milk money, as well as getting the children ready for school and nursery. She noted all this as inefficiency but did not resent it – what else, after all, would she do with her time? Even when she had been promised a free afternoon because the family were going on a visit, she often enough found herself left with the little one because he was too sleepy or cross to go. But the time left was enough for her scanty personal life, and she enjoyed taking the children out to tea and having a chance to compare notes with the other ayahs from Indian and European houses. She never told them she had had a child herself. It helped her not to remember too much.

One day she had requested a Sunday afternoon off to visit the wife of the next-door house servant in the Maternity Hospital. The visit was not cheering. The young mother had lost a lot of blood and had to share a bed with a very fat woman. She looked drained and miserable. Within a week she would probably have to go back to her mother-in-law, since the employer had already made it clear that she would not tolerate the noise of babies crying, and Nyambura had reason not to like leaving Mwangi on his own.

Paulina walked out of the hospital into the blazing sun. The wards

91

had been greatly extended since her Pumwani days and the young midwives had all the self-possession of the modern girl, clicking through the corridors in shiny shoes and with buoyant hair burying their vestigial nursing caps. She turned to catch the bus back to town and came face to face with Amina, her old landlady, now aged with dignity, still voluminously clad in gay cotton, her cheeks a little pinched, her eyes duller than of old, but still quick to recognise, seize, commandeer. Paulina felt herself firmly held by the arm while lengthy farewells to the other Moslem women were completed, then steered towards Section Three.

She protested mildly – she must be back for the children's suppertime – but was glad to meet a friend in such hearty flesh and substance, adding reality to her own tentative hold on life, and so obediently she went along. She followed Amina upstairs above a grocery shop in one of the old Eastleigh streets. The stairs were grimy but the sitting-room, which they entered through a Yale door, was bright and clean, with yellow and red lino on the floor, a sofa set with elaborate embroidered cloths, a fringed tablecloth, a chiming clock and a radio playing at full blast. The young girl lounging in the armchair beside the radio could only be Joyce, though she looked more than her twelve years or so – a hefty young person with gingery hair tied back on her shoulders with a scarf, a long nose, a small mouth and a smile that did not go very deep. She entered politely into the greetings and exchange of news, speaking perfect Swahili but with a mannerism quite different from her mother's.

Paulina did not mean to talk about the baby or about Nyanza at all but Amina's way was at once so compelling and so sympathetic that it all came out, except Okeyo's parentage, of course, which was none of Amina's business but which it was, all the same, likely she would know about already – as indeed she did. Amina was direct in her sympathy – 'See how long I had to wait before I got this one, but you at least have the assurance that you can have another.' – but it was Joyce who surprised her. Tears welled out of her and ran unheeded down on to the expensive stuff of the new armchairs. When she escorted Paulina back to the bus-stop she pressed upon her a tray-cloth she had embroidered at school.

'I want you to remember that there is a child who cares for you,' she said simply.

'I am grateful,' answered Paulina, just as simply, 'and I should like you to remember that I loved carrying you when you were a baby and I did not seem able to have one of my own.'

On the way home Paulina realised – or would have realised, if the thought had not come to her as an intrusion to be speedily repressed – that she had lost the habit of speaking to people. She passed the time of day with servants along the road, enquiring into their household routines and how they were treated. A few of Mrs Okelo's visitors greeted her civilly – she always dreaded that they would know too much of the past. There was a young widow working at the grocery store with whom she would occasionally go to church or shopping if their free times corresponded. But there was no one to whom she would pour out her sorrows and questions as she once had to Rachel or Susanna. There was so much she wished to hide and so little she wished to know, though some kinds of knowledge obtruded upon her.

Her little sister came one school holiday, and by manipulating times and sometimes getting permission to take the Okelo children too she managed to show her Parliament Building, the Post Office, the park, very much as she had shown the club women long ago. And out of her private memories she showed her the museum too, and the open shop doors where young men work at mending carpets in rich colours without leaving a trace of needle or thread, the milliary stone where you could measure your distance from Bahoya in Australia, or the Pyramids of Egypt or the Pope in Rome. But she did not really talk to the sister, only exhort her to study more and help her mother at home. And she did not really talk to the Brethren either: she could not repent of having Okeyo, and she could not repine at staying alone if that was the price of having had him. She chatted in the re-echoing phrases she had grown up with or the more discursive Swahili of the town – 'So you are planting cabbages, are you?', 'Vegetables have got dearer again', 'A la, who would have thought it?' – but no strength went out of her in real converse. She had none to spare.

CHAPTER
FIVE

1

At the end of 1975 the Okelos went to Mombasa on another transfer and talked about taking Paulina with them, but she was in two minds about whether to go. She knew nobody there and feared that in a strange town she would be even more tied by 24-hour-a-day duties. Martin was visiting her regularly now and she felt that to move with the family would confirm her position as a house-servant for the rest of her days. The cook had long since been dismissed and more and more duties fell to her.

It then appeared that the European family the Okelos were replacing had requested them to take over the house-servant as well as the furniture. Nobody enquired whether the man in question was enthusiastic, and Paulina thought he had better reconsider how urgently he needed his job if he supposed he was going to dragoon this family into keeping the same hours and recipes he was used to. But it was hinted that she might prefer to look elsewhere, and as the older children were being sent to boarding-school – it was feared that another move to a hot climate might interfere with their education – and the youngest no longer required close attention, her ties with the family were weakening in any case.

Paulina hesitated. She had been home to visit her mother only once in the four years since she had escaped to Nairobi and it had not been an easy time. People made up to her because of her good clothes and the expectation of gifts, but they sneered behind their hands, she thought, at her childless state and broken marriage. On the bumpy journey down to Kisumu, two old men on the bus – one a retired policeman she remembered with terror from her schooldays, when his uniform and massively protruding teeth were always held up as a threat to the young, the other a small shopkeeper from the local market – discoursed loudly to one another on the blessing of children and the miraculous fertility of their sons' wives. True, not all the progeny were alive, but the Good Lord knew when enough was enough, and so natural deaths were not to be feared like the bringing of someone purposely into a danger zone.

Paulina had shrunk in her seat, the weird rock forms she gazed at through the window now uncanny and repellent where once they had been familiar and amusing. She burned with the knowledge that her uncle had been fined for not digging a pit latrine even after the second cholera scare and that she had caught her own niece going through her handbag. The bats had kept her awake and her sisters-in-law had spotted her aversion to the unwashed gourd in which porridge was offered. And she had no home of her own in which to defend herself against their scorn. Although she sent money and letters when anyone she knew was travelling back, she was not eager to go again. Certainly she could not live there, even if by sewing and teaching she could maintain herself in a separate house, and she felt guilty whenever she heard her friends planning happily for a village retirement, even the Okelos, who would shout to high heaven if the electricity were cut off long enough to damp the fridge or cool the bath-water. She might, of course, look for another community development job, but she had fled from Kano without giving notice, and these days, when all the jobs were localised, you needed to face an appointing officer supported by husband and brother-in-law, dignity and the signs of wealth. Besides, these days there were plenty of girls who had completed secondary school, whereas she herself had not even been right through primary. But, more than anything, she feared going where people would know about Okeyo. Deaths of children are not memorable, but that day of death was stamped on the memory of Kisumu people.

The matter solved itself as the Brethren told her matters offered up in prayer often do. One of the sitting MPs had just moved to a new house in Nairobi. His wife was fully occupied, as big people's wives are, but also more concerned than some about the running of her household. She was looking for a mature woman to keep an eye on the needs of the school-age children and guests, supervise the cook and put the finishing touches to the housework. She herself could speak Luo although it was not the family language and the children were

95

taught Swahili and English as well as their mother tongue. An adequate room was available immediately and Paulina moved in the day after the Okelos left for Mombasa. A few weeks later Martin, on a Sunday afternoon visit, asked her to look after his briefcase and a box of books while he was on a selling safari. He dropped in from time to time to take what he wanted and would bring a couple of shirts for her to mend and iron. Once or twice he stayed the night because he did not feel up to the journey back on the late bus, and the first time she left him her bed and made up her own in the children's room as she would if their parents were away. But soon it was an understood thing that he would stay when he wished. Within six months he had moved all his things to her room. Typically, he was a week away on business and a fortnight in Nairobi. She cooked for him when he was home and asked no questions when he was not. He gave her a hundred shillings towards the food at the end of each month and often brought back cheap bananas and eggs from his safaris. When he first came to stay he bought her a pair of shoes and a dictionary for her little sister in high school.

They were both very deliberately casual about it. He said he did not like to stay alone when he was out of town so often and his goods would not be safe. He had not made out very well sharing with men friends – there were always bottles in the house and disputes over the kitchen items. It would be prudent to move in with her for reasons of security and economy.

She twisted the wedding ring which she still wore. Of course he would be free to come if he wished. She did not assert any right in him but she was still his wife. Neither of them referred to the fact that there was only space for a single bed in the room.

They stored some chairs and the frame of the other bed in the garage. Paulina could not help remembering how they had squeezed into the tiny room in Kariokor so many years ago, and how lavish her present possessions would have seemed to the girl she then was. And, after all, they did not now really have to *live* in the little room, which would once have seemed ample for their needs. As often as not she had lunch in the kitchen and spent the early evening in the children's room or serving guests in the lounge. In the daytime there was the whole garden to sit in, and when the family was out she was expected to be within earshot of the telephone and the doorbell. She had once heard Mr M. explain to an enquiring guest, 'Oh no, she is not a housemaid, she is more of a general factotum', and when she asked the meaning she liked the sound of it.

2

In fact she didn't have much time to ponder over her personal relationships because the election was coming up and she was worked off her feet. She hadn't thought like that about elections, people don't after all, if they are not involved. She remembered the tremendous excitement of 1957 but of course she was not qualified to vote then. People stood in a line to make their mark and drop the paper in a box. Then the papers were counted and the results announced. That was all there was to it, just like counting hands at church council elections. Of course the candidates were running around giving talks and getting photographed for the newspapers, but she hadn't thought that affected anyone else much.

She herself had never voted. For the little General Election of 1966 she did not feel free to go back from Kano to Gem, although by then she had a card. She had no heart to go for the by-election after Argwings-Kodhek's death; in any case the result was a foregone conclusion. The election of 1969 was meaningless to her; it was a fight among survivors. And now – she would have voted for Mr M. if she could, because he was a kind man and seemed to her sensible, but of course his constituency was far from hers. Mrs M. asked if she wanted to go to Gem, but obviously this would be difficult to arrange, with both employers away and the house besieged by callers, so she said no. Martin had not even suggested her going with him. And it was too late to transfer her vote to Nairobi – it only now occurred to her that with her husband nearby and a job she enjoyed she could actually live in Nairobi instead of treating it as a place of refuge.

It started even before Parliament was dissolved, the rush of extra visitors, the meetings and the private talks that followed meetings, the telephone always ringing and glasses, glasses, glasses to wash and put away. She was worried that many people wanted to talk in a language she didn't know.

'Don't get upset,' Mrs M. kept saying. 'If they know how to use the

97

telephone they know how to speak Swahili or English well enough. We want you to keep the home together when it's in danger of busting, not to run the constituency for us. Name and phone number is quite enough.'

'Busting?' She thought she must have misheard.

'Now don't look as though you're going to cry over me. You can't afford to get sentimental just because your Martin's come home to roost. Just wait till this little lot's over and then tell me whether any sane woman would stay married through more than one election campaign.'

'But you haven't any choice, have you?' asked Paulina, bewildered.

'You wait and see! But seriously, Paulina, I shall have to be away a lot and the house will be full of people. I'm relying on you to keep the children steady – that's why I can't do with an old woman who only knows about tying napkins and bathing babies. They will want you to decide whether they can have friends to tea or not. (On the whole not: you'll be run off your feet without that. But you have to keep them from resenting the claims of the election as much as I sometimes do.) And you'll have to see that they get enough rest and finish their homework in spite of the racket going on in the house. It's no joke, I tell you.'

Paulina swallowed hard. 'It's beyond my experience. I'll try to do what you want but perhaps a relation would be better.'

'Every relation we're on civil terms with will be campaigning. And though it's beyond your experience, it's not beyond your capacity. I trust you to keep it all under control.'

'And if people want to stay while you're away? How shall I know?'

'You know the people who come regularly. That is no problem. And if I send anybody there will be a note or a phone call. With a lot of casual callers you'll be able truthfully to say the house is full and if they have election business they'd better contact us at home about it. But if there is something that really looks tricky, phone my sister-in-law – you have her number and she will recognise anyone who really has a claim on us.'

So the weeks passed. Mr M. was away most of the time, appearing suddenly to spend a night and then off again, bringing people for tea and drinks but hardly a solid meal at home. Mrs M. took her accumulated leave and was also away a lot. Paulina kept a list of things they would need to present to her every time she dashed in – the week before the polls Mrs M. wrote a hefty cheque as a deposit at the grocer's so that she would not run out. Even so, Paulina had to use some of her own money for extra milk from the local shops and hot dogs when the little boy caught a chill and wouldn't eat anything else. She tried to keep an account of it but there was just too much to do.

Then the day came that the children's transistor radio disappeared. Paulina was sure at first that they must have taken it into the garden or concealed it in their bedroom to listen when they were supposed to be asleep. But it was gone for good. The children were almost as much upset at the prospect of having to report the loss as at missing the programmes and Paulina also expected a reproof for carelessness, but Mrs M. took it very lightly.

'You know I feel responsible,' said Paulina, 'but the house is never still for a moment, and I think you know that I have always been careful with your things before.'

'Do you think I'm blaming you?' laughed Mrs M., who was buying in yet more material for supporters' uniforms. 'If you came to the other house with me you would cry. I shan't have a teaspoon left by the time the campaign is over, not to say a chicken to breed from. Well, you can't make an omelette without breaking eggs, I suppose. And you mustn't annoy supporters by asking questions, so let's make the best of it.'

By the time polling day arrived Paulina was caught up in the enthusiasm, and she sat beside the TV half the night seeing results in. Martin, of course, had gone home to vote, and the children had fallen asleep in spite of their eagerness to stay up late. She was excited when Mr M.'s victory by a safe majority was announced next day but could not get very interested in the other results.

Mr and Mrs M. were both exhausted when they returned to Nairobi. They asked her if she wanted a few days off to compensate for those she had missed but were obviously relieved when she said she had nothing to do at home. It had not occurred to her that you could take a holiday elsewhere. They bought her a dress instead, but in fact she had enjoyed her time of power rather than resenting the extra work.

'Huh,' said Martin. 'Anyone would think you were going to make the speeches and get the pay, so bucked you are about it. They won't be getting you extra roads or schools for our place, that's for sure. All it means for you is more kitchen work as far as I can see, and running up to the school in case their fine friends with cars forget to bring them home.'

What he really meant, of course, was 'Anyone would think it was your own children you were fussing over.'

3

Martin had opened a shop at home, he told her, a couple of years before, in collaboration with a half-brother and a cousin. He was always grumbling at the outlay – nothing very much seemed to come back from it in relation to the repairs and investment being demanded. It gave him a bit of interest in going home, now that the old folks were no longer there and there was no incentive, she supposed, for improving the little house with no family growing up in it. He never suggested that she should go with him. It was her turn to be the town wife.

And as she – trying to retain him less consciously than Nancy or Fauzia had done – cooked her best, dressed modestly in new fashions, kept up with current events and showed an innocent familiarity with town life, reporting to him where there were men's shirts selling cheap or when a special speaker was expected at the cathedral or the university, Martin the more withdrew. He refused to speak Swahili outside the work situation, impugned the motives of almost everybody in business or politics, had to be reminded to use the outside lavatory instead of passing water in what was, after all, Mr M.'s private garden. The shop seemed to dominate his thoughts when he was not attending meetings of community or clan associations. His world was shrunk to 'home' and everything outside suffered disparaging comparison, whether the price of vegetables, the behaviour of Mrs M.'s children, the weather or the quality of fish.

He did not go regularly to church any more, though he might go if there were a special speaker or if he felt particularly at odds with

100

Paulina's having sometimes to work on a Sunday. The climate had changed from the days when you used to say, 'I am a Christian but I am not yet saved.' To praise the Lord no longer helped you to get a job, and though the top people attended places of worship in surprising numbers they were often eager for a quick getaway. It was another way in which the light was going out. People talked about religion – on buses, in queues, in cafés you heard them talking, but often as though it was something dull, outside themselves. Paulina sometimes envied the white-robed women in their endless, vernacular-chanting processions, whose proclamation of the faith did not seem to come up against communal grouping or standards of living. Or perhaps it only looked like that in a separate compartment, and on Monday morning homesickness and bickering reasserted itself. And yet to see a bus driver, regardless of insults, wearing the turban of his sect with uniform, day in, day out, or those little groups who, ignoring a hand proffered to shake, clapped instead in greeting, this was a reminder of something worth having. Paulina wished, sometimes, that she had not been so carefully schooled to be inconspicuous.

One day, early in 1975, when Martin was away in Nakuru, she had requested time to see off her brother's son who was returning from leave to Dar es Salaam, where he worked with the Harbours Corporation. The long-distance buses were marked 'East African Road Services' but everybody called them OTC as in the old days. The office had never changed much, either, still on that busy corner that marked the beginning of African Nairobi, stretching away from the bazaars and temples towards the plains where an old European lady who came to visit them had told her that long ago she used to gallop her pony and the wild zebra would gallop beside her.

You still crowded into the ticket office, where the clerks barked out their demands from behind high barred windows crowned with a sacred list of routes and starting times. It was hard to imagine any pre-colonial age when the bus timetable did not fit a grid of order across the whole country. Only ticket holders were allowed through the barrier into the great, dusty yard where the tarmac never seemed to hold down the bits and pieces perpetually chased by a man with a twig brush. But it was not very difficult to get round at the back where a chain was being constantly raised and lowered to allow the buses to enter, and this she managed to do, chatting with her young nephew about home matters and asking questions about Dar es Salaam, where working life was ruled by the football results and where Asians worked for you like other people, carrying out their crafts in tiny recesses in the city streets or behind the mud walls of ordinary location houses. She could picture the sleepy, hot streets and the sight of a ship's funnels appearing to pass along in the midst of the town, and after a long period of peace she felt anew the urge to be up and doing and seeing fresh sights, but as she waved her nephew off she remembered that she was now thirty-five and he was young and single with the world before him. The bus left on time, though the coast one was still hanging about to be checked, and the noticeboards were full of names of places she had never seen and could not picture.

She made her way out with the arriving passengers, pushed her way across the road and started up towards the Tusker bus stop. She had not got very far before the bomb went off.

No one understood at first. Her ears hurt and the air was full of smoke and flying dust. It did not even remind her of that day in Kano when a little pop, a tiny piece of metal, were the bearers of death. After a few seconds she began to connect the sound with scenes she had seen on television while waiting up with the children, and as she did so perhaps others did the same, for a voice arose that was somehow a corporate voice, not shouting or weeping exactly but a rumble rising and falling in waves, louder and closer than the rumble which had echoed round Nyanza the day Tom was shot and yet had not made its implication known, and people began to run, some back towards the bus station from which, rumour already began to suggest, the noise had come, some away from it. After standing still for perhaps three minutes, pressed by a surge of bodies in each direction and clutching her bag tightly, Paulina made up her mind. Ignoring the police sirens and screaming ambulances, she set herself to walk steadily in the direction of Parklands, heeding neither the scramble for buses nor the street corner discussions that were bound to be a target for police. Every inch the city dweller, freezing her face to the anonymity which so many in Kisumu had practised five years before, she took methodically the shortest route home on foot.

102

The children were disturbed and excited. She countered their questions stolidly. There had been a big bang, and if they had not heard the bang itself they might have heard the chain of shouts and questions and whispers that spread so rapidly across the city. Perhaps a bus had blown up, but they did not need to worry about their daddy as he would be using his car, not any buses. But they had better stay at home till next day because some traffic would be diverted from the city centre to outlying roads. She did not know how she knew this, but had no doubt of it. Their mother soon came home and was busy on the telephone. Paulina tried to keep the children out of earshot but could not help hearing some of the rumours herself. Eventually she coaxed them to sleep with stories.

4

'Tell us the coast one,' they said. 'The funny one.' And she embarked on one of Amina's Swahili stories, though not sure in her own mind that it was funny.

'Once upon a time, in the northern part of the coast where magic is very strong, there was a whole village haunted by djinns. There were so many of them and they alarmed the people so much that the whole village at last decided to move, and they built a new home on the opposite side of the river.

'My friend's mother had a second cousin called Petro, who was a Christian. He worked away in town and so he was not at home when the move took place. When he came back he was very angry at what had happened and said that no one who believed in God need be afraid of spirits. So he determined to sleep by himself in the old village to prove that he would come to no harm. This is a true story. My friend's mother knew the man and had it from his own lips.

'So Petro went to the village and said his prayers and went to bed. But about midnight he woke up to hear the sound of a whole crowd of people walking from the direction of the river, pat-pat, pat-pat, *pat-pat*, PAT-PAT.'

Paulina told the story as Amina, a master of the craft, had told it, and the whole room seemed to be filled with the tread of damp bare feet coming gradually nearer.

'As they approached, Petro could hear the clinking of the women's bracelets, chigili-chigili, chigili-chigili, *chigili-chigili*, CHIGILI-CHIGILI, growing gradually nearer and the squelching of the men's sticks on the marshy ground, pff-pff, pff-pff, *pff-pff*, PFF-PFF. And then he heard voices coming gradually closer, "Someone's in there, someone's in there, *someone's in there*, SOMEONE'S IN THERE".'

The children huddled together, their eyes rounded with expectation.

'Petro lay quite still on his bed. The door was bolted but he heard ssst-ssst and he knew there was someone in the room. He was sweating in terror and because of this he felt he must get up and pass water. No sooner did he sit up than a shrill voice above his head said, "He wants to pass water" and a gruff voice somewhere near the floor repeated, "He wants to pass water." By now he was so frightened that he could not contain himself any more. "He has wet his bed," said the shrill voice. "He has wet his bed," repeated the gruff voice. "Ha, ha, ha, he has wet his bed."

'Petro lay there and he felt his feet beginning to freeze. Little by little he lost the power of feeling up to his knees. He realised that if he did not make an effort he would never move again. He struggled into a sitting position and cried aloud, "Jesus, save me."

' "Ah," cried the shrill voice above him, "who is he talking to?"

' "Who is he talking to?" echoed the gruff voice.

' "He is calling on his Jesus," they mocked.

' "He is calling on his Jesus."

' "Who is that Jesus of his?"

' "Who is that Jesus of his," they laughed.'

Peals of shrill and gruff laughter echoed while the quiet voice pursued the story. The children joined in but Paulina felt herself hot with the sweat of sympathy.

'But although they laughed they were defeated by the name of Jesus. Petro heard again ssst-ssst and knew that the room was empty. Outside he could hear many voices growing fainter as they moved away.

' "HA, HA. *ha, ha*, ha, ha, ha, ha."

' "HE IS CALLING ON HIS JESUS, *he is calling on his Jesus*, he is calling on his Jesus, he is calling on his Jesus."

' "WHO IS THAT JESUS OF HIS? *Who is that Jesus of his?* Who is that

Jesus of his? Who is that Jesus of his? Jesus – Jesus – Jesus – Jesus – Jesus."

'And he heard the bracelets getting fainter, CHIGILI-CHIGILI, *chigili-chigili*, chigili-chigili-chigili-chigili – and the sticks, PFFF-PFFF, *pfff-pfff*, pfff-pfff, pfff-pfff, pfff-pfff, and the footsteps, PAT-PAT, *pat-pat*, pat-pat, pat-pat, until they faded away into the river.

'As soon as it was light Petro ran to the place where he had left his boat and crossed the river to the new village. And though the Christians were glad that the Name had prevailed, no one has been known to sleep in the place ever since.'

5

When the children were asleep Paulina sat in the big house to watch the news on TV and keep Mrs M. company till her husband should return. He came late at night. He had been going over and over the known course of the event with his political colleagues and everyone was baffled by it. The bomb had been traced and yet no one could discover a reason for its having been planted on the bus. No VIP was about who might have been a target for assassination. One could not find any local connection or revenge motive that made sense. Mourners and sympathisers gathered as the casualties were identified. Rumours flew but not one of them seemed credible.

Paulina was thankful that Martin no longer had to travel by bus outside Nairobi but took the firm's driver with a load of samples. She did not know when to expect him but he arrived back at dusk on Sunday looking tired and shaky. This was no time, he said, to be travelling with other people's property. He would rather risk losing a few orders than get hijacked on the way and asked what a Nairobi van was doing on the road. He ate early, without appetite, and hurried to bed as though his weariness was worldwide.

They later heard that the Dar es Salaam bus was the last to leave before the explosion and so had been stopped for investigation and every passenger cross-examined about his identity and travel plans. Her nephew did not know the reason and assumed some border incident to be in question, but nothing suspicious was found and they were allowed to proceed to Dar es Salaam where the radio and newspapers soon enlightened them.

Paulina had been directed by a sense of the city in retreating from the scene of the explosion to the anonymity of the house. Similarly she became absorbed in the feeling of the city in the next two weeks while everyone wondered and few spoke, while formal statements of investigation were made and not acted upon, when tension became absorbed into the multiple rhythms of everyday life. For in Nairobi you get dressed whether you have clean clothes or not, you eat whether you know where the next meal is coming from or not, you do work, whether the work is a compulsive progression from dustbin to dustbin, from one employment office to the next, or whether it is a ritual with scales or paper clips to dress out someone else's fantasy. In Nairobi you withdraw when someone threatens your personal space, you manipulate the calculations necessary to crossing the road almost without accident, you recognise by a shrug or a lifted eyebrow the appropriate stations of men and gods. So you cannot be said just to hang upon the next event.

And yet you know that there must be a next event, and when the newspapers begin to report the search for J.M. Kariuki you know that in one sense or another the event has happened.

In the days after the bomb went off the air was full of whispers. Paulina knew the sense of them although they were often enough phrased in difficult English purposely in order to exclude her. But she could not be excluded. Had she not lost a child? They said that Kariuki had gone to Zambia, had registered in a hotel there. But the elder Mrs Kariuki was an acquaintance of the house and she did not know of it. Her co-wife also did not know. There had been no preparations for going: there had been no custom of keeping unnecessary secrets. It was small husbands with small concerns who did that.

Whisper, whisper, whisper. They said the police officers had been transferred from here to there. That officers had been consulting with the missing man here and there. That there was a lot of money. That Parliament – whisper, whisper, whisper.

Paulina went about her duties, ironing, setting tables, supervising the servant in the cleaning of the house and the hard washing. Sometimes her belly throbbed with the child who had been so casually taken from her at another time like this and the others who had been denied her. And yet a child was a child with a light hold on life. When it came to a man, a wealthy man, golden tongued, greatly loved, though he was not of her own people she knew this much, that the passing of such a man would be remembered, celebrated. Still not a week passed without someone speaking of Tom.

And when the body was found, discreetly mutilated, you knew what the event was that for weeks you had been expecting, although the real event was still not known. The police officers went about their leave or their business outside the station without referring to it, the mortuary keeper who had a well-dressed corpse of appropriate size and weight and characteristics in his charge did not tumble to it. The airline clerks checking flights to Zambia did not tumble to it. The children playing in the streets did not tumble to it – children who were of the age to have been shot in Kano or Patel flats, children who did not shy away from the sight of a gun or hold their noses against white smoke from a bonfire, children who had been conceived after their fathers had come back from the camps, after the squatters had missed their chance to buy up the white farm settlement plots, after the land titles had been written, children who did not know the eerie stillness of the forest or the KEM prohibited signs. Children of the New Method, who knew John Wayne and the Aga Khan and Bruce Lee and Charlie Chaplin by sight, who knew how to figure on a base of five and counted out diligently in their nursery schools:

'Eeny, meeny, miny mo,
Catch a little baby so,
If he hollers let him go,
Eeny, meeny, miny mo.'

Even those terribly sharp children did not tumble to it.

Nobody really knew how it tied up with the bomb. There was no need to know. Hyenas were there to settle with those who asked too many questions. But while the casualties of the bomb were nameless people absorbed into the daily casualty lists of fire, flood and domestic quarrels, J.M. burst upon the scene as a martyr and a paroxysm of grief ran through the city. The skies were leaden that April and it grew colder and colder. Eyes grew hard in Nairobi and conversations were rounded off with polite, empty phrases, even before the stranger came

107

close. Photographs of J.M. alternated with the Pope and the Sacred Heart on the roadside framing stands. The book was reprinted and within a few months Parliamentary speeches were printed too. A Kikuyu gramophone record was banned. Mr Mwangale remarked bluntly in Parliament, 'This time we cannot be told Njenga did it.' Paulina and Martin did not discuss it. The employers spoke of it in low tones. In May the rains came, chill and steady, a bit late, and in the shanties by the river people squirmed and shivered over the water-logged ground and fires smoked damply at the mouth of airless polythene shelters.

Sometimes Paulina lay awake thinking about it. The district was quiet enough with its big gardens and widely spaced houses, and yet these days it never seemed quiet to a woman who had endured the sounds of eight households mingling over the wooden rafters of Pumwani or the noise of sacks and boxes swaying perilously overhead in Kariokor and latecomers squeezing past folded chairs and unrolled mats in adjacent rooms. Here dogs barked at night suspiciously, on the defence rather than on heat, and, human noise being caged in protective houses or convoyed out in automobiles to vent its passion elsewhere, the distant sounds of traffic hung long in the air, like the early morning bus at home that was heard so far off, amid the unmechanical buzz of night, that you could get up and dress and be ready to catch it at the market. You could hear the car coming as though straight at you, like the looming danger in a gangster film, and then often you heard the opening of padlocks and the creak of gates to show how well protected your quietness was, and the ear was suddenly tensed, the head lifted from the pillow as though you expected to hear a baby cry or a bomb go off. In that anxiety a barrier had been raised again between rich and poor. But between poor and poor a barrier had been broken down. Whatever else might have happened, the force which had become personalised in this man's death was not enmity between tribe and tribe.

The months dragged on and the air did not lighten. The dead man's watch had been found at a police post. A Parliamentary Commission reported but the police declared themselves unable to take any action on the report. The MP and the visitors who came talked in low tones, drank with steady determination, did nothing to bring notice upon

108

themselves. Passenger trains stopped running. Martin had been taught at school that the country had grown up round the railway as a lifeline. Certainly the notion of country as distinct from locality grew where the railway was. It was as though a whole epoch of history had been uprooted, and skilled middle-class workers on indefinite unpaid leave struggled to meet their school fees and to keep their boots in good repair.

In October came another shock. There were high words in Parliament about the state of the ruling party, KANU, and a few days later Mr Seroney, the Deputy Speaker, and Mr Shikuku were taken into detention.

The cloud did not lift. It was as though voices were muffled. Paulina went about her duties as usual, washing linen and glasses – the glasses again seemed to be endless – giving a final polish to the furniture and at the same time answering the telephone, taking messages, helping the cook out when dinner had to be stretched to extra servings. She felt almost like the manager of the house. She was getting the full Nairobi rate of four hundred shillings a month which, with a free room and much of her food provided, made her feel affluent indeed. She did not have to wear a house servant's uniform or be ordered in and out of the rooms. Somehow the household absorbed her without loss of human dignity, and she was sorry for the cook, always being called to account for the eggs or the milk. She could speak English quite fluently now – could listen to the English radio more readily than she could read a newspaper. She had never exactly learned it, but ever since her days in Homecraft more and more of the language had hung in the air around her.

6

Only one person asked a lot of questions about the new detention and that was a single woman MP, a rare bird indeed. Her questions were not fully answered, though rumours buzzed about, and fresh news overtook them as the months passed. Then all of a sudden the girl – Chelagat Mutai was her name – was accused of inciting a crowd to violence in the previous year and sentenced to thirty months' imprisonment.

Thirty months – an unbearably long time, people said. It was about as long as the whole time Paulina had had Okeyo. But time passes. Twice as long as that, more than twice, had somehow been got through since she lost him. Chelagat was tough. She would get through it too. Mrs M. asked Paulina's opinion about getting a cross-section of Kenya women to petition for release. Paulina shook her head. She did not know many women and most were concerned only with their own domestic affairs. It was not her business and yet it troubled her.

All the time she was getting closer to Mrs M., who was herself a high school girl from a generation when high school girls were rigorously selected, and a trained secretary. Mrs M. appreciated the qualities in her 'general factotum' which had been developed without the aid of formal education. She often took Paulina with her to meetings where women's place in society was discussed, pointed her out as a person who had achieved a balanced and contented life without the blessing of children, stressed her great usefulness to society though she was not competing directly in any man's field of achievement. And yet Paulina could not help remembering that her usefulness was secondary to Mrs M.'s usefulness, her contentment, if that was what you could call it, partly derived from Mrs M.'s own motherhood and precariously dependent on Martin's failure to get a child from any other woman. She did not claim to understand it all, but worked, prayed when she could, observed, remembered and held her peace. It was no use getting upset on your own behalf.

Paulina focused all her indignation on the Mutai case, all the complaints of woman in a man's world which she dared not relate to her own commonplace experiences. She even overcame her usual reticence to the point of shouting at Martin when he sat down to eat, without showing any particular emotion, on the day the sentence was announced. Perhaps his public emotions had been used up while hers were conserved. At the time of Tom Mboya's murder she had been too happy with Okeyo to feel much grief: the later 'incident' was swamped by her private sorrow at the loss of her child. She could hardly have told you when the election was held or the curfew lifted. The Sedition Trial had hardly touched her: it was like a stage play in a church hall: one could not really believe that such things were going on. And J.M.'s death had crystallised a feeling of belonging, so that though she herself had dared to go up and take the hand of the widow when she visited the house, and pour out what phrases of consolation she could manage in Swahili (for mourning was something you ordinarily did only in the mother tongue and had to be rethought if your sympathies lay outside), people had thought more of themselves than of the dark terror of those moments, the betrayal by friends, the gradual chopping off of fingers. But Chelagat, a strapping young woman and single, was within her comprehension, cut off from friends and constituents, humiliated in the cell, sent out to dig, kept from the news of other sufferers which she had been demanding before anyone remembered the incitements said to have occurred so many months back, when she had not yet addressed the press conference or posed the awkward statements and the defiant questions.

'We must do something,' Paulina howled at Martin.

'Don't shout at me. I'm not the High Court of Appeal. What do you think we can do?'

'Write to our MPs, make processions, sign petitions, strike . . .'

'You going to strike against Mrs M.? To persuade her to do something she wouldn't have wanted to do?'

'Well, of course I don't have to, but you know what I mean.'

'I know you can't do anything. Anything at all. Only government can do it.'

'But *we* are the government. Mrs M. says . . .'

'If you are the government, you get Mr M. to queue up to put his cross on a bit of paper with your symbol on it: fig-leaf or something, or a militant crochet-hook. I don't see . . .'

'We put them there and we help them to act.'

'Paulina, will you be silent, for I see myself that there is nothing for us but "can't". I used to go to meetings, as you know, and classes, as you know, and read books such as we still have here, but what is there for me to do? When I married you I was selling envelopes and now I am still selling envelopes, maybe a few more and a bit dearer but that's all there is to it. Yes, I have a better suit and eat meat more often, but what of it? If I had six sons to keep I should have less for myself than I had then. And no more to say.'

'You have the shop.' What could she answer to questions about sons?

'So I do have the shop at home, or a half or a third of the shop with my brothers. What do I get out of it?'

'You get the feeling that a bit of Nyanza is yours.'

'If I have no shares in anything I don't fit into the new society. And if I do have shares in it, how can I change it?'

'Then you could . . .'

There would have been no end to it except that they both had their work to do, their separate circle of acquaintances. Their time together was limited, their conversation desultory, but always she was the one demanding to grow, to get out, to do things, and he was tired and disillusioned.

Mrs M. and Paulina thought that a women's petition might secure not a pardon for Chelagat, that was a matter of law, but some mitigation of her sentence. Even if it failed, women might become politically conscious by making the attempt. And whereas six women, or twenty, making a fuss in Nairobi about a court case, might be arrested or harassed, no one in these non-Emergency days could arrest thousands on thousands of women. Tirelessly Mrs M. sought out the leading women in different professions, tribes, communities to assist her.

'Well, of course I would sign if I thought there was any possible chance of succeeding, but since there isn't, why stick your neck out?'

'But of course she *prefers* being a martyr. She would just hate it if anyone else had a hand in getting her freed. I simply couldn't *face* her, you know.'

'I think it's an absolutely marvellous idea and of course you should do it, but me, I've taken far too many risks already: my husband would never allow me to put my name to it.'

'But if you could really get some old Nandi grannies marching about, wouldn't they be in just the position that Chelagat is supposed to have put them into at the beginning?'

'And with so few women in leading positions, wouldn't it be wrong to put a career at risk just for a gesture . . .?'

Mrs M. sighed, reporting one refusal after another.

'But if you went straight to the people,' asked Paulina, 'you, say, to your location and I to mine? Would not the educated women come forward to help? It would be a start at least.'

'Picture it. You go to Gem. You have not lived there for more than ten years, right? Have you any status there? Face it. To the old grannies you are a childless woman whom they admired for a little while when to read and sew – and still stay at home – was a distinction. So you tell them that a Kalenjin girl stood up for the rights of poor people. But faraway people whose needs and rights they do not know. She was convicted in a court of law, and headmen and elders always tell people to respect the law. And to these old ladies, what is so terrible? They have seen women going to prison for illegal brewing and men for tax offences and failing to build latrines, and the people come out much the same, not very much damaged. If the girl has no children to leave behind, no husband to misbehave while she is away, what is the loss? She will dig as other people dig and eat as other people eat. For a girl who has been to all those schools it is not a bad experience, they will say. I do not see how we can do anything without the help of leading women who will stand up to the chiefs and convince the ordinary folk. And even if we did it only in your district and mine, we should be accused of tribalism if we did not get signatures on all sides . . .'

For a little while they let it rest, until one day Mrs M. approached her husband on the subject. He was furious. The Constitution, he pronounced sententiously, was not made for individuals. One person could sink or swim without making it right to put the rest in danger. He intended to keep his head and his seat and his chance of helping people in his constituency, and his wife would be well advised to be a bit more active in collecting funds for a self-help secondary school.

Mrs M. repressed an impulse to answer that there were more secondary schools already than they could find fit pupils or teachers for, but she managed to retreat with dignity to a Red Cross committee meeting. Soon they saw in the paper that an appeal date had been fixed for Chelagat's case, so there seemed no point in doing anything else until the appeal came up, and by the time it was rejected the opportunity for a petition had passed, even if they had had the heart for it. All the same, neither of them was prepared to accept 'can't' as a standing answer. And in insisting so, Paulina for the first time set up her will against Martin's. She had given in to Simon by default, not of set purpose. This was different, and for the first time she felt the same pressure to defend her opinion that Mrs M. and other educated women felt. It was no longer obvious that decisions had been made for her.

The mood was depressing – there was a tension in the house that Paulina could not explain just from public affairs. The one thing everyone got excited about was the Entebbe Raid. Even though most people in Africa took without question the Palestinian side against Israel, still it somehow lightened the heart to hear of an exploit in a neighbouring country that came straight out of storybook fiction. The newspapers rang with it, the books sold in hundreds. 'Scarlet Pimpernel in East Africa,' declared Martin, remembering his schoolboy favourites.

Compared with the humdrum of every day, where most people who got killed died arbitrarily and passed into obscurity, here was romance and gallant sacrifice, and that in the country that had always left a feeling of unease among them compared with the straightforward conflicts of interest elsewhere. Uganda left you with a feeling of dread – its kings, its crocodiles, its martyred history, its excesses of dress, devotion and, in recent years, of devious violence. Martin had once been there to visit a relation at Tororo, where, before the Kenyan Exodus of 1970 more Luo was spoken than Luganda. But even such a little way into the country the roads, the vegetation, the traffic were spectacularly different from Kenya. So there you could imagine rescue swooping from the sky and feel somehow linked with a worldwide network of – what – intrigue, morality, technique, honour, imagination, courage? There was a human existence outside, different from the trickle of experts and equipment that remained impersonal, remote, and acts of force could, at a cost, be reversed. It was something to be going on with.

The months dragged on. Paulina took the children to the Nairobi Show, but she could not get excited about it. They came home with an assortment of cardboard headgear, free tracts and samples of soup which she calculated could have been bought with less strain on her employers' pocket and her own feet, not to say sparing the washing off of candy floss and discussions on the superiority of colour TV. She

114

made the wearisome journey to Kisumu to see her mother who was sick in hospital, but was getting better and Paulina's brother was going to look after her till she was well enough to go home, so she did not attempt the trip to her birthplace or feel any need to do so. Kisumu looked as it used to do, trim, miniature, self-contained, and full of women she had once known with long-legged children in school uniform to shop for them and take the maize for grinding. Their energy in the hot afternoon amazed her. She went down after the hospital visit to catch the breeze from the lake and there were people still manhandling crates and sacks on to lorries. She booked her return ticket from the market-place where turnboys vied for custom and hawkers jostled to be first in with their wares. She saw the medicines – Kamba and even Swahili as well as Luo medicines – spread for sale, to give fertility, vigour, good memory, to protect against coughs, malaria, swelling of the joints, and felt no longer even the faintest temptation to buy. She clambered into her seat on the third day and did not turn away her gaze as they rode past her old house and the schoolroom and the little unmarked grave. She had no impulse to go back, to instruct exhort, tidy, straighten. She sat back, open-eyed, and learned things as she had become accustomed to learn – new names in Kericho streets, abundance of tea plants which, oddly, sometimes left a shortage of tea in the shops, new metal on the road, woolly sheep promising good blankets to come. She turned her head as they pulled up the shoulder out of the Rift Valley. It was so magnificent one could not do other than look. But she did not catch her breath at the sight or covet any of those vast rolling fields, only took note that the road was risky and that Martin crossed it more often than she remembered. That much remained of love in her.

7

At home she was better, with routine work to do and plenty of sewing. The last thing she would have anticipated was a visit to the National Theatre. She had seen films, in church sometimes and now and again in a commercial cinema when there was no one else to take Mrs M.'s children. She liked the news best and the cartoons. And of course she sometimes saw the television, but the National Theatre looked foreign and difficult. She had seen people there lugging about enormous musical instruments when they had stopped the car once or twice to pick up a neighbour's child from ballet class, and the children made ludicrous imitations of that kind of music. But it so happened that one of the young executives from Martin's firm was taking part in a play, and had given out complimentary tickets which Martin said it would be rude not to use, so she found herself, one early evening, in a sober navy-blue jersey dress with three-quarter sleeves, standing outside the theatre waiting to meet Martin. As she waited, the crowd around her laughing and chattering and a line of uniformed schoolgirls led by a harassed young teacher, heavily pregnant, she spotted a figure she half-recognised. Could it be Amina's daughter – what was her name – Joyce, now very grown up, sixteen or seventeen she supposed. She was more surprised to find the girl also looking at her.

'Excuse me, I think you are a friend of my mother's,' she said. 'My mother is Amina and I am Joyce.'

'How clever of you to remember! My name is Mrs Paulina Were, and I was wondering if it was you – so much grown up. How is Amina?'

'All right. Still down in Eastleigh, you know.'

'She didn't come with you to watch the play?'

'Me, I'm not watching, I'm dancing in the play. In the daytime I'm taking a secretarial course.'

'Is that so? You perform every evening? How do you get home?'

'One of my friends will take me home. I'm staying with my friend: she's in the play too. Nancy, this is Mrs Were.'

A tall coloured girl came forward, older and more sure of herself. Martin came hurrying over and there was sudden silence.

'Oh, Mrs Were? You are Martin's wife, then. He was always talking about you. I am so glad to meet you.'

'Really? I thought he never talked much.'

'Why, Nancy, how are you after all this time? Nancy and I used to be neighbours in Kibera,' said Martin stiffly.

'Yes, yes, good neighbours,' chimed in Nancy. 'I think it was my cousin who introduced us.'

'You look as though you have gone up in the world since then.'

'Well, there was no way to go except up, don't you think?'

116

'And you are also in the play, Mrs . . .?'

'Just call me Nancy. I don't fancy sharing anyone else's name. But that's the second bell, kid. We ought to be dressed and the producer will be fuming.'

They ran off, and Martin, suddenly solicitous, showed Paulina to her seat explaining the layout of the theatre (he had been there twice before, once for a music festival and once for a Swahili play) and insisted on bringing a son of his old teacher from the opposite side of the hall to introduce him. Paulina was immediately suspicious, but there is no point in chewing over the past. Everything was so strange and new to her that she was fully occupied with the play. The story was not very clear to her but there were some funny slapstick scenes and she enjoyed the dancing.

In the first interval she remarked, 'Amina's girl has grown up quickly.'

'Time passes.' True enough. She might have had a son in university by now.

'She's a pretty girl too. Do you think she's related to the other one?'

'She's not supposed to know about any relations is she? That was what Amina laid down.'

'I suppose not. Where does the other girl come from?'

'Nairobi, why?'

'I thought you knew her.'

'Yes, I knew her in Kibera and she speaks Kikuyu, but I never heard she had a home outside Nairobi.'

'And how does such a person get married?'

'How? Well, I can't say I've thought about it. It's not difficult to pick up a man in Nairobi, surely?'

'I wouldn't know. But that isn't quite what I meant.'

And she shook herself and knew that what she meant meant nothing any more, for even here in the audience there were people of all shapes and colours, and at home she had received, on Mrs M.'s behalf, brown teenagers who spoke Luo and brown toddlers who spoke little else than German and black children with foreign mothers (or not so foreign) who seemed to speak only English. And you did not ask of these people where they belonged or where they would marry, you only asked it in Eastleigh and Pumwani. At home you never asked, but perhaps it was time to start asking. The music was beginning and they gave their attention to the play. And the young man who had given them the tickets was pointed out on the stage as an old, bent man with white hair and a blanket thrown over his shoulder. Really it was very confusing!

The dancing was well done, again the terrifying, wasteful energy of the young. Paulina was sure they were young although they were made to look otherwise. But then in something very similar to a Luo dance a young man suddenly started jumping up and down on one spot like a Kamba, whom you might see performing in the stadium before a rally started, or again it made you think of the Israeli sect in their white robes and turbans: some were always running but she had seen them jump like this also to the dull drumbeat on a Sunday, head and shoulders appearing higher and higher over the hedge round the flats, while onlookers stopped to stare and shout encouragement: it beat the Salvation Army for a show and offered another hazardous distraction to Sunday drivers. But these acrobatics did not fit with the Luo dance, and then the words suddenly switched to English and the costumes seemed to be coastal wrappers, all bright and strapless, with not a modest Moslem *buibui* in sight. There was nothing to point out what you were supposed to believe.

All the time, she pondered, giving up the effort of finding a story in the play, there seemed to be new things. Not things that had been there before, like Swahili conversation or Parliament Building, that you started to learn about after leaving school, but things that had never effectively existed in one's life. Cracks were even appearing in the customary reticence between husband and wife, so that she could even question her husband, for the sake of guests, on what they kept in the shop, and he could bring her an order for crocheted cloths. She did not mind dealing with the new things, but there was an emptiness where some of the old things ought to have been.

After the play they walked decorously down to the bus stop, with nothing to say about the show which had entertained them without moving them, and had to wait a long time. They were surprised to see Mr M.'s Peugeot passing them – if he had spotted them he would surely have offered a lift – and there was Joyce sitting, smiling and relaxed, in the front seat, with no other passengers. The journey home was slow and they were late to eat and late to bed, but were roused again at two in the morning by the sound of the Peugeot coming in.

CHAPTER
SIX

1

One day Martin asked Paulina to go to the bank. This was something quite new. She had learned how to deal with the big city shops. Government offices in the old provincial style were familiar to her – sentries more or less on guard outside the old colonial buildings, whitened stones, trees, long, cool staircases, desks set in ordinary rooms with high ceilings and green or brown paint like a schoolroom in town or a police station, files that were a long time coming and receipts written tediously by hand. The new officialdom of towering buildings, all lifts and windows, did not exactly frighten her: it belonged to another world, one she had hardly glimpsed, collecting a form, perhaps, from the passport office or delivering a note for her boss to someone whose telephone was out of order. But a bank, that was within her compass and yet outside her experience.

Martin explained where to go and how to identify herself as authorised to collect the money. She had not thought about it before, had always assumed that he collected his pay in cash at the end of the month and kept it in pockets and boxes as small people did – as she herself did, paying in modest sums to the Post Office Savings Bank. Then she saw that there must be accounts for the shop in Gem, goods bought and wages paid. Of course she had not seen that particular shop or, for a long time, the brothers who shared it – the half-brother worked as a clerk at Maseno and the second cousin ran a *matatu* between Kisumu and Eldoret, but in her heart of hearts she knew that local purchases – sugar, soft drinks, cigarettes from a town wholesaler – would be made piecemeal from cash in hand, and scanty wages, she knew also, would be supplemented by borrowings from stock. This was very far from the shiny walls of the bank, the slippery floor and the potted plants. For a moment she could picture herself as if she were a proper wife with a son in secondary school and babies round

120

her knees, standing at the counter, a rough and greasy table that would leave a mark on the front of her dress – bottle-tops and spit-out pith of sugar-cane and lumps of clay brought in by sandalled feet strewing the floor – the smell of rough tobacco and kerosene and hard soap, the air dusty and full of repetitious voices . . . No, it had not been meant to work out that way. Better face the bank.

She was wearing a neat dark dress, flat-heeled shoes and, of course, a watch. No working woman could be seen without a watch. All the same, she felt cowed by the splendour of the building, but she kept her dignity, marched straight to the right counter, queued, signed, completed the transaction without mishap. She was surprised, then, to hear her name hissed, 'Paulina.' She could see no one she knew. And no one she knew, except the Brethren, would be likely to call her by her baptismal name in a public place. Unless – she saw the cashier in the next compartment gesturing to her. The woman was enclosed in glass and stone, immobilised by the sheafs of bank notes and bags of silver around her. Her hair was straightened and stuck out from her head like a wire brush. She had an ample figure swathed in patterned jersey and heavy beads bounced upon her bosom and from her ears.

'You don't know me, Paulina? Your mother asked me to look out for you in Nairobi.'

There was a little scar, the shape of an arrow, on the forehead and the weal of an old burn on the forearm. Paulina racked her brains.

'It can't be – Rhoda?'

'Indeed it can be Rhoda. Do you forget that we started school together?'

Rhoda indeed, who had left her in standard two, had plodded on to finish primary school the year Paulina got married and then gone away to teacher training. How long – Paulina wondered suddenly – since she had seen any of the girls from that class, how long since she had thought of the mud-walled classroom with holes cut out for windows, the half exercise books and stubs of pencil on the floor, the ba-be-bi-bo-bu on the blackboard.

Rhoda had lived very near them, so they had continued to recognise one another till full grown, though a girl taking examinations (in boarding school she was by then) was set apart from the maids-of-all-work around the homesteads. And then when Paulina was at

121

Homecraft Rhoda had been a young teacher coming into Kisumu on Saturdays for shopping, and once had brought a netball team to play against them, and during the later years she heard that Rhoda had married a senior teacher and so, perhaps, had come in for this glamorous job and this glamorous outfit.

'It is so long,' said Paulina awkwardly, when the customer waiting had been served. 'I did not know you were in Nairobi. And how are things at home?'

'We are well,' said Rhoda, a little uneasily. 'My husband is in the Ministry now, and we have five kids – one doing CPE this year and three others in primary and one in nursery. And my goodness, the expense of that. It is enough, I tell you.'

Paulina's heart sank, but no questions followed. Rhoda already knew from home that there are things one must not ask.

'You are working here? You are not with Community Development any more?'

'Yes, I am working with a family.' She named them – she could be proud of them. 'And Were is here some of the time, but his work takes him travelling a lot.'

'Oh, I am glad, really glad.' Rhoda evidently had not known of their coming together. 'Otherwise after work there is nothing. Life in Nairobi is hard.'

'Hard?' Paulina gazed at the fancy ceilings and the bobbing beads. 'When I first came I found it hard. You were in school then. The closeness of things and the noise and the smells. But if you have a nice place to stay it is not so bad. Life can be hard anywhere.'

Rhoda nodded, and signalled Paulina not to go away while she attended to another customer. Paulina's attention was on a man at the next desk weighing little bags of money one against the other as though they were beans in a shop, and then deftly pulling out soiled notes from a bundle and writing on them – writing numbers actually on the notes that were real money. It looked unholy.

'When are you free? You must come and see us at home. Saturday afternoon?'

'Saturday?' Paulina had to think hard. 'Yes, I think I can be free in the afternoon. In the evening they are having a party. I must be back to serve drinks. I'll let you know if I can't get off.'

'Saturday, then. Meet me outside here at one o'clock. We stay at Kariokor. Not far . . . Yes, sir, twenty shillings for a pound this morning. Fair enough.'

Paulina crept away. Kariokor? Life hard in Nairobi? Kariokor? She almost slipped on the broad, shallow steps as she remembered creeping round the door that would never quite open, trying to scrub the tiny window clean, the passing buses spraying dirt over your washing and your pots and pans. Taking a firm hold on herself she marched into a tea-shop for tea and cake, the consolation befitting a mature Kenya woman, before collecting the children's record-player which had been left for repair and taking the bus home.

On Saturday she met Rhoda outside the bank as promised, and wriggled after her on to a rush-hour bus which was full beyond her experience, jabbed with elbows, knees and shopping baskets until she was almost breathless.

'Sometimes James collects me in the car on Saturdays,' Rhoda said, 'but today he is off out somewhere – you know.'

'Yes, I know,' said Paulina, uncertainly.

She nearly missed getting off at the right place as Rhoda squirmed her way ahead to the exit door, but there were shouts to the driver and she scrambled off under the arm of a youth who was holding both sides of the door. She knew, of course, that there were flats you passed on the bus going to Eastleigh but it had not struck home to her that this was in fact the new Kariokor.

The flats towered high. There were many vehicles about and good stout washing lines. The stairs could have been cleaner but the flats inside were spacious and convenient. Rhoda's was comfortably furnished and curtained, with a gas stove and a fridge.

'Children, did I ever tell you to have this mess out of my way by lunchtime,' she bellowed in English. A game of ludo was set out on the table, a mess of crayons and comics on the floor. The radio was playing very loudly.

'I always tell them to be ready, but, you know,' said Rhoda.

'Yes, I know,' answered Paulina.

Lunch was served by a teenage maid who recalled the children to their duty by a series of blood-curdling yells over the stairwell. Paulina admired, whole-heartedly, the children, their drawings, the house, the furnishings, the food.

'I am so glad you came,' enthused Rhoda. 'Otherwise it is so dull at home you are longing for Monday morning to get back to work again.'

'Dull? But with the children here you must have so much to do – so much to talk about.'

'The children? They are not babies any more to want nursing. I assure you, my dear, at the end of ten years of teaching you have had enough of children – Emma, sit up and eat properly. The visitor will think you don't know how to use a knife and fork.'

'You like your present job better, then?'

'Oh, it pays much better than teaching, yes. And less botheration. But these people eat it all, of course. Nothing left for poor mother. Frank, just look at that mess on your shirt, be careful now.'

'But you have beautiful dresses. I am surprised you can bear to wear them for work.'

'For work? Where else would I wear them? That's the one thing you get out of it, being able to look a bit decent. You see all sorts of big people, coming and going. Then you get home, put on your old dress, spend an hour telling the girl what to do, go to market, very likely, if you can't trust her to save your money for you. I tell you, it's a treat to have a visit from someone from home. These single girls have the best of it – pictures, dances. Me, I don't know what the inside of a hotel looks like in Nairobi.'

'But you have the car . . .'

'My dear, in Nairobi you have either a car or a husband at home occasionally, not both. Oh no, I'm thankful I have a job where I meet some decent people. Otherwise life in Nairobi is hard, I tell you.'

'But don't the children want to go out? I see a lot of interesting things with Mrs M.'s children if sometimes the family can't find time to go together.'

'Oh, they go out quite enough – only last term you went to the museum from school, didn't you, Frank, and they have their sports days and all that. They do all right. But Kariokor, day in, day out, if you didn't have a job you couldn't stand it.'

'Did you know I used to live here once upon a time?' asked Paulina, turning to the children.

'I hear the flats were very good when they were new, but oh! they are so messy now. We keep on saying we are going to move, but we don't get around to it.'

'There were no flats when I lived here. That was in colonial times and there were just little red-brick barracks then. You know, children, what the Carrier Corps was?'

The children looked at her and went on eating steadily. She wondered for a moment if they did not understand Luo, but remembered that the maid had been speaking to them quite freely: perhaps they just did not expect to speak with adult visitors.

'I thought the flats had been here for ages,' said Rhoda. 'They look so beaten up by now. But of course I've only been five years in Nairobi.'

'But I was in Nairobi eighteen years ago. You can't imagine how things have changed since then.'

'Time flies,' said Rhoda, still the schoolmistress at heart. 'To think that it's longer than that since we were at school together. You see, children, you must make the best of school time. It soon gets finished. They come to CPE,' she added, turning to Paulina, 'ready for secondary school, and you have hardly noticed that they are out of their cradles. You know?'

'I know,' answered Paulina dejectedly. What else could be said to a schoolmate with whom one had shared those early years? And yet she hugged a kind of knowledge which Rhoda would never share and could never be asked about.

Beside the bus stand where they waited to go back to town an old beggar reclined on a blanket.

'Don't be frightened,' said Rhoda. 'He is always there. Aren't they everywhere nowadays? But he won't bother you.'

Paulina had had no thought of being bothered. The old man with his majestic bearded head looked well in control of the situation. Someone had given him a cigarette and he was smoking it with a flourish between two fingers, like some of the university visitors, not like a workman closing his hand over the stub in his mouth. He might have been challenging the young layabouts to snatch the fag out of his hand. Style, he was saying to them, is important if you are to make the best of what you have, and that was the lesson they were learning from this old beggar who did not look under-nourished or humiliated

125

either. The panache with which a teenage turnboy hung out of a *matatu* or a country bus, expending on those spectacular leaps and quite unnecessary delays energy which might more profitably have been used in the classroom or on the football field, was all part of the same complex, the rakish angle at which a barefoot parking boy put on the tattered remnants of a hat picked up from some gutter after a fight, the theatrical bow with which an urchin had once offered her a seat before jumping off the city bus warily ahead of the conductor's demand for a fare. The boys seemed better at it than the girls. Perhaps woman's life was so arduous at bottom that only the most leisured and wealthy had time to cultivate the seeming spontaneities of style.

2

All the way back Paulina was thinking about the other beggars of Nairobi. There seemed to be so many of them, and a few of them glued to the same spot they had used long ago when she first came to the city. Had there always been so many or was it just that she had then less knowledge of the affluent streets? Some of them used to go home to Pumwani, the blind led by a child or a lame man pulled on a trolley by little boys: some, too, who could straighten their shoulders and speak with normal voices once they were at home. Some could afford to use the buses nowadays, and generally the conductors were patient and would give them time to scramble in on hands and knees before telling the drivers to start. But there were those just like half bodies, head and trunk, whom you could lift with one hand like a baby, and she shuddered to think how these were looked after for, even though some had been given wheelchairs, you could not ever see them making use of them or imagine them heaving themselves up or propelling the chair along with those tiny arms. It did not bear thinking of. At home the only beggars were those half-crazed who hung around bus stops and bars and were steered away gently by the headman if they looked like getting out of control. But there was the other kind of begging too, the hands held out for soap or tobacco money, the long whine of complaints . . . Even at home people were not secure in what they produced, not confident, not content. Would someone, then, feel at home in any place?

She reached what she now called home in time, put on an apron and

126

bustled about setting out trays of nuts, crisps and biscuits. The cook was finishing off the sticks of grilled meat and then going off for the evening.

She did not exactly share in the party but moved in and out, opening bottles and emptying ashtrays, greeting those who were regular guests of the house. The coloured girl they had seen at the theatre – Nancy, Martin had called her – was there with one of the civil servants, very much made-up, wearing a midi-skirt, a low-cut blouse and calf-length boots. She greeted Paulina civilly and seemed to be looking her up and down. Then she worked her way close to the MP and spoke to him in confidential tones.

'Joyce isn't coming today?'

'Joyce is a kid. This isn't the sort of place for her.'

'Isn't it? I thought it might be.'

She turned aside and Paulina filled her glass. Mr M. was looking a bit uneasy. In someone's own house, she thought, people should not embarrass him like that. Mrs M. was chatting determinedly with a big group in another corner, chiding one of the Commission members for not having brought his wife. The man rallied back as well as he could, saying that in such delightful company one should not be tied to the same face one saw at breakfast every morning, but there was a hint of something more than humour in Mrs M.'s persistence, and she was not sorry to turn her attention to Paulina's request to take some refreshments to the children's room as they were obstinately awake and calling for her.

'We never get any fun,' asserted the eldest.

'Not much fun for you there,' rejoined Paulina. 'A lot of grown-up people standing about and talking. You've got as good to eat as they have and you can hear the music from the gramophone just as loudly.'

'We can't even see the TV.'

'Well, for one night that won't hurt you all that much.'

'Is Joyce there?'

'Joyce? What Joyce?'

'The pretty one. Nearly white one. She works in Daddy's office.'

'Does she now? I don't see anybody there from the office.'

'Yes, she was with Daddy when he came to pick me up from school. Mummy had asked Daddy to come because the other car was out of

127

order, and she said she worked there, and she was nice and played I Spy with me. And she said she wants to be an MP herself when she grows up – well, she is grown up, of course, but not very. Her mother keeps a hotel in Eastleigh, she said.'

'A kind of hotel, perhaps. I think I know her mother. But she's not at the party. They're mostly old people.'

'Really old people? Older than you?'

'Perhaps some of them are even older than me. Now eat up and be quiet. I have to go now – it sounds as though your father wants me in the kitchen. And wipe your hands before you get grease all over the sheets, mind.'

'Paulina – where the hell did you get to? Find me another bottle. They think your taps run neat whisky, these people, as soon as you get "The Hon." in front of your name.'

'Half a minute. Here you are. I was just attending to the children.'

'Children! Good Lord, aren't they old enough to go to bed by themselves? Now find me some more glasses. Two are broken already.'

He was not often that sharp with her. After all, he had the right. But the question about Joyce nagged at the back of her mind and the wastefulness of it all, and the hard looks of the women in expensive frocks, keeping themselves up, of course, just as the Pumwani wives used to do, against the competition of pretty youngsters who had never had to liven up election rallies after a hard week's work and forbear from counting the spoons and knives after the victory party.

'My God, why do we do all this?' cried Mrs M. after the last guest had gone, kicking off her high-heeled shoes as Paulina swept up the broken glass. 'No need to wash anything now but for heaven's sake tell the cook not to make breakfast for us in the morning. You can see to the children and get them off to church, only get me a flask of tea about nine o'clock and see that no visitors disturb us – none at all. Oh Lord, why don't we go back to the village?'

'Because you would be brewing the beer and carrying the man's chair for him if you did,' answered Paulina boldly, and Mrs M. made a face at her to show she knew she was out of sorts and out of character.

Martin was fast asleep. He woke with a sore head, perhaps because he had had to go and share supper with the cook, perhaps because he had caught a glimpse of Nancy and was harking back to a relationship Paulina could only guess at, perhaps just because he had missed the whisky and the deep talk of public affairs. He flounced out without saying where he was going and she fell to work, cornflakes and tea for the children's breakfast, stacking away the glasses and linen after Juma had washed them, counting the empties for return. She tidied up the lounge, leaving the hard cleaning for Juma to do next day, took a couple of 'call-back' messages and saw him started on the lunch before the first delegation arrived.

The first delegation consisted of a couple of elegantly suited young men whom she recognised as coming from the constituency. She sat them under a tree in the garden and gave them tea. The second delegation was made up of five rather older and shabbier men who said they came from a co-operative. She had a bench brought out for them and promised more tea, while a basket of whole maize lay delicately on the grass awaiting presentation. The third incursion was a carload of ladies wanting to take Mrs M. off to a rally somewhere. They said they would call back in an hour when, Paulina said, swallowing hard, the family might be back from church. At this point she discreetly tapped on the bedroom door.

Mr M. emerged a little later, informed the delegates that he could spare them just twenty minutes, as he had a lunch date at 12.30 and noisily drove away. Mrs M. decided to remain 'in church' but the ladies did not in fact come back till four o'clock, by which time she had gone to visit a friend in hospital. Nobody ate lunch except the children, and Paulina spent the rest of the day crocheting in the garden. She liked doing things with her hands and enjoyed seeing good work done by others. Perhaps women's work was like that – the word for creation was the same one you used practically for knitting or pottery. Men's work was so often destructive – clearing spaces, breaking things down to pulp, making decisions – and how often did the decisions amount to anything tangible? Words in the air, pious intentions, rules about what not to do. She was glad that a lot of her work lay in making and mending things. This was more satisfying to her than those nebulous women's meetings where you were expected to keep your hands still but weave and work your mind laboriously through a tangle of words.

3

A relation of Mrs M.'s kept a tailor's shop just off Cross Street: Paulina had been there with her to check on a fitting and sometimes went to pick up a finished garment or a bag of beans sent in from the country. She liked going there in a nervous kind of way – she was moved by the immense vitality of the district, every little shop front spawning new business, enterprises taking shape on the pavements, the young and strong thronging corners, seeking a way to employ their overflowing energy, preferably for profit but at least to use up some of the exuberant time which they could not picture running out, could not pin down in cartons or padded jackets till the unimaginable day when someone would want to buy it off them. She was still amazed by the contrast with the languor of small town streets, their ponderous slowness and paucity of conversation.

She liked the square at the bottom of the hill with trees and iron balconies in unevenly climbing flats, like the pictures of old European cities she had seen in travel agents' windows. True, the space under the tree was not neatly planted but a sleeping place for drunks and vagrants and also, perhaps, for disheartened and hungry jobseekers. Of course the saris and *shukas* fluttering from the railings were not like Paris or Italian dress seen in newspapers, and the pastel-painted turreted temple altered the skyline, but still Paulina felt herself in the presence of something sophisticated and immeasurably old.

She might smooth her skirts away and clutch her handbag tightly, for all these twenty years she had remained fastidious, disturbed by the more raucous aspects of the town, the gobbets of raw meat, the repetitious rows of the same watches, the same transistor radios, the same suitcases and schoolbags, the letters stencilled, here and there reversed, on the insides of shop windows, shirts flung open to the waist, babies' tasselled berets or cut-down ladies' felt hats on bejewelled young men, platform soles and wedges strapped like fetters on girls' feet, as ungainly as lip plugs or facial scars from remote countries. She steeled herself against the strident music, Hindi or Congolese, pouring from open shop fronts, the shouts across the street in one language or another which always seemed, half-caught, to contain a word or two of your own, the husky pleas of street-sellers, the whistles which could not, any more, be aimed in her direction but which she must not even appear to be curious about, the honk of horns which might mean come in or get out of the way, the whirring of machines, an occasional chortle of pigeons. But still she enjoyed going there, with the same detachment, perhaps, as the ochre-haired moran or cloaked Turkana watchmen with their intricate ear-rings who were always gazing haughtily into windows of electric torches or striped socks, and still she came back, dazzled with activity, to the good order of the residential districts, where occasionally a gap between houses, a servant's shack under the trees, a shrub in flower or the high painted gates of an embassy took you into the fairytale world of the children's picture books.

It was on a visit to the tailor's that Paulina found herself briefly in the news. She was on her way to pick up a suit of Mr M.'s that had been made larger, and paused to stare in a shop window at one of those ornaments where a bird dips and raises its head without visible mechanism over a seeming pool of water. From a side alley came shouts and scuffling, then the sound of a small boy crying. One or two people stopped to stare, then hurried on. Paulina peered round the corner. She saw two big boys, perhaps eleven and twelve, holding down a smaller boy on the ground, a few coins clutched in his hand. One of the big boys had his foot on the child's chest and was trying to prise open his fist: the other was slapping his face.

'Let me go, let me go,' the little one howled. 'It's my money. You can't take it.'

'But I bet you on the next lorry in the garage. You owe me eighty cents.'

'No, no, I don't,' wailed the urchin. 'You took the twenty cents I had then. I never bet a shilling. You can't take what I didn't have then.'

The little boy was wearing a ragged pair of shorts and an oversized T-shirt that read, between holes, 'University of California'. His head was cropped almost bare and he was reasonably sturdy. The boy threatening him was tall and skinny, with stick-like arms and legs. Every rib showed under his buttonless shirt and his shorts were made up of patches. His eyes were red and sore, his hair long and gingery with wisps of straw and wood shavings adhering to it. The princely

131

character with his foot on the victim's chest wore, with an air of condescension, odd sandals, one red, one blue, knickerbockers to mid-calf, a Blue-Band Margarine T-shirt and an eye-shade on a piece of elastic. A one-inch fag-end hung from the corner of his mouth.

'Stop it,' said Paulina firmly in Swahili. 'Let the little boy alone.'

They took no notice, nor did passers-by. Paulina was surprised at herself.

'I told you to stop it,' she repeated. 'Two big boys against one little one. That's not fair.'

To her surprise the slapping stopped, though the arrogant foot remained in place.

'It's my money, missus,' said a small voice. 'A man gave me. I didn't steal it. I want to eat, not to bet with it.'

'Betting is wrong.' Paulina could hear herself, sententious, like a very young curate. 'And also silly when you have so little. Keep the money for food.'

A crowd was beginning to collect.

'They can go to Kariokor,' said a man in messenger's uniform. 'They get looked after there if there really isn't any family: if there is, they have to go home. But some of these Nairobi boys are just sent out to beg.'

'He's got a mother and a room to live in,' announced the skinny one, pointing at the small boy. 'He don't have to work for his food like some of us.'

'But she doesn't come till night-time, Che,' cried the small one. 'You think I'm going to stay hungry till then?'

'You got something, Johnny,' the possessor of the eye-shade pronounced judgment: someone in the crowd addressed him as Muhammad Ali. 'But Che ain't got nothing. That's why I've got to help him more than you. It isn't just a matter of size.'

This philosophic statement impressed the onlookers.

'What about you?' asked a big boy in the crowd.

Muhammad Ali removed his foot, acknowledging himself outnumbered, but kept a firm hand on Johnny's shoulder when he bounced to his feet.

'Me? I can work when I have to. I got a brother sells things.'

'Oh yes, we know what kind of things,' said a shopkeeper, menacingly.

Paulina felt the initiative slipping from her and for the first time in her life she resented it.

'You three – would you like something to eat?'

They did not need asking twice and suddenly small, ragged, doubtless hungry boys bristled from the pavement. They seemed to appear from nowhere.

'You and you and you,' she repeated. 'I can't treat everybody. But no more fighting now. Let him keep his money.' And she led them off to a snack bar with wall paintings of smartly dressed customers with forkfuls of chips and mugs of tea. She was surprised to find someone at the edge of the crowd taking photographs, deeply offended when he asked for her name and her opinion on child vagrants. Haughtily she turned her back on him and led her charges to a table where, despite raised eyebrows behind the counter, they were served with tea and large sticky buns, after much splashing of hands under a running tap.

Muhammad Ali, she discovered, lived in a shanty with his brother and a couple of friends.

'It's not bad when it's dry. When it's raining, though, it's hard to keep warm: even if you put ⸜ardboard on the floor the damp seeps up into your blankets and all that. And the rats. My brother makes some money selling things from door to door. Vegetables? Well, odd things he picks up, like. One of his friends helps a man who runs a handcart from the country bus stop and the other one sometimes gets work on a building site. Not regular, of course, but still we can eat. Only you can't leave food over because of the rats. You need to bring a bit every day.'

'And can you leave your things safely?' asked Paulina, who had seen the wretched humps of cardboard and polythene down by the river. 'Don't people try to take your blankets in the day-time, or your cooking things?'

'Oh no, neighbours don't do that. Someone from outside might try to ferret around, but probably there's someone we know there most of the time. We help one another, you see, don't dirty near someone's shanty and that. It's the City Council you have to watch out for, but we've been in the same place nearly a year and not got burned down. Some of the people used to fold all their stuff up every Saturday and stow it in a ditch in case of a raid, put the house up again in the

133

evening, but it's a waste of time that. If they burn, it will go anyway.'

'I saw a fire,' put in Johnny. 'Last year I saw a fire down by the tea-shanty they call "Hilton No.2". The smoke was bad.'

'Yes, it was bad, and they pulled out a lot of things, but one house they said they had a lot of stolen clothes and they had to let'm burn because the askaris were watching to see what you brought out. All the dustbins people had scoured out for brewing had to go – of course they belonged to City Council to start with, before they were hired out to houses.'

'But you feel safe enough?' asked Paulina.

'Oh yes, we can look after ourselves. Only if they move you, of course, then you write off your vegetables. One of our friends has a little patch he digs down by the river. And they come sometimes to look for bhang – police that is, not City Council. Then sometimes they come with horses because people say the horse can smell the bhang.'

'But you could go home if you had to.' Che made the statement wistfully.

'Yes, my people are there – my dad and my second mother and the smaller children. But there are too many people to feed from the plot. Far too many. Here is better. When I've started to pick up casual work, like my brother's friend, I'll send home for my next brother. Life is better here. Let the girls stay there. We managed to get uniform, pencils and things for the bigger one to go to school. They don't have to pay fees for the first classes now. I only went for two years myself.'

'I only went to standard two myself,' said Paulina, and was horrified to hear herself saying it. For years it had not been said. 'But I have learned a lot of things since. If you try hard you keep on learning.'

The boys nodded agreement.

'And what about you, Che?' she asked. 'Did you go to school? I think you must have to get a name like that.'

'Yes,' he said slowly. 'I went to school when my mother was alive. She died when I was nearly finished class two. I was nine then, going on ten. I had a uniform and she always patched it and kept it clean. And we always had enough to eat. Nothing fancy, not meat and that but regular. And hot porridge before we started for school. My sister was in standard one. Then there were two that died, and then a

134

brother and the baby died too when she had it. My dad had a job as night watchman in Nakuru. He didn't come often, but when he came he used to bring us bread and maybe a pencil or something like that.'

'You keep thinking back, Che,' said Muhammad Ali. 'That's no good. You've got to learn to look after yourself in town. Get a nice doorway with a wind break early before they're all taken up, like I showed you. Not go mooning about and then just lie down in a corner where it will rain on you.'

'She used to call me Kariuki,' the boy continued. 'But there was this student came to teach at the secondary school during the holidays, and he said I had to be brave and strong like Che. He was a soldier. Do you know about him?'

'Not much,' said Paulina. 'He was on an island somewhere. But I see students talking about him and one of them uses the name – university students, I mean.'

This passed them by.

'So my dad said we couldn't go on to school for a while because he needed all his money to get another woman to look after us. And when he was there she was all right to us, but she started going queer when she got her own baby: then she hated the sight of us and used to keep beating us for every little thing. And then last year she started saying that she didn't get married to come and live in a back-of-beyond village with a load of kids, and not any rice or hair oil or nice soap like her friends had for their babies, and only seeing her man one day or two in the month, and then she started to drink. And then she didn't cook every day, and never early in the morning, and started saying it was our fault that my dad didn't pay her attention. He only wanted his first wife's children and all that. In the end my little brother got so hurt he ran off to his granny: she doesn't have much, but she likes him and tells him stories. But my sister had to stay to help look after the baby, so my dad said. But me, she said I didn't do anything around the place but eat, and so one day when she beat me worse than usual I ran to my friend's big brother who is conductor on a country bus, and he talked with his dad and put some ointment on the bad places and gave me a ride on the bus free. That was about two months ago.'

'He didn't know anything,' put in Muhammad Ali. 'Lucky for him

I found him wandering about. I showed him the temples, where they give you free food if there is a celebration going on. And how to find the eating places, where good food sometimes gets thrown out when they close, and how – well, all sorts of things I showed him. He just didn't know how to stay alive.'

'Well, you're not very fat yet, Che. What about that place the man said at Kariokor? I know where it is.'

'Oh, we all know where it is,' Che replied, for the first time claiming the fellowship of the down and out. 'But if you take their free meals and their bed, within a fortnight you've got to be sent back where you came from. No thank you! She'll kill me rather than take me in, and if I can manage for myself long enough I'll kill her, and take my sister away, and get a place for her to stay and proper dresses and all that. You think I'm thin? You haven't seen my sister.'

'And couldn't you get a message to your father?'

'My father is sleeping on some doorway in Nakuru. The difference is that he gets paid for it. But my father is finished. Is that what having a wife does for you? He drinks too, now that he finds her with the stuff, and he's too far gone even to listen to our side of it. No, you learned a lot since you came to Nairobi and you're all right, aren't you? I'm going to learn too and however hungry I am I'm keeping well away from that Kariokor place. Nobody's going to say I come crawling back.'

His bewilderment and resentment frightened Paulina. Was he right in suggesting that all her lessons had been learned in Nairobi? She had resented her own time in Kariokor, escaped from it but never fundamentally questioned it. But for these children return meant renouncing their brave adventure into town and a new world, facing, after an interlude of feeding at the Save the Children Centre, recriminations at home, hunger, renewal of humiliation all the more bitter for glimpses of life that looked from the outside so different. No wonder so many of them refused to go, listened to the false bells pealing 'Turn again, Whittington', as the lucky boy in the story had – but then the stories were always about the lucky ones – or went into the refuge pondering all the questions and possibilities that to most people do not become apparent until their course of life is irrevocably set. Perhaps, after all, that was what it all meant, this turmoil and

136

change that had beset her ever since getting married, that act which the grannies, like the story-books again, regarded as so simple and inevitable that after it there was nothing left to tell.

She roused herself: the boys were still chattering and looking hopeful. She called for second cups.

'Me,' Johnny said simply, 'I only have to live in the day-time. My ma makes me tea in the morning and in the night-time she brings me chips or cassava or something, and I have a blanket to sleep on behind the curtain. I'm not to come out till the morning, out round the curtain I mean. Then there's only me and my ma.' He paused. 'Where do you live, missus?'

'I live on the other side of town. I work in a big house. I look after the children and the visitors. So there is a little house for me and my husband.'

'You got children, missus?'

'I had a little boy but he – died – a long time ago.' She had said it. She choked a little but she had got it out, and these children could understand it, because to them grief and deprivation was commonplace.

'You don't want another little boy like me?'

'Don't be silly, Johnny,' Che snapped at him. 'She wants her own one. Only natural, isn't it?'

'What happened to him?' asked Muhammad Ali politely, showing sympathy the only way he knew.

'There was a big crowd. I was living near Kisumu then – and he got – shot.'

The boy nodded, age-old and knowing – he made her think of the old man saying, 'We left our dead . . .'

'I had an uncle shot in the Emergency,' he said. 'Of course, I didn't know him – my auntie told me. They never found out who did it, but he crawled back half a mile, bleeding, before he finally passed out. So my dad had to pay school fees for his kids, see, after he came out, and then they kept his part of the land for themselves. That's why there isn't much left . . .'

Paulina looked at her watch.

'My goodness, I have work to do, you know. I must get on.'

'Thanks for the·tea, missus.'

137

'That's all right. But no more fighting, mind. I know it's hard for you, but knocking one another about won't help.'

'And look out for that watch of yours, ma – missus I mean – that big boy who tried to get in with us, regular for watches he is.'

'I'm sorry,' said Che quietly. Then, afraid of being misunderstood, 'Not sorry for anything I've done, mind. I mean I'm sorry about your little boy.'

Paulina hurried off to the tailor's, feeling she had learned something that both clarified and complicated things. As she came out with the parcel she saw Johnny, eyes wide and appealing, scampering along to keep pace with a well-dressed man who had just got out of his car.

'After all,' Johnny was saying, 'for all you know you might be my father.'

4

It was late. She was behind time with the children's supper and the oldest had skipped his homework, so she did not speak to the family about the incident but mentioned it to Martin that night.

'Damn silly,' he growled. 'You can't do anything. Show sympathy and they're only after what they can get out of you.'

She neither retorted nor acquiesced and he appeared to forget about it until the Sunday paper came out with a picture of her haranguing the little boys on the middle page.

'Discipline by kindness,' read the headline. 'This lady, whom our reporter overheard urging a group of parking boys to stop a fight, afterwards took them to a restaurant for a meal to remember. Refusing to give her name or comment on the situation, this good lady has given a practical lesson in charity that many of us only talk about.'

Martin was angry with a tight-lipped fury that she had not seen in him for many years.

'Making fools of us all,' he shouted. 'Now every beggar in Nairobi will come flocking after us expecting to get something. Just drawing attention, that's what it is.'

Mrs M. was overjoyed.

'You should have given them your name,' she said, 'and a lecture on responsible parenthood.'

'Me give a lecture! You're joking!'

'No joking! You used to teach women to knit and crochet, which doesn't by any means come by the light of nature. Ways of keeping families together, poor or not, surely ought to come easier.'

'But I who haven't . . .'

'That didn't stop you getting along with these kids. Look at their faces.'

'Well, I'm glad you didn't name any names,' said Mr M. 'Might have been embarrassing for us and landed you with a whole lot of begging letters. I know you feel sorry for these children but palliatives don't help much.'

'And what is there except palliatives?' demanded Mrs M. 'The kids would be dead before you could alter the system to provide residential care for all of them. What you can give them right away is a crumb of self-respect.'

'Not necessarily charitable care. Just jobs and homes for their fathers.'

'*Only* jobs and homes – and a ticket to the moon each! In any case how many of these particular kids have a father who's not drunk, dead, sunk without trace or just plain unemployable?'

'I don't think it's self-respect they're lacking in,' said Paulina. 'It's other people's respect. And therefore they find it hard to respect grown-up people themselves.'

Mr M. stared at her and nodded agreement.

'All the same, Paulina, you must think before you act.'

'I reckon I've had a lot of time for thinking – years and years for it,' said Paulina, slowly and deliberately. 'And these kids have more thinking-time than is good for them, too. It's my business who I buy a cup of tea for, and who I give my name to, if it comes to that.'

She picked up the late breakfast dishes and swept off to the kitchen with them. Mr M. whistled.

'It looks as though you've got yourself a new woman, all right,' he said in his own language.

'Good for her.'

'Indeed, good for her. I hope Martin knows his luck.'

'I doubt it,' replied Mrs M., 'but she makes the best of it.'

Martin did not come in till ten at night. He refused the food that was ready for him and insisted on having the light turned out straight away though his wife was still sewing.

Next time Paulina went to the tailor's Mrs M. gave her some outgrown shirts for 'her' boys. She didn't run into Che or Johnny, but Muhammad Ali was stalking about in a shirt that still read faintly, after many washings in the river, 'Stings like a bee' and a crown of cardboard with the newspaper photograph mounted on it above a band that read 'Pride of Kumasi Street'.

On the way home she ran into Nancy, making for a bus stop. Paulina would have passed with a quick greeting but Nancy was determined to talk.

'I saw your picture in the paper,' she said.

'Oh, that. The photographer must have been just passing.'

'It was good, though. Don't be bashful about it. Anything that helps readers to see those kids as people is good.'

'One of them considers himself "people" all right.' She told Nancy about the cardboard crown.

'I like that. You see – I know you don't approve of me, but you ought to know – I could easily have been like that. Only my mother worked hard for me and even got me started in secondary school, but I didn't finish. You have to be tough, you know.'

'I don't know how tough you are. You don't sound it today. But I know what you mean also. Did Martin ever tell you about what happened to me in Kano?'

'He didn't. But Joyce did. I'm sorry. You know – all that time I wasn't seeing Martin, honest. I left Kibera the day Tom Mboya died – I was just a kid: I couldn't stand all the weeping and wailing. And it was afterwards that – it happened – wasn't it. After we met you at the theatre, then Joyce told me. I hadn't known her very long then: she was doing a secretarial course the same place I was doing a refresher course: my boss gave me day-release to do it. So of course she didn't know I'd ever been friendly with Martin.' They were looking straight at one another, Nancy's handsome light brown face, with high cheekbones and hair elaborately pinned back was just beginning to show wrinkles at the corners of the eyes, to need that vivid lipstick to gain attention. She is, what, ten or twelve years younger than me, thought Paulina, and soon she will be old. Why do we look at these young things as though they are a challenge to us for ever? And Nancy

140

was thinking, she doesn't make much of herself. She thinks she doesn't care any more. But what dignity she has, good features, good sense. A decent girdle and a bit of colour about her, if you got rid of that awful headscarf, and Martin could be in for a bit of competition again.

'But the point is – sorry, the buses are going but I need to talk to you – Joyce, she's not so tough.'

'She had a good home, I know, ever since she was a baby.'

'But me, I've always had my eye on the main chance. Not that it's done me any good. Any security I've got comes from my own hard work, and if you let the time go for getting married . . . well, when I first knew Joyce she'd just left school with a third grade, and so when that boss of yours came stalking round her I thought she was on to a good thing. I didn't arrange it, mind you, but I didn't try to stop it either. And now I see that she's really upset about it. Is his wife cutting up rough?'

'I've no idea. We are on good terms, but not as close as that. If we had been I'd have warned the wife myself. I felt a bit bad when I saw Joyce in his car once. But I suppose Amina – Joyce's mother – always had an eye on the main chance, as you say, herself. I wouldn't have expected her to encourage the girl, but I thought it was not up to me to interfere.' There was a silence between them while the babble of early office leavers, late hawkers, urgent traffic and military helicopters at practice continued all round.

'There was sometimes a kind of – strain – in the house,' went on Paulina. 'You know what I mean? People are fed up over their work – they say so. They're bawling the kids out for making too much noise – you know it. Something wrong with the bank balance, they let it drop. But sometimes there's something else and you wonder whether you imagined it, or brought it in, or whether they even know it's there.'

'I do know. Certainly something made him cool off on Joyce pretty quick. I think she has got the message, but I'll try to see that she doesn't call him up any more. You can tell the lady so if it seems necessary. OK?'

'OK. Thank you.'

'And . . .'

'And?'

141

'I'd do the same for you if it were necessary. But as far as anyone I know goes, it isn't necessary.'

'I know,' said Paulina cheerfully. 'But it would be no good the pot calling the kettle black.'

'Look who'd be calling me black!'

You could talk like that. It wasn't taboo any more. So they parted cheerfully, and at that moment Paulina heard a little voice piping up Tom Mboya Street. 'After all, you might be my father.' She was too embarrassed to break up the act and present Johnny with his prep school shirt.

The next day somebody rang up Paulina and asked for an interview. It frightened her to think that someone could track her down just from a photograph and find the house and the telephone number as well as the name. She was a little flattered but instinctively refused the interview.

'Perhaps,' she said vaguely, 'some other time, when I've done something. This was only an incident.' And she took down the lady reporter's name and number. 'When I have done something.' She wondered what in her life she had ever expected to do. But it bore thinking about.

CHAPTER
SEVEN

1

For the beginning of 1978 they had a New Year's Eve party. Paulina had come to think of parties in the house as always something to do with business. They occurred when somebody was coming into office or somebody going abroad, they sometimes ended with a little group talking, talking, talking in Mr M.'s study, or with plans for some enormous self-help collection or occasionally with a sense of disappointment if some important person had failed to turn up.

But New Year's Eve was going to be different. Mr M. had just been seeing a delegation of squatters asking for someone to take a case about their land rights.

'What's the use? They can never get anything out of it,' exclaimed Mr M. looking weary. He ordered a big meal to be served to the old men but hurried off in the car before they tackled it. 'This is a day for us to remember,' said the leader of the delegation courteously, as Paulina served them under a tree (Juma took a poor view of feeding people who were 'not proper visitors'), but what else was there for them except a sympathetic memory? Mrs M. had just succeeded in getting homes for two orphaned babies, but for dozens of others there had been no success. There seemed no end to it. Paulina herself was putting aside secondary school fees for her elder sister's child, should she get a form one place, as the father was out of work, and wondering how she would manage if the rest of the family were also going to demand help. Okeyo would have been going into the examination class – well, no good going back over it.

'Damn it all,' said Mrs M. 'Let's have the party and hope for better things. I'm having a new dress in any case. Let's drown our sorrows. The little that we might save would not put anything to rights.'

'Little by little fills the measure,' quoted Paulina soberly, but she also shared their mood. 'No aprons today,' said Mrs M. 'This time it isn't to impress anybody. Bring Martin over too.'

So Martin put on his best suit and sat steadily drinking beer and getting more and more depressed. They sang. Some of them danced to the gramophone. They listened to the peal of midnight. They lay long awake, seeking comfort for a restlessness they could not explain. And the first newspaper to come out after the holiday weekend told them that Ngugi had been arrested. They all – hosts, guests and neighbours – told one another that they couldn't have known, that New Year was a holiday and one couldn't keep wondering and anticipating. But they all knew that there was nothing to celebrate, and kept telling one another what a good party it had been. None of them were great readers, but everybody knew about Ngugi: after all, if his books were set in school you could be sure they were good.

For eleven days they waited, and there was silence in Nairobi behind the clamour of voices, the feeling partly of expectation, partly of fear, as when a vehicle is overdue. On the eleventh day news of the detention order was released. At least you knew where you were.

Paulina supposed at first that it was the January heat and the general tension that made her feel specially tired and irritable. Martin came home at the end of the month with a copy of Ngugi's *Petals of Blood* – he who had almost stopped buying books and was sceptical even of newspapers – and sat down solidly to read it, so there were long evenings with hardly a word spoken.

Paulina had spent years enough alone not to be worried by silence. She hugged her thoughts to herself. She was at home now. And at home, though news comes to you of meetings and proclamations, of trials and conflict and achievement, home does not change for that, Nairobi does not change for that, whisper, whisper, whisper, the hum of traffic and the undertones of bargaining, the quick breath of pushing carts and the slow breath of sleep, the unbroken round of terms, of seasons, of fashions, of celebrations. There is always something to do, always something to talk about, if you gave yourself time to learn, always something to depend on too and to live by.

It was in March that Paulina met Amina. She had gone to town to get the electric iron repaired and to match some curtain material for the children's room. She found herself fingering the nursery designs, peering into cots. This would not do. She must not yet again set her

144

heart on it. And she had not even spoken to Martin, dared not face him with it. Leaving the shop she found Amina staring intently into the window, obviously figuring in her head. The two women greeted one another warmly.

'Are you buying the shop up?' asked Paulina cheerfully. 'Doing up your apartment house?'

'Not only that,' Amina confided proudly, 'I'm going into partnership in a small private nursing home. Maternity and all that, you know. Lady staff. Not all those men poking the women about.'

Paulina nodded, amused at Amina's contempt for male skills. Still, she knew it would help to get her clients.

'So we have to furnish the wards. Everything nice, you know, pretty. Nice for the mothers, nice for people to work in, nice they will pay for it too. But it has to be good stuff. All that washing – my, have you any idea of the washing?' Paulina was seized with a vision of Pumwani, Amina's motto-ed wrapper and embroidered tablecloths hung out on a string, her own constant battle with white crocheted chairbacks.

'Where I work now we have a washing machine,' she offered.

'Of course, of course. But the material has to be strong to stand all those detergents.' And bars of soap they used to stack in the cupboards to get hard so that there would be less waste when you scrubbed with them.

'I haven't seen Joyce for a long time. How is she getting on?'

'No, I guess you haven't seen her since that long-faced boss of yours let her down. But she's getting on fine. Got established as secretary grade two now. American boy wants to marry her. I don't mind as long as she doesn't go so far away. He wants to find his roots, she says. Well enough, I told her, let's see what roots he's got six months from now. What he's found so far is a fancy hairstyle and a temporary job. Still, better than the old ones promising and promising and never getting around to anything. Besides, she's a Christian: she's not supposed to be going for a second wife. It's not the same as it would be for me. And that madam you work for wouldn't be welcoming her either.'

'Indeed not. I didn't know there was ever . . .'

'Well, least said soonest mended. You and I know not to judge an old lion by the loudness of his roar,' she added companionably, 'and

145

we've made our way in spite of that.'

Paulina knew she was being offered a compliment but she dared not confess her hopes of a quite other congratulation.

'We have learned to take what comes and make the best of it,' she said.

'To *make* what comes and to *take* the best of it,' answered Amina firmly. 'But there's my bus coming: I must go. Greet the big man for me and tell your friends to come to my nursing home.'

'Goodbye. Give my love to Joyce.' But underneath Paulina was saying, 'No, not a nice little nursing home but the big hospital, the biggest, where everything can be taken care of. And the next thing is to put it in words and see if it will still be there.'

She was free that evening after the children's supper, and when she had set Martin's food out and prepared tea for herself she began cautiously:

'I met Amina today.'

'Amina? My goodness, she must be feeling her age a bit by now. What's she up to these days?'

'She's opening a maternity home.'

'Well, good luck to her.'

'An all-female one.'

'Well, I suppose the other half has already discharged its duty. Let the women care for the women. She has gone up in the world, hasn't she?'

'Yes, indeed. Do you remember when we stayed in her house in Pumwani? She was good to me then.'

'She was, and fair as landladies go. And do you want to tell me that no one else was ever good to you? Because I thought we'd decided to leave all that crap behind.'

'Yes, I thought so too. It wasn't that. I wasn't throwing anything up at you. Only I couldn't help remembering, the first day I came to that house. It was all so strange to me, and I told you I was three months on and you didn't believe me.'

'Well, you were and then you weren't. There's no use bringing that up again.'

'But I found it hard to tell you then, Martin, when we had been so little together. And if I were to tell you now again, Martin, that it was the third month, would you believe me this time?'

'Believe you – woman, what are you saying? It's impossible. We are getting old. It is more than twenty years . . .'

'My husband, I am younger than your mother was when your last two sisters were born. I am the same age as my brother's wife, who is still bearing children. I would be old to have a first child, but you know it is not a first child. And though I hardly dare to hope, I must give you also this hope, after giving you disappointments so many years. Or do you no longer care?'

Martin was beside himself, half embracing her, half standing back to look at her.

'I have no reason not to be happy. All has not been well with us. You know it. I know it. There were women, and none of them gave me a child. You had another man and his child was lost to us. I thought you were only eager now to become a new woman – perhaps to go into Parliament.' They both burst out laughing. 'Or to get your photograph in the paper again waiting at one of Mrs M.'s parties.' He swallowed. 'Do I understand what you are telling me, or have I got it wrong?'

'You understand it, Martin. This is your baby. Since I came to Nairobi – in fact since I was carrying Okeyo – there has been no possibility of its not being yours, and I hope you will help me to take good care, so that even if one of your safari wives gives you a dozen children still you need not be ashamed of your home in Gem.'

'And you want to go off to Amina's little two-bit nursing home without a proper man doctor in the place. Is that it?'

'That is not it. I want to be near the biggest hospital so that everything can be done. Even if they cut me up I don't care so long as it is all right.'

'I'll sell the shop if necessary. I'll tell my people to take me off safari work. Anything. Do you want to move away from here?'

'No. No. Now you are getting excited. I keep house here as though it were my own house. The work is not too hard. The family is always here – the car, the telephone. If you are away I can't get sick without anyone knowing.'

'Have you told Mrs M.?'

'Not yet. She will be happy for us but she will pretend to be

147

disappointed because she likes to present me to her clubs and classes as the lone woman, independent of domestic ties.'

They laughed until they were tired and then were almost too tired to sleep, overcome with joy, surprise and an unexpected trust.

Mrs M. was indeed at first alarmed by this reactionary event, then moved by it, then actively excited.

'I'll use it as an illustration for my family talks. Do not rush to marry young. Satisfaction for the older couple. Happiness through persistence, mature maternity.'

'Say what you like afterwards,' laughed Paulina, 'but just now let's keep custom, eh? No boasting, no getting things in advance. Believe me, I've suffered enough disappointment not to want to shout too soon.' And in her heart she thought, 'perhaps then I could ring back the lady reporter after all.'

The clinic was enormous and part of a still vaster hospital complex. How much easier to lose her way now than all those years ago when she had lost her first baby there. True she had gained in confidence and the place had gained in skill and equipment, but, if one dared think about it, how much more she knew about the possibilities of loss and being lost. How confident girls still were in that simple alternative, blood or no blood, and how she would have trembled, that long-lost girl-like Paulina now sealed deep under layers of propriety and habit, at these formidable questionnaires, this gleaming array of diagnostic instruments. There were a few girl-brides scattered about the benches, but all better clothed, better informed, no doubt, than she had been, yet not better prepared for actively pressing towards motherhood. But many others were smart working ladies, secretaries perhaps, mindful of their figures as they swelled in discreet pleats behind their barrier desks, or teachers whose classes had been merged with others for the morning in the blur of noise. Some may have been simple housewives but experienced now, prompt with their little bottles, adept with numbered cards. The unpartnered had of necessity to deploy most skill, eager to return to work on time, to calculate correctly to define dates and claim for expenditure.

Paulina found it interesting. She was not sorry to be without the magazines or the knitting which (ahead of time and regardless of custom) occupied so many of these young women. She was not lost in

148

ecstasy – she had been already too scarred by hope for that – but keen to observe, as she had long missed observing in such a setting, those of her sisters, weary and sagging with protracted maternity, who had got so far ahead of her, those who might have been her daughters, firm-breasted, well-nourished, curiously shod, who were catching up. Not often here the thin limbs and tattered garments of the rural clinic, and not often here either the vociferous joys and woes of 'home'. A tired lady in uniform, herself vastly protruding, gave out leaflets headed 'Planned families are happy families' and healthy faces beamed over them from calendars advertising every kind of baby food and appliance. On one of the doors hung a notice announcing 'Breast is best'.

A pram, Paulina thought suddenly, would be a help. Baby out on the lawn while I am busy in the kitchen. Baby going out shopping with me, not left with a little nursemaid. In any case my employer doesn't hold with little nursemaids and has quarrelled with some of the other big ladies about it in the name of education for girls. A pram or a pushchair with a canopy for sunny days; it was no longer just a daydream, and in any case she would no longer find it easy to carry the weight.

At last Paulina's turn came to be interviewed at the table. She was questioned by a buxom woman of about thirty with dark shadows under her eyes and a telltale smear issuing from the left nipple under her white uniform.

'Age?'

'Thirty-eight.'

'Number of children?'

'None.'

'A la! How many live births have you had?'

'One.'

The woman looked at her strangely. 'Year?'

'Nineteen sixty-seven.'

'Cause of death?'

'He was shot.' It did not now much disturb her to say it. The nurse swallowed her next question and looked down at the paper. There was a sudden silence among the women waiting their turn at the nearest bench. One muttered under her breath, 'Holy Mother of God.'

'Date?' The woman was still not looking at her.

'Nineteen sixty-nine.'

'I am sorry,' the woman whispered. 'I know. I was a schoolgirl and we had to stand by the road. How long married?' she suddenly shouted, making a mark in the column 'accidental death'.

'Since 1956.'

'How many other pregnancies?'

'Four or five. I am not sure.'

'But you must be sure. You know whether or not . . .'

'People know what they wish and sometimes they come to believe what they wish.'

Again the nurse hung her head. 'Any discomfort?'

'Nothing special. But a very great hope.'

'Take your card to door number three. She always does her best for people like you, people who have cherished their hope a long time. I hope for you too. . . . Next!'

AFTERWORD

Marjorie Oludhe Macgoye has had a profound impact on the literature of Kenya, her adopted homeland. To date, she has published seven novels, two collections of poetry, children's stories, historical studies, and cultural criticism. Regardless of the form they have taken, all of Macgoye's works at their most basic level share a common theme: they explore the challenges, especially for women, of negotiating a changing world. While these challenges take a particular shape in postcolonial Kenya, Macgoye likes to remind her readers that movement, migration, and social change have always been part of the human experience.

Macgoye's writing has won her literary recognition in East Africa and abroad. In Kenya, her poems are read by schoolchildren, her novels are part of the university curriculum, and her work has become the subject of graduate-level dissertations. On the basis of artistic accomplishments alone, therefore, Macgoye ranks in the top tier of first-generation writers from East Africa, alongside other leading figures like Ngugi wa Thiong'o, Grace Ogot, and Okot p'Bitek.[1] But her influence has a significant personal side, as well. Macgoye has been the model and inspiration for many East African writers, thanks to her tenacious and principled commitment to promoting the literature of the region. She has been an active member of the Kenyan literary community in its various manifestations over the decades, and the writers' groups, meetings, and readings that Macgoye organized in Nairobi during the late 1970s have become the stuff of legend. In her early seventies at the turn of the millennium, Macgoye is regularly characterized in feature stories in the Kenyan press as the mother or grandmother figure—even the "doyenne"—of the country's literature. One such profile, in East Africa's longest-lived newspaper, describes her simply as a "national treasure" ("Catching Up").

Coming to Birth is Macgoye's second novel to be published and her best-known work. For a Kenyan audience, the story is all too familiar: A naïve young woman from rural Western Kenya joins her new husband in the city at a time of social unrest. Far from her familiar support structures, she is initially overwhelmed in this alien environment, but eventually manages to adjust to the exigencies of urban living, and in the end even finds that the city offers her some measure of emancipation. In Paulina, Macgoye offers an ordinary, unpretentious protagonist, who knows not to expect too much from life, but who must come to terms with dramatic social change. As the story of Paulina's transformation, then, *Coming to Birth* depicts very real concerns, and it has the distinction of being one of the first Kenyan novels to present these concerns from a woman's perspective. But there is more to *Coming to Birth* than Paulina's story, since hers is merged with the national story—the story of Kenya. As Macgoye herself has put it, *Coming to Birth* presents a personal narrative set against a particular historical backdrop:

> It attempts to show something about the consciousness of women which was emerging during those years. Something about the emergence of the concept of being a Kenyan, and a good deal about the consciousness of town life. (Troughear)

The novel's title alludes to births on various levels. There are literal births, of course, including the anticipated birth that closes the story, but Paulina's gradual transformation symbolizes a coming to birth as well—the birth of a confident and self-reliant woman. And wrapped around Paulina's story is the birth of Kenya as an independent entity. The tale begins in the troubled 1950s—the gestation and labor period leading to the birth of the new nation in December 1963—and continues through the first fifteen years of independence. Not surprisingly, Macgoye infuses the novel with the imagery of childbearing: gestation, labor, miscarriages, growing pains, and the emotions that accompany them. The present progressive of the title suggests that for

152

Paulina and Kenya alike, birth is a process rather than the work of a moment, and that this process is ongoing. Consequently, *Coming to Birth* offers a rich thematic repertoire. It is a feminist story about a woman overcoming great difficulties to make her way in a male-dominated society. It is about national identity and history, exploring the birth and early life of a new nation. It also suggests that life, like history, appears simple in retrospect, but is enormously complex and uncertain when we are living it. Life and history involve a complex series of difficult decisions, in which flawed and imperfect people, buffeted by forces beyond their control, try to make the most of their lives with limited knowledge and resources.

Coming to Birth was an immediate success when it was first released by the British publisher William Heinemann and by its Nairobi-based affiliate, Heinemann Kenya (now East African Educational Publishers), in 1986. Because its subject matter and style suited it to various educational levels, the novel soon appeared on the reading lists of Kenyan schools and universities. Heinemann Kenya quickly released a supplementary study guide for students, authored by the Ugandan writer and critic Austin Bukenya. In the year it was published, Macgoye's novel won an international award, the Sinclair Prize, and was released in yet another edition (now out of print) from the London-based feminist publisher Virago. This new edition of *Coming to Birth* from The Feminist Press is a welcome event, as it brings this important Kenyan novel within reach of a wider audience outside of East Africa.

Marjorie Macgoye defies easy categorization, as a writer and as an individual. British by birth but Kenyan by choice, she arrived in Nairobi in 1954 at the age of twenty-six, as a bookseller for the Church Missionary Society (CMS), the mission arm of the Anglican Church. Six year later, she quit her job to marry Daniel Oludhe Macgoye, a Luo medical officer to whom she had been unofficially engaged for two years. Along with 9 million others, she became a citizen of the new Republic of Kenya soon after it received its independence from Britain in 1963, and except for a four-year stint in Tanzania she has lived and worked there ever since, and raised four now-grown children.

Because of this background, Macgoye is an unusual, perhaps even a unique, figure in the literature of Kenya and of Africa. She certainly does not fit any of the typical categories of African writers. She is naturalized rather than native-born, so that while she is undoubtedly Kenyan, and while her marriage into a Luo family gives her special insight into that community's experience and sensibility, Macgoye clearly occupies a position very different from that of Kenya's indigenous black writers. At the same time, while there is a large community of white Kenyans— many of them former settlers or their descendants—this category seems even less apt, if only because Macgoye has consistently rejected the privileges that go along with being white in a place like Kenya. Writers from this group, who produce what is referred to in Kenya as "expatriate literature," include Elspeth Huxley, whose works describe growing up in a settler community in central Kenya, and Isak Dinesen, the pseudonym for Karen Blixen, whose book about her experience as an unsuccessful coffee farmer outside of Nairobi was made into the popular film of the same name, *Out of Africa*. Literature of the type produced by Huxley and Blixen is written from an outsider's point of view, with outsiders' concerns in mind, and it displays a consciousness of being part of a European colonial diaspora. Macgoye, by contrast, writes from a fundamentally different point of view and with radically different ends in mind. As a result, she is a Kenyan writer, but sui generis.

Macgoye's unusual life is best understood in light of three influences: her working-class background, the emancipating role of education in her life, and her commitment to a socially active Christian faith. She was born Marjorie Phyllis King in Southampton, England, on October 21, 1928, the only child of working-class parents. Her father, Richard Thomas King, was a clerk in a shipyard. As the oldest boy in his family, he had been forced to leave school and go to work at age twelve, and missed the more satisfying and lucrative artisan training that his younger brother enjoyed. Marjorie's mother, Phyllis, did complete school and was

154

a teacher before she was married, a job which she did not enjoy. When Marjorie was growing up, Phyllis did not work outside the home, but she later took in paying boarders. Marjorie's maternal grandparents lived with the family during Marjorie's early years, until their deaths in the mid-1930s, and her paternal grandparents lived nearby. Her childhood was affected by the Great Depression and by two wars: World War I was a recent memory that had left its mark, and World War II over-shadowed her teenage years. The wars affected all of British society, of course, but as an important passenger and cargo port city, Southampton was a prime military target; in her memoirs, Macgoye recalls two severe attacks, along with constant disturbances.[2]

Writing and reading were always part of Macgoye's life. She describes herself as being "fed on books" as a child, and a poem she wrote at age seven won publication in the *Daily Mirror*. She made it to secondary school on a scholarship, graduating in 1945 and taking university entrance exams when World War II was in its final stages. Marjorie had always assumed that higher education was beyond her reach—the only person that she knew who had been to university was the neighborhood doctor—but again she was awarded a scholarship, this time to the Royal Holloway College of the University of London, a small women's college in Egham, Surrey, just outside London. The college experience opened a new world to Macgoye, bringing her into contact with the current scholarly debates of the day, as well as international political and social issues. It was here, also, that she sensed a call to the mission field.

Macgoye's parents were churchgoers, although her grandparents were not. At college, Macgoye became what she now describes as "an earnest member" of the Student Christian Movement, a theologically and socially liberal alternative to the more evangelical Intervarsity Fellowship. When she felt the call to missionary work, she assumed that it would be in Africa: "It was not a burning desire to see people baptized," she says, "but rather to be a witness" (personal interview). The mission field was booming at the time, but for various reasons—which in retrospect, Macgoye

155

identifies as partly class bias and partly her own idiosyncracies—it would be six years before a missionary society took up her application. Following graduation in 1948, Macgoye spent those six years working in bookshops and other stores in London, involving herself in Labour Party politics, and at the same time completing a Master's degree from Birkbeck College, which catered to part-time students. She wrote a thesis on Thomas Carlyle and periodical criticism of the nineteenth century, and she published some of her academic work. Fully expecting to be sent to West Africa, Macgoye prepared by studying Yoruba. But when her call came, it was for a post that had unexpectedly opened in Nairobi, where CMS needed someone to work in the agency's bookstore.

The sudden nature of the opening meant that Macgoye never passed through the traditional one-year training that CMS required of its missionaries. This untraditional route is typical for Macgoye, who as a missionary was always something of a maverick, never following the standard path. When she arrived in Nairobi, for instance, she soon realized that the mission compound on Bishop's Road, on the summit of the elite Nairobi Hill, was far removed from the daily lives of the people she was supposed to serve. Within the year she moved instead to the mission house on the edge of Pumwani, the large "African location" that had grown up on what was then the city's outskirts. Today, the city has surrounded and absorbed Pumwani, but it remains one of Nairobi's major slum areas. Pumwani provides the early setting in *Coming to Birth*; in fact, Macgoye and another CMS worker who lived in the house with her appear in the novel as Ahoya and her assistant, Macgoye being "the short one with glasses and a bicycle" (30–31). From her new home, Macgoye would ride her bicycle each day to the CMS bookstore in Church House—at the time, the tallest building in Nairobi.[3]

It was during a visit to a Sunday school at Remand Prison, on the edge of Nairobi's industrial area, that Macgoye met her husband-to-be, then a medical assistant for the Ministry of Health. The two were married at the Anglican Church in Pumwani on June 4, 1960. Interracial marriages were not unheard of in Kenya in this era, but when they did occur they tended to involve leading Kenyan political figures. Jomo Kenyatta, Kenya's first president, had an English wife, and it was the marriage of the lawyer-politician C. M. G. Argwings-Kodhek to an Englishwoman that had caused the miscegenation law to be changed. Macgoye's marriage, as she notes, was "rather different from politicians who were bringing back white wives. I had been in the country for six years before marrying" (personal interview). Furthermore, she was not marrying into the Kenyan elite; Daniel Oludhe Macgoye was a junior civil servant.

The couple immediately moved to Western Kenya where they would live for the next eleven years close to the hospital where Daniel was posted. It was during this time that Macgoye was integrated into her husband's family and into Luo customs and attitudes, and she credits her mother-in-law, Miriam, with a spirit of generosity and welcome that made this adjustment successful.[4] Macgoye gives herself a second cameo appearance in *Coming to Birth*, when Paulina travels to Kisumu to observe the Independence Day celebrations in December 1963:

> Paulina spotted the little white girl who had been in Pumwani, with two children now and a black husband, and, though they did not really recognise her, they greeted her civilly in Luo and exchanged congratulations on the occasion. (52)

Macgoye indeed had two children at the time of independence: Phyllis Ahoya was born in Kisumu in March 1961, and George Ng'ong'a was born in May 1963, during a visit to England. Two more sons were born while they lived in Kisumu: Francis Ochieng' in January 1965 and Lawrence Thomas King Odera in March 1966. For the rest of the decade, Macgoye occupied herself with raising her children, teaching part-time at Kisumu Girls High School, and writing steadily, placing a number of her poems in East African literary journals.

Kisumu is located on Kenya's western edge, on the shores of Lake Victoria and close to the borders of Uganda and Tanzania. It is Kenya's third-largest town, after Nairobi and Mombasa, which meant that while Macgoye was not at the heart of the nation's cultural life, she was nonetheless well connected to contemporary developments. Makerere University in Uganda was at the time the leading higher education institution in the region, having produced many of East Africa's first-generation writers and academics. Because the East African Community was still intact, communication and travel between Kenya and Uganda was routine.[5] In *Coming to Birth*, Kisumu is where Paulina begins her journey to independence, by enrolling in the Homecraft Training School. She learns to know Kisumu quite well—it's smaller than Nairobi, after all—and through Paulina, Macgoye evokes the atmosphere of the town in the 1960s: "Sunny in the morning, scorching in the afternoon, with a wind suddenly blowing up before dark, thunder storms sometimes and dust devils nearly every day" (42). The lively marketplace, the religious rivalries, the constant threat of changes in the level of Lake Victoria—all of these are elements of her own Kisumu experience that Macgoye writes into Paulina's story.

It was during this era that Macgoye came to know the Ugandan poet and academic Okot p'Bitek, whose influence on her writing was profound. In 1966, Okot had energized the East African literary community with the publication of *Song of Lawino*. The poem is about the seduction of Westernization, a key issue for African societies in the 1960s. Even more significant, it offered a radically new poetic form for East Africa, a free-verse style based loosely on oral poetry from Okot's Acholi community, in eastern Uganda. East African writers quickly took to the new style and tone of the poem. Okot himself followed up with *Song of Ocol* (a sequel to *Song of Lawino*), as well as the less successful "Song of a Prisoner" and "Song of Malaya" (published together in the volume *Two Songs*). Macgoye had the opportunity to hear Okot recite the original, Acholi version of *Song of Lawino* at a 1965 reading in Nairobi before its publication in English, and during 1968 and 1969 Okot lived in Kisumu, where he was associated with the University of Nairobi's Extramural Centre. Although she is famous for her willingness to challenge aspects of Okot's literary vision, Macgoye gives a nod to his influence in the title of her own major poem, *Song of Nyarloka*.[6]

Living in the largest town in Western Kenya, Macgoye was at the epicenter for Luo political aspirations, which were becoming increasingly frustrated during this time. Despite the rhetoric of national unity and the call for Kenyan identity to supercede tribal loyalties, the major political story in the decade following independence was the struggle for control of the Kenyan state by leaders of the Luo and Kikuyu communities. It was a struggle that the Luo were to lose, as the Kikuyu consolidated their position under Kenya's first president, Jomo Kenyatta (even though they were unable to secure the presidential succession, carried off in 1978 by Vice President Daniel arap Moi, a Kalenjin). The first major blow for the Luo came in 1966, when one of their leaders, Jaramogi Oginga Odinga, was forced from his post as vice president. Odinga formed a new political party, the Kenya People's Union (KPU), the first serious challenge to the ruling Kenya African National Union (KANU) in many years. Not surprisingly, the KPU's base of support was in the Luo area of western Kenya, and the two-party structure smoldered uneasily until 1969, when the conflict came to a head. Two leading Luo politicians were killed that year: Argwings-Kodhek died in a suspicious motor vehicle accident in January, and in July an even more important figure, Tom Mboya, was assassinated in broad daylight on a Nairobi street.

A few months later, yet another important event took place in Kisumu—an event which Macgoye places at the heart of *Coming to Birth* (and also grants a prominent role in the poem *Song of Nyarloka*). In October 1969, in a politically charged atmosphere, President Kenyatta and his entourage made a rare trip to Kisumu to preside at the opening ceremonies for a new hospital. Whether the unrest at the Kisumu rally was incited by Kenyatta's entourage in order to provide an excuse for retaliation, or whether it was invented after the fact to justify the shootings that occured, the result was that Kenyatta's motorcade made an abrupt departure, with soldiers firing tear gas and bullets into the crowd as they left town. Among the dead were schoolchildren who had been required to stand by the roadside to salute the president. A news blackout meant that the shooting and deaths were not publicized. Macgoye rushed to Nairobi, where she tried without success to inform the international press. "Song of Kisumu," her poetic response to the aftermath of the incident, was originally published in the *East Africa Journal* and later appended to the first section of *Song of Nyarloka*—the only segment not originally written as part of that longer work. She puts the incident in the central chapter of *Coming to Birth*, where it marks a crucial turning point. In the context of the story as a national allegory, the fatal shooting abruptly terminates the life of Paulina's firstborn just as it terminates Kenya's initial hopes for a harmonious and just political life. "The country had eaten its people," the narrator concludes (84). Immediately afterward, Odinga's KPU was banned, and Kenya returned to being a one-party state.

Following the Kisumu incident, Marjorie and Daniel Macgoye were understandably eager to remove their children from the Kisumu schools, where they might be required to stand by the roadside for presidential motorcades. Macgoye immediately took up the offer of a post managing the University of Dar es Salaam bookstore, moving there with the children in 1971 (shortly before the publication of her first novel, *Murder in Majengo*). Macgoye's four years in Dar es Salaam, her only years spent outside of Kenya, turned out to be among the most intellectually stimulating and artistically fruitful of her life, in part because she was now free of obligations to her extended family. For the first time in a decade, she recalls, she was able to write in the evenings after the children were in bed. More importantly, Macgoye was now in the thick of the Dar es Salaam academic community, which in the early 1970s was a hotbed of African intellectual debate, especially for leftists attracted by President Julius Nyerere's vision of African socialism. While relishing the intellectual stimulation, Macgoye often felt at odds with the more extreme Tanzanian activists. In Kenya, Macgoye's poetry had at times been criticized for being too political; in this more radical climate it was deemed insufficiently committed to a progressive political agenda. In Dar es Salaam, Macgoye finished *Song of Nyarloka* and wrote *Victoria*. In *Coming to Birth*, she includes a nostalgic nod to her memories of the Tanzanian city, with its "sleepy hot streets and the sight of a ship's funnels appearing to pass along in the midst of the town" (102).

In 1975, Macgoye returned to Kenya for good. The family settled in Nairobi, and for five years she managed the S.J. Moore bookstore—at the time the richest source of quality literature in the city, according to Austin Bukenya. For Kenyan literature, these were dynamic, eventful years. New titles were appearing from Ngugi, Ogot, and other established names, and there was a concurrent explosion in popular literature—thrillers and romances, often based on European and American models and often excoriated for their lowbrow aspirations, but very successful commercially. This was also the time of Ngugi's now-famous literacy and drama work with a peasant cooperative at Kamiriithu, which led to his arrest and eventual exile. Along with the poet Jonathan Kariara, Macgoye instigated monthly poetry readings at her bookstore for several years. She also worked on *Coming to Birth,* completing it in 1979. Ngugi himself read an early draft and encouraged Macgoye in the project.

It took seven more years before the novel would appear in print, during which time Macgoye quit her post at S.J. Moore, working as a publisher's sales representative (which allowed her to travel throughout East Africa) and as editor for the University of Nairobi's correspondence courses. By this time, Macgoye was widely known within the Kenyan literary community, but the 1986 publication of *Coming to Birth,* and its subsequent receipt of the Sinclair Prize, a British award for works of social and political significance, boosted awareness of Macgoye to new levels. The novel's success opened the door to publication of more of Macgoye's works, among them the novels *The Present Moment* (1987), which is also being republished by The Feminist Press; *Homing In* (1994), the story of a settler widow, which won second place in the Jomo Kenyatta Prize for Literature in 1995; and *Chira* (1997), the first serious Kenyan novel to highlight the issue of AIDS. Her husband died of stomach cancer in 1990, and today Macgoye continues to live in her modest flat in Ngara, near Nairobi's city center.

Coming to Birth has a methodical and uncomplicated structure,

161

with each of its seven chapters relating a significant stage in Paulina's development and each corresponding to a distinct, chronologically arranged period in Kenyan history. Chapter one covers 1956 and 1957, two particularly unstable years. At the time, British rule was under unprecedented challenge, and independence, if not imminent, at least appeared inevitable in the long run. The narrative, reflecting the general view at the time, suggests that independence seems likely within twenty years (1)—far beyond the seven years that it actually took. Since none of Britain's African colonies had yet taken that step, the twenty-year scenario would have seemed realistic to many. What was peculiar to Kenya, creating much of its instability, was the challenge to colonial rule from the armed insurgency known as the Mau Mau movement. The rebellion flourished in the central highlands, where settlers had appropriated large tracts of the country's most desirable land from the Kikuyu community, and when Macgoye describes the "accepted fact" of the Emergency (1), she is referring to the heightened security measures taken by the colonial administration between 1952 and 1958, in response to the Mau Mau insurgency.[7] These measures were designed to restrict the movement and association of the Kikuyu and of the related Embu and Meru communities (indicated as "KEM" in the signboards prohibiting entry). In the rural areas of central Kenya, many Kikuyu were forcibly evicted from their homes and moved into centralized and more controllable "villages." Prison work camps were set up for suspected rebels and sympathizers. In Nairobi, curfews and pass laws restricted movement, and entire sections of the city in the so-called "African locations" were cordoned off by barbed wire.[8] Pumwani and other such "locations" with a high density of Kikuyu residents were of particular concern for colonial authorities. Their "Operation Anvil" forced many Kikuyu from these areas, resulting in housing opportunities for members of other communities— like Martin Were, a Luo.

Fresh from her village home in western Kenya, and possessing limited political awareness, Paulina is understandably disoriented when she arrives on the morning train in Nairobi. This is her first experience with urbanization, and while Nairobi in 1956 was nowhere as large as it is today, it was certainly large enough to be confusing. Readers who remember colonial-era Nairobi will see that Macgoye has carefully replicated the cityscape and its ambience, from the "khaki longs" that Martin is wearing (1) to the placement of the railway station and its *landhies* (railway worker's housing) in relation to the rest of the city, and even the types of housing in Pumwani itself. The main events in chapter one are Paulina's shocking plunge into city life and her miscarriage, events that parallel the nation's awakening to the volatility and violence of the Emergency. By the end of this chapter, however, the Emergency seems to be easing and Paulina is slowly adjusting to the rhythms and requirements of city living.

Chapter two covers 1957 to 1962, the era immediately preceding Kenyan independence, when the movement toward self-government was becoming inexorable. The Emergency restrictions were lifting, and Jomo Kenyatta was emerging as the leader of a group of Kenyan politicians who were to lead the country to independence from Britain, following the model of Ghana, which in 1957 became the first British colony in Africa to receive its independence. For many Kenyans, this was an era of optimism and promise, carrying the hope that independence would usher in a new era of freedom, justice, and prosperity for all Kenyans. Politicians had not yet lost the common touch, as the narrative suggests by highlighting how Moi and Ngala lodge in Pumwani.[9] For Kenyan readers today, there is considerable irony in this passage, given the disappointing behavior of the political elite since independence. As the novel shows, many of the promises of independence were never fulfilled—they were barren hopes, to use the imagery of the novel. The police raid that contributes to Paulina's miscarriage reminds readers how the government in postcolonial Kenya uses force against its own people in the same way that the colonial administration did.

Just as the period of self-government presages the nation's fate, the events in this chapter offer a taste of what is in store for Paulina: The intimations of Martin's infidelity with Fatima precede his more public affair with Fauzia, the hints by some of her relatives that Paulina should conceive with another man—a practice, Macgoye

163

suggests, that "custom was not too hard on" (35)—paves the way for her later affair with Simon, and Paulina's visit to the Homecraft School leads to her eventual enrollment there. Paulina's miscarriages do not bode well, particularly given their metaphorical implications for the nation at large, and Martin's prospects, which were so promising at the start of the narrative, are in decline, as evidenced by his downwardly mobile move to Kariokor. Some things are going well, however. Paulina begins her journey to financial independence, first by crocheting and then by joining the Homecraft School. Martin and Paulina confirm their wedding in a church ceremony. Paulina's second, confident arrival in Nairobi is a sharp contrast to her first, suggesting a new level of maturity and competence. Despite the series of miscarriages, there is a significant birth in this chapter—the mixed-race child Joyce, who offers Paulina a pretext for friendship with Amina, a woman whose example gives Paulina both inspiration and warning. Like Fatima and Fauzia, Amina is from the coastal Swahili community. Her friendship with Paulina, like biracial Joyce herself, suggests the hope for a new, multicultural Kenya.

Related to the idea of multiculturalism is the tricky role languages play in the birth of this nation. With forty distinct ethnic groups and languages, forging a genuine and just national identity from Kenya's remarkable diversity has been a dilemma for the country. Swahili is a mother tongue on Kenya's coast, but has historically been adopted first as a trade language and later as a national language, throughout the country. Most Kenyans, especially those with a limited education like Paulina, know Swahili only on a relatively rudimentary level, which is why she feels at a disadvantage against the savvy ways and language of women like Fatuma and Fauzia, who know the "deep" Swahili so well that "they could always make it too hard if they wanted to" (34). Their advantage backfires when Martin beats Fauzia, whose cries in Swahili are ignored by neighbors because "true disaster can only proclaim itself in the tribal language" (58). Even though this is a "tribal language" for Fauzia, most Kenyans would think of it as a second or even third language.

The actual moment of Kenyan independence is surprisingly

164

anticlimactic, as Macgoye turns the focus of chapter three, which covers 1963 through 1968, away from political events and onto Paulina's inward, personal development. The June 1, 1963, celebrations are for Madaraka, or internal self-government, which was a step on the way to Uhuru, the complete political independence that came six months later. For Paulina, however, the celebrations contrast with her personal experience: This "great year dragged on" (51), and even as the new nation comes into being, "something had died in her" (52). Paulina's relationship with Martin is disintegrating, and it is telling that while she is seen attending the celebrations, he is not mentioned in relation to independence at all. Martin, in fact, is worse off than he was at the start of the novel; Paulina, by contrast, is more autonomous.

Chapter four, which covers 1969 to 1971, constitutes a pivotal period in the story. Political events return to the fore, but they are almost exclusively setbacks, as the euphoria of independence withers in the face of power struggles and economic stagnation. The period was a difficult one throughout the region: the novel makes reference to the assassination of Eduardo Mondlane, the founder of the Mozambican independence movement that eventually won the nation independence from Portugal in 1974 (72), and to Idi Amin's overthrow of the Ugandan president, Milton Obote, in a January 1971 coup d'etat that ushered in an era of terror and chaos for that country (90). In Kenya, as we previously noted, 1969 was a year of retrenchment for Luo political aspirations and for national unity. The trial of Njenga, Tom Mboya's alleged assassin, becomes a transparent cover-up, since the "one question which would have made sense of the trial" (82)—the question of which highly placed politicians were behind the assassination—was not allowed to be aired. Martin is experiencing the equivalent of a midlife crisis, growing but not maturing (78), his autonomy shrinking in relation to the growth of his cynicism. Amina greets him as Bwana Mkubwa—"Mr. Big Man"—a friendly but satirical salutation which only serves to remind him of his dashed aspirations (80). Above all, the tragic death of young Martin Okeyo in this chapter recapitulates the death of East

Africa's economic and political aspirations. With her son's death, many of Paulina's hopes are killed, just as the optimism of independence is irrevocably put to rest. It is a barren moment, as Paulina contemplates her prospects: "He would go to the earth, like herself, unperpetuated and unfulfilled" (84). There is a poignant irony here, as young Martin has just been described as a child who, like "a real Luo," was "more keen in a funeral than anything else" (73). He ends up in the Kenyan equivalent of a pauper's grave—a public plot rather than a burial on the homestead—without any of the usual rituals and observations (85). As the chapter ends, Paulina, like her country, feels that her life has reached a dead end.

As Austin Bukenya points out, the date that opens chapter five should probably be 1973 rather than 1975, since Mr. M's campaign for reelection to Parliament would have occurred in the general election of 1974 (*Notes* 36). In any case, the action in this chapter moves through the end of 1975, Kenya's most politically volatile year since 1969, and the result is an increased level of background tension and anxiety. There had been a coup attempt in 1971, which was easily squelched, but in 1975 cracks were appearing in the formerly solid rule of KANU and of the aging President Kenyatta, who was to die three years later. The bomb blast at Nairobi's major bus terminus was a real event, from March of that year, but it was the disappearance of the Kikuyu politician and businessman Josiah Mwangi Kariuki, generally known simply as "J.M.," that suggested the high level of jostling for power, even within the Kikuyu elite. Although wealthy, Kariuki had a reputation for being on the side of Kenya's poor, and he was a hero of the independence movement; the book that was republished following his death (108) is *"Mau Mau" Detainee,* his 1963 account of being imprisoned during the Emergency. After Kariuki was reported missing, rumors about his fate, including the suggestion that he was merely visiting Zambia, did not end until his mutilated body turned up at the city mortuary, where it had lain unidentified for several days. As in the Tom Mboya assassination, and as in the unsolved murder in 1990 of the Luo foreign minister Robert Ouko, the general consensus was that high powers in the government were behind J. M.'s death, although none was convicted.[10] Macgoye's narrative turns bitterly lyrical in denouncing the culture of fear, whispers, and silence that prevents Kenyans from "tumbling to" the truth, even when that truth is obvious (107). In the meantime, the ruling party, KANU, was having internal power struggles of its own, as evidenced by the detention of its deputy speaker, the Nandi politician Jean Marie Seroney, and his Luhya counterpart, Martin Shikuku, for publicly criticizing their own party. Chelagat Mutai, a young female member of Parliament, was imprisoned for more than two years, ostensibly for an old offense but actually for criticizing their detention.

For Macgoye's plot, the most significant developments during this era are the steady expansion of Paulina's world and the concurrent shrinking of Martin's. While the two are reunited in this section, it is on terms strikingly different from the terms of their original relationship. Working in a politician's household, Paulina grows in political awareness and even shows the first signs of political activism with her unsuccessful campaign to challenge Mutai's imprisonment. Nairobi is now her home in a way that it had never been before; in fact, her rural home now seems an alien environment. Martin, meanwhile, is increasingly cynical and disillusioned, a far cry from the politically active young man we saw in the novel's first pages.

When Macgoye began writing *Coming to Birth* she planned to end the narrative in 1976, thereby rounding out the tale with a neat, twenty-year span of the nation's life. But the years 1976 through 1978, which provide the backdrop for the novel's last two chapters, turned out to be the final moments of a distinct era in Kenyan history—the Jomo Kenyatta era. Extending the narrative for two additional years lends Paulina's story an even more effective allegorical punch than Macgoye had initially anticipated. Kenyatta died in August 1978, concluding a presidency that covered all fifteen years of Kenya's existence as an independent nation. The jostling for power following his death, won by then–Vice President Moi, has been recorded in dramatic fashion in *The Kenyatta Succession,* an unusual work of Kenyan

167

investigative journalism coauthored by Joseph Karimi and Philip Ochieng. Ochieng's reputation as a leading journalist is attested to by the special mention Macgoye gives to his editorial following the Mboya assassination (82). *Coming to Birth* never actually mentions that succession struggle, since the story ends in March 1978, five months before Kenyatta's death. Paulina is in her third month, meaning that her child—the "very great hope" that concludes the novel—would be due in September, a date that for Kenyan readers would be pregnant with meaning, to say the least. How would the birth of a new political era affect the nation?

In chapters six and seven, the increasing corruption and cynicism in the political realm contrasts with Paulina's remarkable new personal involvement in social concerns. Political detentions continue, most notably the year-long incarceration of the novelist and playwright Ngugi wa Thiong'o, whose writings had become increasingly critical of the Kenyatta regime.[11] The government is doing relatively little about the growing number of children who are living and surviving on the streets.[12] Meanwhile, Mr. M, who had seemed a decent man when Paulina first went to work for the family, is betraying his wife and family through his sexual affairs. As a parliamentarian, Mr. M should take the lead in addressing social problems, but instead it is Paulina who takes tangible steps on behalf of the street children. Although she is still a servant, Paulina is more confident than she has ever been, willing to speak up for what she believes is right—both to her employer and to the nurse who sees her in the final scene. She is indeed, as Mr. M notes, "a new woman" (139). Even Martin, roused from his cynicism by Ngugi's arrest, "sat down solidly to read" *Petals of Blood*—Ngugi's longest and most complex work (144). In the end, this new woman, on the edge of a new era in the nation's growth, waits for the future with a mixture of uncertainty and hope. By any standards, Paulina's transformation is remarkable.

Jonathan Kariara, Macgoye's friend and fellow poet, once asked her why she seemed so obsessed with birth and its associated imagery (Macgoye, personal interview). His premise is astute; this

type of imagery is central in *Coming to Birth* and runs throughout Macgoye's work. It symbolizes not only personal and national development but also the artist's creative process; the act of
writing, for Macgoye, constitutes an artistic bringing to birth. This
is by now a familiar formula in postcolonial literature, even literature by men. For instance in *A Grain of Wheat,* the definitive
literary statement on Kenyan independence, Ngugi concludes the
narrative with the hope of a child for Gikonyo and Mumbi. In
Midnight's Children, Salman Rushdie pulls together the loose
ends of his sweeping vision of postcolonial India by giving
Salim Sinai a son who represents the prospects for a new national future, following India's own Emergency.[13] The difference is
that for these male writers, evocations of labor, birth, miscarriage,
and so on remain strictly metaphorical (and they are only one
metaphor among many—for Ngugi, for instance, biblical imagery
or the footrace at the end of his novel carry even greater sym-
bolic significance, while Rushdie uses a stunning array of
metaphors, including chutney-making, to explore his ideas
about history and art). For Macgoye, childbirth carries a more
personal burden, since it describes female reality; the device
becomes metonymic rather than metaphoric.[14] In any case,
Macgoye's answer to Kariara was simply that she writes about birth
because it is fundamental to a woman's experience.

It might surprise some readers, then, to know that Macgoye
resists defining herself and her work as feminist. Among African
women writers, however, she is by no means unique in this regard.
The Botswanan writer Bessie Head, who like Macgoye established
her writing career in an adopted homeland and whose works also
explore female emancipation in a male-dominated society, is similarly famous for insisting that she is not a feminist. Like Head,
Macgoye says she wishes to be remembered simply as a writer,
rather than as a woman writer. There may be several reasons for
this stance, the first being simply the writer's instinct to avoid
restrictive categorization. Especially for someone like Macgoye,
who has lived her life consistently against the grain, resisting obvious labels may be instinctual. More fundamentally, despite the
fact that her theology is decidedly progressive in other ways,

169

Macgoye finds certain facets of feminism in conflict with her religious principles. Specifically, she views sexual differences as divinely established and believes any attempt to eradicate those differences to be ill-advised. In one of her essays in *Moral Issues in Kenya,* she urges readers to retain a sense of those things she considers unique to the female experience—"the joy and responsibility of motherhood, the gift of nourishing and healing, the artistic insight" (74). She especially objects to anyone rejecting the validity of motherhood, as some of the more radical colleagues from her Tanzania days apparently did.[15] Finally, Macgoye is no doubt affected by the fact that mainstream feminism, as it has been translated into Africa from its European and American roots, too frequently reflects the concerns and biases of those alien origins, and is not always attentive to the specific issues of African women. For African women, siding with feminism has sometimes meant siding with colonial or Western ideology. As Chandra Mohanty famously argues, Western feminisms too easily gloss over cultural difference, making European forms of patriarchy (and European forms of resistance to it) appear as universal norms, when in fact they are not.

Despite Macgoye's reticence about the term, it is difficult to read *Coming to Birth* as anything other than a distinctly feminist story, at least in the broader sense that it explores a woman's experience of maneuvering through and eventually overcoming, in however limited a fashion, the constraints of a profoundly patriarchal society. The story, as Macgoye herself emphasizes, is about the growth of a woman's consciousness, and in this respect the contrast in the trajectories of Martin's and Paulina's lives is striking: *Coming to Birth* relates the empowerment of Paulina, who ends up a "new woman," and the concurrent diminution of Martin's status as a man. At the end of the story, their roles are dramatically reversed. Instead of Paulina moving into his home, as custom would require, Martin is taken into hers, and on her conditions. She is the political activist, at ease in the city and its various social settings, while he is cynical and depressed. Paulina, who in the novel's opening pages could only resign herself to being locked in a small and strange room—"Being married was, it seemed, a whole history of getting used to things" (6)—is now "the one demanding to grow, to get out, to do things, and he was tired and disillusioned" (112).

The novel also highlights political events of significance to Kenyan women. In 1969, a year that is otherwise already full of tragedy, Kenya's Parliament retracts the Affiliation Act (72), a colonial-era piece of legislation beneficial to some women because it required fathers to take responsibility, including financial responsibility, for their children born out of wedlock. For Kenyan women, its annulment was a serious setback. The imprisonment of Chelagat Mutai, one of Kenya's few female members of Parliament, drives Paulina to a new level of political action, which leads to the first time that she "set up her will against Martin's" (111–12). In the end, the novel suggests that Kenya's first attempt at nationhood has been a disastrous failure under male leadership, and it may be time for a different approach that would draw on a life-embracing, female ethic:

> Perhaps women's work was like that—the word for creation was the same one you used practically for knitting or pottery. Men's work was so often destructive—clearing spaces, breaking things down to pulp, making decisions—and how often did the decisions amount to anything tangible? Words in the air, pious intentions, rules about what not to do. She was glad that a lot of her work lay in making and mending things. (129)

Similar ideas about women and their role in society wind through all of Macgoye's work in various guises, and she is enough of an insider that she can credibly challenge patriarchal elements in Kenya and in Luo tradition. Macgoye is famous for her attack on what she terms "domestic slavery," the practice of exploiting (usually female) household servants. This is the burden of her well-known poem, "Song of Freedom," which tells the story of an urban family's mistreatment of a young, rural, female relative in this way, and it resurfaces in *Coming to Birth* in her criticism of the Okelo family's treatment of Paulina (91).

Macgoye is also famously critical of what she considers an undue obsession with extravagant funeral rites among the Luo; she takes on the issue directly and at length in *Moral Issues in Kenya,* and touches on it in passing in *Coming to Birth* (73, 89). Macgoye's works—fiction and nonfiction alike—offer a consistent vision of these sorts of issues and of how they affect Kenyan women. Taken as a group, Macgoye's protagonists represent the richest and most compelling collection of female characters in Kenya's novelistic tradition. They include Lois Akinyi (in *Murder in Majengo*), Wairimu, Rahel, and Sophia (in *The Present Moment*), the eponymous Victoria (in a sequel to *Murder in Majengo*), Ellen Smith and Martha Kimani (in *Homing In*), and of course Paulina.

Beyond this specifically feminist vision, Macgoye's works offer a thoughtful analysis of how ordinary people are affected by history, and the possibilities of affecting it in turn. Bruce Berman, in his study of the colonial state in Kenya, suggests that an appropriate way to understand any history, but especially the history of the colonial system, is not as "melodrama, with the forces of good arrayed against the forces of evil," but rather as "tragedy, in which the great majority in each group did the best they could according to their various and often conflicting values and interests, and within a context they only dimly, and frequently quite inaccurately, understood" (xii). This is precisely the perspective on Kenyan society that permeates all of Macgoye's writing. Toward the end of *Coming to Birth,* Paulina meets up with Amina, whose pluck and assertiveness she has always admired. The two women share their news, and their concluding comments sum up their contrasting ways of viewing the world:

> "We have learned to take what comes and make the best of it," [Paulina] said.
> "To *make* what comes and to *take* the best of it," answered Amina firmly. "But there's my bus coming: I must go." (146)

Neither view, the novel suggests, is entirely accurate. People are not completely passive and helpless in the face of world events, but neither is it possible to transcend these events completely. There is an echo of Marx here: People make history, but not always under the conditions of their choosing. Macgoye's novels explore the various stories and events that combine ("enfold" is actually her favored verb) to create "the present moment"—which serves as the title for her subsequent novel.

If *Coming to Birth* has a weakness, it is undoubtedly the dialogue, which at various points is less than convincing, taking on vocabulary and cadences that seem more natural to Southampton than to Nairobi. The conversation between Martin and Amina in chapter four, for instance, where Amina urges him to rent her "nice rooms, furnished, water laid on" (81), or the surprisingly standard grammatical constructions of the street children in chapter six, do not quite ring true. Characters end up sounding too much like one another. When the dialogue becomes ironic rather than earnest, it is far more successful. The exchange with Rhoda, for instance, is quite good. Like a colonial mistress whining about the difficulty of finding good help, her complaint that "life in Nairobi is hard" (122) elicits little sympathy from her former classmate Paulina, and her tiring refrain, "you know," reveals Rhoda's pretentiousness.

What tends to be more effective than the dialogue is Macgoye's frequent use of a narrative technique known as free indirect discourse.[16] To express what a character is thinking, writers have several choices. They may state a thought indirectly, putting it in the narrator's voice, but clearly identifying it as the character's internal reflections. An alternative is to quote a character's thoughts directly, in the same way that one would quote the character's speech. A third way, which Macgoye deploys throughout *Coming to Birth,* is to use what is sometimes called free indirect discourse, which presents a character's thoughts and expressions as part of the narrated portion of the text (therefore indirect), clearly from that character's perspective but not explicitly tagged or marked as coming from that character (therefore "free"). This technique allows an unusual closeness between the

173

more objective voice of the narrator and the subjective mind of the character, and it is therefore less crucial than in directly quoted speech to get the wording or phrasing exactly right for that character. In the third paragraph of *Coming to Birth,* for example, the first and fifth sentences of the paragraph are from the external narrator's perspective, but the second through fourth are Martin's interior monologue, even though the shifts are not denoted by direct quotations, and the third-person voice remains the same:

> The overnight train from Kisumu had not yet pulled in. It would be her first time on a train. She could probably count the number of times she had been in a motor vehicle, even. How Nairobi and his mastery of Nairobi would overwhelm her! She was sixteen and he had taken her at the Easter holiday, his father allowing two cattle and one he had bought from his savings, together with a food-safe for his mother-in-law and a watch for Paulina's father. (2)

The use of this free indirect discourse gives Macgoye narrative possibilities that she exploits quite effectively. In the first place, it allows her to present characters sympathetically but also ironically. We sympathize because of the direct access we get to a character's emotions, but we are also struck by the irony of how those emotions do not always correspond to reality. Sympathy and irony mingle particularly well in the novel's opening, where we are struck by Paulina's vulnerability and naivete as, for example, when she notes that "Being married was, it seemed, a whole history of getting used to things" (6).

Free indirect discourse is also effective in revealing the minds of characters who find themselves at a crucial juncture, hanging between reflections on the past and anticipations of the future. Macgoye uses this to good effect at the novel's close, where Paulina is caught in precisely such a moment, suspended between the disappointments of her past and the fragile hope for a new future:

174

A pram, Paulina thought suddenly, would be a help. Baby out on the lawn while I am busy in the kitchen. Baby going out shopping with me, not left with a little nursemaid. In any case my employer doesn't hold with little nursemaids and has quarreled with some of the other big ladies about it in the name of education for girls. A pram or a pushchair with a canopy for sunny days; it was not longer just a day-dream, and in any case she would no longer find it easy to carry the weight. (149)

A final advantage to this technique is that it allows the narrator to range freely and intimately from the mind of one character to another. In *Coming to Birth,* the consciousness that dominates the opening pages is Martin's, but by the fifth page the emphasis shifts to Paulina, whose consciousness dominates the rest of the book. Macgoye also uses the technique to insert a more subjective narrative voice that does not belong to any character, but rather seems to express a communal or even national consciousness, which is another way of linking the story of Paulina to the story of Kenya. An excellent example appears in the description of the aftermath of the murder of J. M. Kariuki, where the voice is not that of an objective narrator, but also not that of an identifiable individual:

And when the body was found, discreetly mutilated, you knew what the event was that for weeks you had been expecting, although the real event was still not known. The police officers went about their leave or their business outside the station without referring to it, the mortuary keeper who had a well-dressed corpse of appropriate size and weight and characteristics in his charge did not tumble to it. The airline clerks checking flights to Zambia did not tumble to it. The children playing in the streets did not tumble to it—children who were of the age to have been shot in Kano or Patel flats. . . . Even those terribly sharp children did not tumble to it. (107)

175

Macgoye's prose finds its best moments when her poetic instincts shine through, which often happens in the aftermath of a crisis. In the passage above, for instance, Macgoye uses parallel syntax and repetition, understated allusion, and an angry but lyrical tone to express the national outrage in a particularly effective manner. Another outstanding example appears after young Martin Okeyo's murder in the Kisumu incident. Macgoye describes Paulina looking from the wrinkled face of an old man to her own reflection and finally to her dead son's features, in a passage that powerfully captures the grief and loss of the moment (84).

Coming to Birth won the Sinclair Prize the same year that Wole Soyinka became Africa's first Nobel laureate in literature. It was published in Britian in a new series from Virago Press that included major works of fiction by African women writers, such as Zoë Wicomb's *You Can't Get Lost in Cape Town* and Mariama Bâ's *So Long a Letter.* So it was natural that the novel, and its author, should come to the attention of the international literary review circuit, especially in Britain, Australia, and South Africa. In addition to praising its lyricism, many reviewers recognized the novel's sense of authenticity—what one called "its scrupulous precision and its intensity of tone" (Hinds). *Coming to Birth,* suggested another, "is modern Kenya's response to *Out of Africa,*" meaning that its relevance and truthfulness contrast with Dinesen's nostalgic fantasy representation of the country (Sinclair). A few critics objected to the novel's overt political focus. The reviewer for the *Times Literary Supplement* found this aspect of the novel simply unconvincing (Maja-Pearce), while others considered it downright unartistic, including the critic who lamented that in the novel, "obstetrics . . . are soon absorbed by mere politics" (Hawtree). Not all critics would preface the word "politics" with the word "mere," of course, and one even faulted Macgoye for being insufficiently politicized, her vision for Paulina too limited (Nri). Most, however, found the balance of personal and political to be effectively executed; the story of Paulina and the story of Kenya, Hinds suggested, "interweave: they do not run parallel." In the end, of course, it was precisely the political significance of *Coming to Birth,* combined with its artistry, that appealed to the judges for the Sinclair Prize.[17]

By contrast, critical commentary by Kenyans seems to take the novel's historical and political vision as an uncontroversial given.[18] What these critics find far more noteworthy is its commentary on contemporary women's issues. As Kibera points out, Macgoye's female protagonists "present a kind of Kenyan 'herstory' in which private necessity or inclination mesh with widening public opportunities to afford women the means of controlling their lives" ("Adopted Motherlands" 312). Bukenya offers an interesting analysis in his contention that *Coming to Birth* invites a feminist deconstructive reading, if one examines the novel's deployment of childbirth and of language. Viewing childbirth as production, the novel shows that women like Paulina can produce without a man. By creating her own home, Paulina stands Luo notions of correct social order on their head—yet there remains the paradox that producing children also reproduces the social order (Bukenya, "Narrative").

In contrast to some international reviewers, who find the feminist message of the novel to be undermined or at least muted by a conclusion that valorizes Paulina only through childbirth (and perhaps in contradiction to Macgoye's own commitment to the importance of motherhood), both Masinjila and Kibera argue that despite Paulina's longing for a child, her womanhood—her discovery of her potential and a sense of self—are not achieved through marriage or even motherhood. "Childlessness almost seems a necessary qualification for women desiring or even being capable of living a full life," Kibera argues: "Paulina's childlessness constitutes the very reason she must and can undertake her odyssey in search of an identity" ("Adopted Motherlands" 325).

In the end, it is Paulina's ordinariness that makes her story so compelling for all readers, but especially, perhaps, for Kenyans. Again it is Kibera who puts it well: Paulina stands for all Kenyan women, and to the other births in the novel we must add this one:

Ranged behind Paulina is a cross-section of Kenyan women, differing in status, tribe, consciousness. But all, some hesitantly, others boldly, are seeking their way to a new consciousness, yearning to be participating, not peripheral, members of their communities. ("The Story of Paulina" 29)

Her coming to birth is also theirs.

J. Roger Kurtz
State University of New York, Brockport
May 2000

Notes

1. Ngugi, East Africa's best-known writer, produced the first Kenyan novel in English, *Weep Not, Child* (1964). Ogot, who has combined writing with a career in politics, became Kenya's first woman novelist with *The Promised Land* (1966). The Ugandan Okot wrote the major poem *Song of Lawino* (1966), a work that dramatically impacted East African literature.

2. In addition to the published sources cited, the biographical information presented here draws on my own conversations and correspondence with Macgoye. It is also informed by an unpublished autobiography, read with her permission, which Macgoye intends for posthumous publication.

3. As its name suggests, this building housed the administrative offices for the Church Missionary Society in Kenya and many tenants. It stands on a central location on what is now Moi Avenue, directly across from the former site of the U.S. Embassy, which was destroyed by a bomb blast in August 1998.

4. A section of *Song of Nyarloka,* titled "For Miriam," celebrates her mother-in-law's ability to meet social change with grace and integrity.

5. In 1967, Tanzania, Kenya, and Uganda established a set of agreements that eliminated trade and labor barriers among the countries, essentially creating an East African common market. Known as the East African Community, this arrangement included a common airline, railway, postal service, and other such cooperative efforts. The chaos in Uganda created by Idi Amin effectively dismantled the organization, which was officially disbanded in 1977.

6. The connection between Okot and Macgoye is additionally strong because the Acholi, Okot's tribe, and the Luo, the tribe into which Macgoye

had married, are historically and culturally related, with similar Nilotic languages and customs. In fact, Macgoye reports that Okot would refer to her as "my elder sister," an important title in the Nilotic tradition because it is the older sister whose dowry enables the younger brother to marry in his turn. (She was three years his senior.) But like siblings, they had their differences. Macgoye wrote the poem "Letter to a Friend" in a pique, in response to public comments by Okot that offended her. She intended it for Okot alone, leaving a copy for him on his desk. The poem offers a pointed challenge, but despite this (according to Macgoye, he admitted that the poem hit home), Okot liked "Letter to a Friend" well enough to insist that it be published in the East African literary journal *Ghala*. It also appears in both of her poetry collections.

7. In addition to the enigmatic name Mau Mau, fighters referred to themselves as the Land and Freedom Army. While Mau Mau was defeated militarily, it played an important catalytic role in the achievement of independence. The experience was a divisive one for many Kenyans, especially Kikuyu, and the official discourse about Mau Mau in the postindependence era has been a complicated one, as many of the political elite in independent Kenya were loyalists rather than rebels. The reality is that few active participants in Mau Mau have benefited from the fruits of independence, which has led to a contentious struggle over the portrayal of the movement in the country's literary and historical texts. For historical analyses, see Kershaw and also Maloba, and for a discussion of the ideological issues at stake in the literary representations of Mau Mau, see Maughan-Brown's study.

8. Macgoye describes the ubiquitous barbed wire as one of her first impressions of Nairobi when she arrived in 1954, and Paulina soon learns of it as well (8). The first Kenyan edition of *Coming to Birth* features a prominent strand of barbed wire in its cover design.

9. Daniel arap Moi went on to become Kenya's longest-serving member of Parliament, and his tenure as president (beginning in 1978) was to last longer than Kenyatta's. Ronald Ngala was a cabinet member when he died in an automobile accident in 1971.

10. Kariuki's disappearance still looms large in the Kenyan consciousness.

In March 2000, on the twenty-fifth anniversary of his disappearance, his family and political pressure groups made national headlines with their efforts to reopen an investigation into his death. The government, lauding Kariuki as a lost patriot, gave lip service to this effort, although no new information or convictions resulted.

11. While he had always been an outspoken activist, it was Ngugi's involvement in peasant literacy and drama, specifically the production of the play *Ngaahika Ndeenda* (*I Will Marry When I Want*), that was the immediate catalyst for his arrest. He was released a year later, following an international outcry. For useful sources on Ngugi, Kenya's best-known writer, see Sicherman, Cantalupo, and Ogude.

12. The street urchin, based on characters like Che, Johnny, and Mohammed Ali, has become something of a stock figure in Kenyan literature of urban life. For examples, see Meja and Maina in Meja Mwangi's *Kill Me Quick* or Eddy Onyango in Thomas Akare's *The Slums*.

13. India's Emergency, unlike Kenya's, was a postcolonial phenomenon, referring to the martial law imposed by Prime Minister Indira Gandhi in 1975. In Rushdie's novel, it is a defining moment for the new nation; like the Kisumu shootings in Macgoye's novel, it terminates a period of national growth and optimism.

14. In *The Madwoman in the Attic,* Gilbert and Gubar argue that images of imprisonment and of enclosure in nineteenth-century British and American literature remain mere images—"metaphysical and metaphorical" in writing by men, but represent something deeper—"social and actual"—in writing by women(86). I am suggesting that the same observation applies to the common use of birth imagery in postcolonial literature.

15. Macgoye tells of her anger at the suggestion, bandied about in the academic community, that the primary reason for raising children is to offer more bodies for the liberation struggle. The poem "For Adeola—Militant," which appears in the collection *Song of Nyarloka,* is addressed to Adeola James, the Guyanese academic and feminist who had articulated this idea. The poem begins, "Certainly not."

16. The use of free indirect discourse has a long history in English-language literature. Major writers who are typically cited in examples of its use include Jane Austen, Henry James, James Joyce, and Virginia Woolf. While critical attention to this narrative technique is long-standing and well developed in the French and German critical traditions (which refer to it with the respective terms *style indirect libre* and *erlebte Rede*), it is a more recent subject of discussion in the Anglo-American tradition. Even the term itself is still under discussion: "free indirect discourse" is a direct translation from the French, but Ann Banfield prefers the term "represented speech and thought" while Dorrit Cohn calls it "narrated monologue."

17. For other reviews of *Coming to Birth* in the international press, see Adolph, Bryce, Forshaw, Hough, Khan, MacLeod, Neville, Pullinger, Sen, Walters, and Winstanley.

18. For reviews and commentary in the Kenyan press, see Karmali, Kibera, Gethiga Gacheru, Margaretta wa Gacheru, Ikonya, and Soper.

Works Cited

Adolph, Fiona. "A Poignant African Tale." Rev. of *Coming to Birth. West Australian* 3 January 1987.

Akare, Thomas. *The Slums.* Nairobi: Heinemann Kenya, 1981.

Banfield, Ann. *Unspeakable Sentences: Narration and Representation in the Language of Fiction.* Boston: Routledge and Kegan Paul, 1982.

Berman, Bruce. *Control and Crisis in Colonial Kenya: The Dialectic of Domination.* Nairobi: East African Educational Publishers, 1990.

Bryce, Jane. "Women Writing." *Southern African Review of Books* July/October 1991.

Bukenya, Austin. "Narrative as Feminist Deconstruction in Macgoye's *Coming to Birth.*" Staff Seminar Presentation. Kenyatta University, Nairobi. 4 March 1993.

———. *Notes on Marjorie Oludhe Macgoye's* Coming to Birth. Nairobi: Heinemann Kenya, 1988.

Cantalupo, Charles, ed. *Ngugi wa Thiong'o: Texts and Contexts.* Trenton, NJ: Africa World Press, 1995.

———. *The World of Ngugi wa Thiong'o.* Trenton, NJ: Africa World Press, 1995.

"Catching Up with MOM, the Author." *Sunday Standard* (Nairobi) 23 May 1999.

Cohn, Dorrit. *Transparent Minds: Narrative Modes for Presenting Consciousness in Fiction.* Princeton: Princeton University Press, 1978.

Dinesen, Isak. *Out of Africa*. London: Putnam, 1937. New York: Random House, 1984.

Forshaw, Thelma. "Black and White Portraits." Rev. of *Coming to Birth*. *Weekend Australian* 20 September 1986.

Gacheru, Gethiga. "Task of Woman Writer." *Standard* (Nairobi) 29 December 1990.

Gacheru, Margaretta wa. "One of a Kind." *Nairobi Times Magazine* 16 July 1978.

Gilbert, Sandra M., and Susan Gubar. *The Madwoman in the Attic: The Woman Writer and the Nineteenth-Century Literary Imagination*. New Haven: Yale University Press, 1979.

Hawtree, Christopher. "Uneasy Idyll." Rev. of *Coming to Birth*. *Daily Telegraph* (London) 18 July 1986.

Hinds, Diana. "A New Spirit." Rev. of *Coming to Birth*. *Books and Booksmen* (Surrey), June 1986.

Hough, Graham. "Afro-Fictions." Rev. of *Coming to Birth*. *London Review of Books* 3 July 1986.

Huxley, Elspeth. *The Flame Trees of Thika: Memories of an African Childhood*. New York: Morrow, 1959. New York: Viking Penguin, 1982.

Ikonya, Philo. "Marjorie Macgoye, the Evergreen Author." *Sunday Nation* (Nairobi) 1 May 1994.

Karimi, Joseph and Philip Ochieng. *The Kenyatta Succession*. Nairobi: Transafrica, 1980.

Kariuki, Josiah Mwangi. *"Mau Mau" Detainee: The Account by a Kenya African of His Experiences in Detention Camps, 1953–1960*. London: Oxford University Press, 1963.

Karmali, Joan. Rev. of *Coming to Birth*. *Msafiri* (Nairobi) 2:1.

Kershaw, Greet. *Mau Mau from Below*. Nairobi: East African Educational Publishers, 1997.

Khan, Sonia. "Leafing Through." Rev. of *Coming to Birth*. *Times of India* 15 May 1988.

Kibera, Valerie. "Adopted Motherlands: The Novels of Marjorie Macgoye and Bessie Head." *Motherlands: Black Women's Writing from Africa, the Caribbean and South Asia*. London: Women's Press, 1991.

———. "The Story of Paulina." Rev. of *Coming to Birth*. *Weekly Review* (Nairobi) 12 September 1986.

Kurtz, J. Roger. *Urban Obsessions, Urban Fears: The Postcolonial Kenyan Novel*. Trenton NJ: Africa World Press, 1998.

Macgoye, Marjorie Oludhe. *Chira*. Nairobi: East African Educational Publishers, 1997.

———. *Coming to Birth*. Nairobi: Heinemann Kenya/East African Educational Publishers and London: Heinemann, 1986. London: Virago, 1987. New York: Feminist Press at CUNY, 2000.

———. *Homing In*. Nairobi: East African Educational Publishers, 1994.

———. *Make It Sing and Other Poems*. Nairobi: East African Educational Publishers, 1998.

———. *Moral Issues in Kenya: A Personal View*. Nairobi: Uzima Press, 1996.

———. *Murder in Majengo*. Nairobi: Oxford University Press, 1972.

———. Personal interview with the author. 18 June 1996.

———. *The Present Moment*. Nairobi: Heinemann Kenya/East African Educational Publishers and London: Heinemann, 1987. New York: Feminist Press at CUNY, 2000.

———. *Song of Nyarloka and Other Poems*. Nairobi: Oxford University Press, 1977.

———. *Victoria* and *Murder in Majengo*. London: Macmillan, 1993.

MacLeod, Sheila. "Love Hurts." Rev. of *Coming to Birth*. *New Statesman* (London) 13 June 1986.

Maja-Pearce, Adewale. "Work and Rule." Rev. of *Coming to Birth*. *Times Literary Supplement* (London) 5 September 1986.

Maloba, Wunyabari. *Mau Mau and Kenya: An Analysis of a Peasant Revolt*. Bloomington: Indiana University Press, 1993.

Masinjila, Masheti. "'To Make What Comes and Take the Best of It': The Coming to Birth of a New Woman." Seminar Presentation. British Council, Nairobi. 17 June 1995.

Maughan-Brown, David. *Land, Freedom, and Fiction: History and Ideology in Kenya*. London: Zed Books, 1985.

Mohanty, Chandra. "Under Western Eyes: Feminist Scholarship and Colonial Discourses." *Feminist Review* 30 (autumn 1988).

Mwangi, Meja. *Kill Me Quick*. Nairobi: Heinemann, 1973.

Neville, Jill. "Judged on Their Merits." Rev. of *Coming to Birth*. *Sunday Times* (London) 8 June 1986.

Ngugi wa Thiong'o. *A Grain of Wheat*. Nairobi: Heinemann, 1967.

———. *Ngaahika Ndeenda* [I will marry when I want]. Nairobi: Heinemann, 1980.

———. *Petals of Blood*. London: Heinemann, 1977.

———. *Weep Not, Child*. London: Heinemann, 1964.

Nri, Monique Ngozi. Rev. of *Coming to Birth*. *Women's Review* (London) September 1986.

Ogot, Grace. *The Promised Land*. Nairobi: East African Publishing House, 1966.

Ogude, James. *Ngugi's Novels and African History*. London: Pluto Press, 1999.

Okot p'Bitek. *Song of Lawino*. Nairobi: East African Publishing House, 1966.

———. *Song of Ocol*. Nairobi: East African Publishing House, 1970.

———. *Two Songs*. Nairobi: East African Publishing House, 1971.

Pullinger, Kate. "Dire Straits." Rev. of *Coming to Birth*. *City Limits* (London) 13 August 1987.

Rushdie, Salman. *Midnight's Children*. London: Jonathan Cape, 1980.

Sen, Veronica. "Paperbacks." Rev. of *Coming to Birth*. *Times* (Canberra, Australia) 27 September 1987.

Sicherman, Carol. *Ngugi wa Thiong'o: A Bibliography of Primary and Secondary Sources (1957–1987)*. London: Hans Zell, 1989.

———. *Ngugi wa Thiong'o: The Making of a Rebel: A Source Book in Kenyan Literature and Resistance*. London: Hans Zell, 1990.

Sinclair, Andrew. "Out of Africa Something True." Rev. of *Coming to Birth*. *Times* (London) 12 June 1986.

Soper, Jane. "Marjorie Gets Her First Real Break." *Daily Nation* (Nairobi) 17 July 1986.

Troughear, Tony. "Kenyan Author Wins Top Literary Works Prize." *Sunday Times* (London) 6 July 1986.

Walters, Margaret. "Russian Roulette." Rev. of *Coming to Birth*. *The Observer* (London) 8 June 1986.

Winstanley, Terry. "Corruption in Emerging African Society." Rev. of *Coming to Birth*. *Sunday Tribune* (Durban, South Africa) 3 April 1988.

HISTORICAL
CONTEXT

Precolonial African Societies

The Luo people at the center of this novel live in western Kenya, around Lake Victoria, and are part of the third-largest of the forty ethnic groups that make up contemporary Kenya. The Kikuyu form the largest single group and live in the central highlands. Both communities combined subsistence agriculture with raising cattle and small stock. Their societies were governed on a fairly small scale: Members lived in scattered settlements organized around men related by lineage ties and ruled by councils of elders. The senior man in the extended family had the right to control land and other resources and to reallocate them when necessary. A new bride came to live in her husband's homestead, often from a considerable distance, and was given fields to farm from lands claimed by the lineage. The husband's relatives paid "bridewealth" to her family in recognition of the loss of her productive and reproductive value. These were polygamous societies, and when a wife failed to produce children within a few years, the husband's family would exert pressure on him to marry a second wife. When a married man died, the new widow was expected to marry one of his brothers and keep the man's children and his property within the patrilineage.

These were by no means isolated societies in the precolonial period, even if they were small in scale. Regular patterns of trade and intermarriage forged links between neighboring peoples; ceremonies of blood brotherhood created fictional kinship ties across ethnic lines to stimulate trade. Ethnic identities thus tended to be rather fluid, as changing patterns of trade, rainfall, drought, or enemy raiding parties might prompt families to move away and join a different group. Colonial political and economic

structures later tended to freeze these rather loose associations into more permanent ethnic identities and often to pit them
against one another.

The Imposition of British Colonial Rule

The British ruled Kenya for sixty-eight years, from 1895 to
1963—a period covering only two or three generations—but their
long-term impact on African societies was substantial. For the Luo,
the two aspects of colonial rule with the greatest effect on their
lives were the constant demand for cheap labor and the active
presence of Christian missionaries. They were not faced with the
large-scale alienation of their land to white settlers, as were the
Kikuyu.

British interests in East Africa were originally commercial
and strategic. Thus, one of the first colonial projects in Kenya was
the construction of a railway from Mombasa through the central
highlands to Kisumu on the shores of Lake Victoria to provide
regular access to Uganda and a transportation route for products
grown there, especially cotton. Begun in 1896, the Uganda
Railway ultimately shaped the economic geography and greatly affected the social and political history of the Kenya colony.
Alarmed by the ongoing expenses connected with railroad construction, colonial officials hoped to generate revenue by using
the railroad to carry more and more agricultural products for export.
They assumed that only white farmers could adquately develop
the territory and set out immediately to attract immigrants from
Britain and from South Africa. More than five thousand settlers had come by 1914; they were rewarded with large tracts of
the best agricultural land, the so-called White Highlands of
central Kenya, at very low cost. The White Highlands covered rough-
ly 7.5 million acres of the most fertile land in the colony, including many areas that had been farmed by the Kikuyu and their
neighbors. At its height in 1950, white settlement in Kenya
probably included some twenty thousand people.

In addition to attracting white settlers and giving them access
to land, British colonial officials helped provide the cheap
African labor that settlers demanded through a set of government

190

policies which restricted land available for African use, imposed "hut taxes" on the African population, and instructed to local colonial officials to "encourage" men in their area to meet the labor needs of local white settlers and businessmen—encouragement that sometimes involved the use of force. A formal labor registration system was developed in 1921, whereby all African men over sixteen were required to carry a *kipande*, a labor pass, which listed the dates and terms of their current employment. Especially in the early years, men who were found without their pass or whose card showed they were not currently employed could be rounded up and forced to work on white-owned plantations. African farmers were also prevented from growing the most profitable cash crops, particularly coffee and tea, keeping these firmly in the hands of white farmers until the mid-1950s.

White settlers who had difficulties obtaining regular supplies of labor for their plantations often solved the problem by allowing Kikuyu "squatters" to live on their farms—to build temporary huts, plant small gardens to feed their families, and keep a number of livestock—in exchange for working a specified number of days during the year. It has been estimated that by 1945 nearly one-fourth of the Kikuyu population was living and working as squatters on white land.

Africans living near the Mombasa area were able to work for white employers on a daily basis, as "casual labor," at the port of Kilindini and elsewhere, allowing them to remain actively involved witih their their own farms and families. But men from central and western Kenya, particularly the Kikuyu, Luo, and Luyia peoples, were forced to travel long distances and to work on contracts that usually lasted from three to six months. Wives were generally left behind in the rural areas and were expected to maintain the same levels of agricultural production despite the withdrawal of male labor. In later years, a number of men began working year-round in cities, on the railroad, or on white plantations. Wives left in the rural area protected their husbands' interests by keeping up a viable farming operation to which the men could return if necessary. In the absence of their wives, some

191

men developed informal liaisons with single women in town, and sometimes these relationships lasted for years.

There had been a small European missionary presence on Kenya's Coast since the mid-1800s, and by the early 1900s small mission stations had appeared throughout western and central Kenya. Christian missionaries poured into Kenya from Europe and North America, representing many different denominations. In the early years they were often members of the Church Missionary Society (Anglicans), the White Fathers (Roman Catholics), or the Church of Scotland Missionary Society (Presbyterians). Despite the importance of African lay teachers in the spread of Christianity, mission churches kept key positions within their hierarchy firmly in in the hands of white missionaries, a tendency that later sparked the growth of many separatist African churches.

In addition to propagating the faith, missions were critical suppliers of education, health care, and social services in rural areas. While government efforts in both education and health care were oriented toward the needs of the white population, mission stations operated schools, rural clinics, and orphanages for Africans. Africans who persevered in mission educational systems had access to better-paying white-collar jobs, but African families knew the mission schools would turn their children away from traditional beliefs. Despite African demands, a network of government-supported schools free of missionary control did not become a reality until the 1950s, and by the time of independence, the majority of both Luo and Kikuyu families were Christian.

Girls were much less likely than boys to have had more than just a few years of elementary education, and there were few job opportunities for women in the urban areas. Most white families preferred to hire men, even for domestic service, and for much of the colonial period few women had the training for semiskilled or clerical jobs. Those women who moved to Nairobi, Kisumu, or other cities looking for work to support themselves — or to escape an unhappy marriage—sometimes had few alternatives to informal prostitution, and women living on their own faced a great deal of criticism and suspicion about their activities.

World War I and the Interwar Period

The demand for African labor escalated dramatically in 1914 when World War I came to East Africa. Despite a few German raids across the border, most of the actual fighting took place in neighboring Tanzania—then called Tanganyika and controlled by Germany—and in Mozambique. Some 250,000 Kenyan men were conscripted into military service for the war. While a few served with the prestigious Kenya African Rifles (KAR, or "Keya"), the great majority served as porters in the Carrier Corps. Neighborhoods in East Africa still named "Kariakor" reflect the location of these wartime barracks. About one-fifth of the Kenyan men conscripted for wartime service never returned home, dying more often from malnutrition and disease than from bullets. Those who survived came back to Kenya with a new willingness to demand political and economic change. Colonial officials feared these new attitudes and determined to attract more white settlers to maintain the status quo. An official "soldier-settler" scheme offered qualified British veterans a chance to take up substantial farms at nominal cost, and more than twelve hundred additional farms were allocated under the scheme.

Despite the increased settler presence and demands for labor, many African farmers prospered during the 1920s as they grew cash crops for local markets and for export. The Great Depression greatly reduced those chances for prosperity, however, as worldwide demand for agricultural exports declined, jobs for Africans dried up, and white employers slashed wages. Meanwhile, European settlers demanded and got a series of measures giving them increased control over African squatters. A 1937 ordinance, for example, allowed settlers to limit the number of acres that squatters could cultivate on their own, eliminate squatter livestock, and increase the number of working days per year from 180 to 270. The interruption of the Second World War gave the squatters a certain grace period, but settler pressures for control resumed with a vengeance after 1945, forcing many squatters back to the reserves and provoking their participation in the resistance movement known as Mau Mau.

World War II and the Rise of African Nationalism

The difficult years of the Depression were soon followed by the crisis of World War II. Kenyans were required to fight with British forces against the Italians in Ethiopia and Somalia and against the Japanese in Burma. This time most of them were trained in the use of weapons in combat. Kenya's primary contribution to the war effort, however, was to provide extensive food supplies for the troops. African homesteads were ordered to sacrifice livestock and crops as "voluntary" contributions to a war effort they understood little about. The war years also witnessed government attempts to silence potential opposition by banning African newspapers and political movements.

The years following World War II saw a great increase in racial tensions and political conflict. Kenyan soldiers who returned home had a new sense of European vulnerabilities and expected to be treated with greater respect for their war service; they also returned with substantial pay packets and great expectations. At the same time, white settlers who had enlisted, or who had stepped in to replace colonial officials called up for the war effort, fully expected to be rewarded for their sacrifices and to have a greater say in the colony's affairs. These conflicting expectations would collide violently in the late 1940s and throughout the 1950s as white settlers confronted greater African militancy in both labor organizations and political movements.

While Nairobi was overwhelmingly a British colonial city, with clusters of African neighborhoods and shantytowns scattered around a white official and residential core, Mombasa remained very much a cosmopolitan African town, as it had been for centuries. That is perhaps why the organized Kenyan labor movement seemed centered around the workers of Mombasa, under the able leadership of men like the Luo Tom Mboya and the Indian Makhan Singh. Labor protests at the port of Mombasa beginning in the 1930s culminated in widespread general strikes in 1939, 1947, and 1957, each of which effectively shut down the port and other public operations within Mombasa, and often spread to Nairobi as well.

The roots of Kenyan political nationalism reached back to the 1920s, when a range of locally based organizations were formed to protest such issues as land alienation, the kipande system, hut taxes, forced labor, and the appointment of African chiefs who lacked local legitimacy. The best known of these protest organizations was the Young Kikuyu Association, led by Harry Thuku. Thuku's arrest for sedition in 1922 led to a riot when policemen opened fire on the crowds demanding his release. Thuku was then exiled to Somalia and his organization banned, though a newly named Kikuyu Central Association, with similar concerns, was formed in 1925. Similar organizations in western Kenya included the Young Kavirondo Association (founded in 1922) and the Kavirondo Taxpayers' Associations (founded in 1923).

Following the wartime clampdown on African political activities, the nationalist movement gained momentum with Jomo Kenyatta's return to Kenya in 1946 after years of study abroad. Widely recognized as the leader of Kikuyu nationalism, Kenyatta was president of the new Kenya African Union (KAU). The Luo and other ethnic groups shared many of the same colonial grievances, but Kikuyu dominance of KAU and the the shaping of the culture of resistance by Kikuyu traditions—including the widespread use of traditional oaths to recruit new members and bind them to secrecy—meant that the Mau Mau revolt was primarily, though not entirely, a Kikuyu affair.

The Mau Mau Revolt and Kenyan Independence

The Kenyan government declared a State of Emergency in 1952, following sporadic outbreaks of violence targeting Europeans and African loyalists (those who had declared their support for continued British rule). The widespread anticolonial revolt that followed is known as Mau Mau. Under martial law, colonial police arrested nearly two hundred Kikuyu political activists in the Nairobi area, including Kenyatta himself. Losing their key leaders at one blow, the movement went underground and developed a more decentralized leadership in the rural areas. Thousands of Kikuyu men and some women fled to the forests of Mt. Kenya and the Aberdares, where they formed the military arm of the Mau Mau

195

movement, the Land and Freedom Army, and staged guerrilla raids on British command centers and loyalist farms.

In Nairobi, Operation Anvil forcibly "repatriated" thousands of Kikuyu, Embu, and Meru (sometimes referred to by the British as "KEM") to the rural areas in the hope of breaking up the core of urban opposition. One side-effect of the campaign against Mau Mau was to open new windows of opportunity for other ethnic groups in Nairobi, particularly for the Luo and Luyia, who were often able to move into the jobs and housing left behind by the detained or repatriated Kikuyu.

While several white settler families were attacked, and other African groups had to deal with curfew violations and sometimes arbitrary police brutality, those who suffered most during the 1950s were the Kikuyu themselves. Perhaps 100,000 Kikuyu men and women were arrested and sent to detention camps, where they were beaten and required to perform hard labor. Great hardships also faced those who remained on the land—a campaign of "villagization" forced perhaps a million Kikuyu into stockaded villages, usually surrounded by barbed-wire fencing and a deep trench and guarded by armed loyalists.

Most of the fighting had ended by late 1956, but the State of Emergency was not formally lifted until 1960. After nearly a decade of struggle, some fifteen thousand Africans had died, while at most a hundred Europeans had been killed. But while the Land and Freedom Army might have lost the battle, they had essentially won the war, in the sense that it accelerated British withdrawal from Kenya. The costs of continued colonial control were simply too high for British officials, and negotiations began to settle the terms and process of the transition to Kenyan independence, including the immediate election of African representatives to the Legislative Council (LegCo) for the first time. Most white settlers gave in bitterly and withdrew at this point, selling their farms and leaving the country. (The independent Kenya government would purchase many of those white farms, ostensibly to make them available for landless peasants; in practice most farms were purchased by government ministers or high officials, who relied on tenant farmers to provide labor.)

196

In December 1963, Kenya became an independent nation with Jomo Kenyatta (nicknamed "Mzee," a term of respect for an elder) as prime minister and a democratically elected Legislative Council dominated by the Kenya African National Union, or KANU. Less than a year later, the British model of parliamentary government was abandoned in favor of a republican government with a strong president. Despite the rhetoric of the radical nationalists, the new government declared its commitment to capitalism and to private property. Kenyatta assured world leaders that his would not be a "gangster government" and urged Kenyans to forget the past. Those who had supported the more radical goals of the Land and Freedom Army suppressed their misgivings in the first heady years of independence, but eventually tensions grew between two ideological camps within KANU. With Luo politician and former vice president Oginga Odinga (nicknamed "Jaramogi") as their primary spokesperson, the leftists argued for land reform, domestic equality, and international nonalignment. When Kenyatta purged KANU's left wing, some twenty-nine members of Parliament defected to join the Kenya People's Union (KPU), a new opposition party formed by Odinga in 1966. This political cleavage, which dominated national politics for at least the next decade, largely followed ethnic and regional lines: Kenyatta's greatest support came from the Kikuyu, Embu, and Meru people of central Kenya, while Odinga's support was found primarily among the Luo and Luyia of western Kenya. The Luo and other non-Kikuyu groups felt that Kenyatta, his Kikuyu allies within KANU, and his home district benefited disproportionately from official economic development. Most Kikuyu felt that they were the only ones who had really fought for independence and that they deserved most of its rewards. These ethnic tensions only deepened during the following decade.

The 1969 assassination of Tom Mboya, the most prominent Luo in government, provoked riots in Kenya's major cities. Further riots broke out several weeks later during Kenyatta's first visit to Kisumu, the unofficial Luo capital of western Kenya. When members of the special forces opened fire on the crowds, many innocent bystanders died. Kenyatta blamed the riots on the

197

KPU and immediately banned the opposition party, arresting Odinga and other leaders and cracking down on political dissent. Others accused government supporters of inciting the riot in order to discredit the KPU. Conspiracy theories and allegations of corruption flourished. Other outspoken critics of the government were murdered, including J. M. Kariuki, the popular ex–Mau Mau fighter turned member of Parliament; student leaders disappeared; and prominent members of Parliament such as Martin Shikuku and Jean-Marie Seroney were arrested, along with Ngugi wa Thiong'o, East Africa's best-known writer and novelist.

When President Kenyatta died in 1978, a smaller ethnic group, the Kalenjin, came to enjoy the fruits of power under his successor, Daniel arap Moi. Kenya's population has increased rapidly in recent years, while the changing terms of trade for agricultural products since the early 1980s have led to a generally stagnant rural economy. A coup attempt in 1982—the most serious threat faced by the new nation—was sparked by air force officers who attacked Moi's government for corruption and economic mismanagement. Forces loyal to the government restored order after a few days. Since the end of the Cold War, the United States and other Western nations have pushed the Moi regime to reduce corruption, impose economic reforms, and permit a more open political system. Moi capitulated to international pressure in late 1991 and announced that opposition political parties could form and compete in national elections. In the face of the relative weakness of the ethnically fragmented and underfunded opposition, the regime has continued its repression of dissent, including the use of government-funded ethnic violence to convince ordinary Kenyans that they are safer clinging to the status quo.

CONTEMPORARY WOMEN'S FICTION
FROM AROUND THE WORLD
from The Feminist Press at The City University of New York

Allegra Maud Goldman, a novel by Edith Konecky. $9.95 paper.

Almost Touching the Skies: Women's Coming of Age Stories. $15.95 paper. $35.00 cloth.

Apples from the Desert: Selected Stories, by Savyon Liebrecht. $13.95 paper. $19.95 cloth.

Bamboo Shoots After the Rain: Contemporary Stories by Women Writers of Taiwan. $14.95 paper. $35.00 cloth.

Bearing Life: Women's Writings on Childlessness. $23.95 cloth.

Changes: A Love Story, a novel by Ama Ata Aidoo. $12.95 paper.

Coming to Birth, a novel by Marjorie Oludhe Macgoye. $11.95 paper. $30.00 cloth.

Confessions of Madame Psyche, a novel by Dorothy Bryant. $18.95 paper. $30.00 cloth.

David's Story, a novel by Zoë Wicomb. $19.95 cloth.

An Estate of Memory, a novel by Ilona Karmel. $11.95 paper.

A Matter of Time, a novel by Shashi Deshpande. $21.95 cloth.

Mulberry and Peach: Two Women of China, a novel by Hualing Nieh. $12.95 paper.

No Sweetness Here and Other Stories, by Ama Ata Aidoo. $10.95 paper. $29.00 cloth.

Paper Fish, a novel by Tina De Rosa. $9.95 paper. $20.00 cloth.

The Present Moment, a novel by Marjorie Oludhe Macgoye. $11.95 paper. $30.00 cloth.

Reena and Other Stories, by Paule Marshall. $11.95 paper.

The Silent Duchess, a novel by Dacia Maraini. $14.95 paper. $19.95 cloth.

The Tree and the Vine, a novel by Dola de Jong. $9.95 paper, $27.95 cloth.

Truth Tales: Contemporary Stories by Women Writers of India. $12.95 paper. $35.00 cloth.

Two Dreams: New and Selected Stories, by Shirley Geok-lin Lim. $10.95 paper.

What Did Miss Darrington See? An Anthology of Feminist Supernatural Fiction. $14.95 paper.

Winter's Edge, a novel by Valerie Miner. $10.95 paper.

With Wings: An Anthology of Literature by and About Women with Disabilities. $14.95 paper.

Women Working: An Anthology of Stories and Poems. $13.95 paper.

Women Writing in India: 600 B.C. to the Present. Volume I: 600 B.C. to the Early Twentieth Century. $29.95 paper. *Volume II: The Twentieth Century.* $29.95 paper.

You Can't Get Lost in Cape Town, a novel by Zoë Wicomb. $13.95 paper. $42.00 cloth.

To receive a free catalog of The Feminist Press's 200 titles, call or write The Feminist Press at The City University of New York, The Graduate Center, 365 Fifth Avenue, New York, NY 10016; phone: (212) 817-7920; fax: (212) 987-4008. Feminist Press books are available at bookstores or can be ordered directly. Send check or money order (in U.S. dollars drawn on a U.S. bank) payable to The Feminist Press. Please add $4.00 shipping and handling for the first book and $1.00 for each additional book. VISA, Mastercard, and American Express are accepted for telephone orders. Prices subject to change.